POINT
BLANK

Books by Fern Michaels:

Wishes for Christmas
About Face
Perfect Match
A Family Affair
Forget Me Not
The Blossom Sisters
Balancing Act
Tuesday's Child
Betrayal
Southern Comfort
To Taste the Wine
Sins of the Flesh
Sins of Omission
Return to Sender
Mr. and Miss Anonymous
Up Close and Personal
Fool Me Once
Picture Perfect
The Future Scrolls
Kentucky Sunrise
Kentucky Heat
Kentucky Rich
Plain Jane
Charming Lily
What You Wish For
The Guest List
Listen to Your Heart
Celebration
Yesterday
Finders Keepers
Annie's Rainbow
Sara's Song
Vegas Sunrise
Vegas Heat
Vegas Rich

Whitefire
Wish List
Dear Emily
Christmas at Timberwoods
Fancy Dancer

The Sisterhood Novels:

Point Blank
In Plain Sight
Eyes Only
Kiss and Tell
Blindsided
Gotcha!
Home Free
Déjà Vu
Cross Roads
Game Over
Deadly Deals
Vanishing Act
Razor Sharp
Under the Radar
Final Justice
Collateral Damage
Fast Track
Hokus Pokus
Hide and Seek
Free Fall
Lethal Justice
Sweet Revenge
The Jury
Vendetta
Payback
Weekend Warriors

Books by Fern Michaels (Continued):

**The Men of the
Sisterhood Novels:**
Double Down

The Godmothers Series:
Classified
Breaking News
Deadline
Late Edition
Exclusive
The Scoop

E-Book Exclusives:
Desperate Measures
Seasons of Her Life
To Have and To Hold
Serendipity
Captive Innocence
Captive Embraces
Captive Passions
Captive Secrets
Captive Splendors

Cinders to Satin
For All Their Lives
Texas Heat
Texas Rich
Texas Fury
Texas Sunrise

Anthologies:
When the Snow Falls
Secret Santa
A Winter Wonderland
I'll Be Home for Christmas
Making Spirits Bright
Holiday Magic
Snow Angels
Silver Bells
Comfort and Joy
Sugar and Spice
Let It Snow
A Gift of Joy
Five Golden Rings
Deck the Halls
Jingle All the Way

Published by Kensington Publishing Corporation

FERN MICHAELS

POINT BLANK

ZEBRA BOOKS
KENSINGTON PUBLISHING CORP.
http://www.kensingtonbooks.com

ZEBRA BOOKS are published by

Kensington Publishing Corp.
119 West 40th Street
New York, NY 10018

All Kensington titles, imprints and distributed lines are available
at special quantity discounts for bulk purchases for sales promo-
tion, premiums, fund-raising, educational or institutional use.

Special book excerpts or customized printings can also be created
to fit specific needs. For details, write or phone the office of the
Kensington Sales Manager. Attn.: Sales Department. Kensington
Publishing Corp., 119 West 40th Street, New York, NY 10018.
Phone: 1-800-221-2647.

Zebra and the Z logo Reg. U.S. Pat. & TM Off.

First Kensington Books Hardcover Printing: September 2015
First Zebra Books Mass-Market Paperback Printing: January 2016
ISBN-13: 978-1-4201-3593-0
ISBN-10: 1-4201-3593-7

eISBN-13: 978-1-4201-3596-1
eISBN-10: 1-4201-3596-1

10 9 8 7 6 5 4 3 2 1

Printed in the United States of America

I would like to dedicate this book to my wonderful friend, Sister Julie Brandt, SOSF

Prologue

Three months earlier

The round little monk waddled out to the mini fruit orchard behind the monastery. He was huffing and puffing as he reached for a low-hanging plum that looked so perfect that it was a shame to pluck it from the tree. He did it anyway because he needed to do something to take his mind off what he had just seen and heard.

The small orchard, located behind the Shaolin Monastery, was a peaceful place, with small stone benches scattered under the trees. It was a place where the monks liked to go to sit and watch the fruit grow, as they put it.

It was a beautiful day, with golden sunshine,

not too warm, not too cool. Just perfect. Lazy, fluffy clouds were dotting a sky that was blue as the ocean. A gentle breeze was whispering through the fruit trees.

Unfortunately, the little orchard didn't seem peaceful and tranquil at this particular moment for Brother Hung, because his insides were in total turmoil. It wasn't that he had deliberately eavesdropped. It was just that he was in the library, minding his own business, when the Abbot made an appearance. At first he'd been tempted to announce himself, but a heartbeat later, when the door opened a second time and he heard the harsh greeting directed at the Abbot, he'd changed his mind. He supposed that he *could* have put his fingers in his ears to avoid hearing the conversation, but he hadn't. Or he *could* have made a noise or said something to alert the two men to his presence, but he did neither of those things. Instead, he withdrew even farther behind one of the bookshelves and remained as quiet as the proverbial mouse. And listened as carefully as he could, his heart thundering in his chest.

When the door finally closed behind the Abbot and the man with the surly voice, the little monk didn't move. He felt paralyzed. Finally, after an agonizingly long wait, he was able to make his limbs move, and his feet had taken him outside to the little orchard behind the monastery, where he had just plucked what looked like a perfect plum. He glanced around to see where the nearest bench was and how far from it he had strolled.

He spotted it almost immediately, trundled over to it, and gingerly lowered his bulk onto the hard stone. He started to polish the plum on his robe until he could see his reflection in the fruit. How, Brother Hung mused, was it possible that this piece of fruit from the orchard could be the exact same color as the eggplant in the garden? It was a strange thought, and he could not help but wonder where it came from.

Strange. Everything here at the monastery was strange of late. Strangers appearing at all hours of the day and night. Film people desecrating the sacred grounds. Cursing and shouting. And the Abbot! In his heart and mind, Brother Hung thought of him as some sort of imposter. He'd been tempted to mention his suspicion to the council but was too afraid. What if he was wrong? What if, what if, what if? But he wasn't wrong, and he knew it full well, felt it in every fiber of his fat little body. He was absolutely certain that something bad was going to happen, and it was going to happen right here at the monastery.

Brother Hung's hands, which were holding the perfect purple plum, started to shake. His heart pounded, then his heart raced. He stared at his reflection in the purple plum, wishing he were forty years younger and eighty pounds lighter.

Brother Hung was so deep into his thoughts

that he almost fell off the stone bench when he heard Brother Shen, a fellow monk at the monastery, say to him, "Are you going to eat that plum? Or are you going to stare at it till it goes all soft and mushy?"

Brother Hung held out the perfect piece of fruit. "Add this to your basket, Brother Shen. I guess you are making plum tarts today. Take it."

Brother Shen, taller but a man of the same girth as Brother Hung, lowered himself to the stone bench. "Tell me what is troubling you, Hung. Do not tell me it is nothing, because your angst is written all over your face. Sometimes talking aloud helps to sort things out. I have sensed for weeks now that something is troubling you. How can that be, I asked myself. This monastery is a place of tranquil serenity. There are no worries here. All our needs are met, physically as well as spiritually. And today we are having plum tarts for dessert at our evening meal. Your favorite, I might add."

The words shot out of Brother Hung's mouth like bullets. "I believe the Abbot is an imposter! Something terrible is happening or about to happen. I know it. I sense it in every pore of my body. I can almost smell the disaster coming upon us."

There, the words were out, and he couldn't take them back. He stared at Brother Shen, expecting to see horror on his fellow monk's features. Instead, he saw his friend nod. Brother Shen reached out and over the basket of plums to pat Hung on the arm. The simple touch worked its magic on the disturbed monk, calming him immediately.

"So, are you saying you agree, or are you humoring me, Shen?"

Brother Shen looked around, then lowered his voice. "The rest of us have been talking about it over the past few weeks. In private, of course. If I am not mistaken, it all started when Lily Wong first came to us. Then Jun Yu visited too many times, more than is allowed, to check on his children, Hop and Gan. That's when our old Abbot left, and this current . . . ah . . . person arrived to take his place. I agree with you entirely; he wears the robes, but he is no more an Abbot than I am a scholar of the Han dynasty.

"But even if we were to protest his policies, there is nothing we can do about them. As Abbot, whatever his credentials, he has absolute authority over this monastery. We are to obey, never to ask questions."

"But the students . . . It is suspicious, Shen. Three children, Lily, Hop, and Gan. Children of two of our alumni. Jun Yu and Harry Wong. I suppose I should call Harry by his Chinese birth name of Wong Guotin, but Harry Wong, in the American style of naming people, seems so much easier for some reason. Whatever is going on has to do with Jun Yu and Harry. I feel it here," Brother Hung said, thumping his chest with a plump fist.

"And I agree. Do you see a solution or a resolution, Hung?"

"The only thing I can think of is for one of us to get in touch with Jun Yu and perhaps find a way for him to visit one more time. And to do it in secret, of course. I do not know how we could manage that. We have no access to the telephones or computers. I work in the gardens, and you work in the kitchen. How can we make that happen?"

"Perhaps we could ask Brother Dui to help us. He does help the Abbot out in the office, and I know that he was taught how to use the computer and the phone system. I also know for a fact that he does not like the new Abbot. He said the Abbot speaks down to him, demeaning him. He said that the man lacks a gentle spirit and all he thinks about is money. I will find a way to speak to him either today or tomorrow. Possibly later tonight after procession. I can try to get him alone. Dui is a good man. Very, very spiritual, as you well know. If it is in his power to help in any way, I definitely think he will.

"I must go now, Hung, so I can prepare the tarts for tonight's dinner. Classes will be finished in a few minutes, the bell will ring, and this little orchard will be trampled by many feet. It is best if you return to the monastery with me now."

Brother Hung heaved his cumbersome body off the stone bench and fell into step with

Brother Shen. "Before I came to the orchard, I was in the library, and the Abbot and a strange man were having an intense conversation. Though I stayed out of sight, I could hear them talking. I think . . . Shen, I think the Abbot was talking to one of our old students."

"And what is so terrible about that? Old students visit from time to time, you know that."

Hung looked over his shoulder. "Yes, yes, I know that. But this particular student was expelled; and he has never before to my knowledge returned to the monastery. I will never forget him or the ugly threats he made the day he departed the monastery and Song Mountain."

Brother Shen stopped in his tracks. Now there was fear in his soft brown eyes. "There is only one person that could be, Hung. Wing Ping. Am I right, Brother Hung?"

"Yes. I believe it was indeed Wing Ping in the library conversing with the Abbot, Shen, and he was extremely angry. The Abbot said little other than to agree with everything that Wing Ping, or whomever the person was, had to say. It was almost as if the Abbot was taking orders from a superior of some kind. I could hear the voices but could not make out the actual words. My hearing is not what it used to be. I feel safe, however, saying that the person doing most of the talking was angry and controlled the conversation."

"That is a cause for concern. Several weeks

ago, Brother Tung casually mentioned that he thought he saw Wing Ping entering the Abbot's office. But he was also quick to say he had not seen the renegade in many, many years, so he couldn't really be certain that it actually was Wing Ping. I do not like to repeat gossip, and it is forbidden, so I said nothing. Brother Tung and I were just having a normal conversation about the children, and he was remarking on one of the students. He said that he had to be extra stern with one in particular, or he would turn out to be our second Wing Ping. Let us keep this to ourselves for the moment, Hung."

"Yes, yes, of course. Shen, do you think we should . . . I don't know how to phrase this other than to just blurt it out. Should we perhaps put a plan into action in regard to Jun Yu's children, Hop and Gan, and Harry Wong's daughter, Lily? My instincts tell me that whatever is going on involves those three children. Wing Ping blamed Jun Yu and Wong Guotin for getting him expelled."

"Enough! Enough!" Brother Shen hissed. "The Abbot is approaching. Lower your head and do not look at the imposter."

Brother Hung did not have to be told twice. He and Brother Shen both stepped to the side to allow the Abbot to pass. No words were spoken. There was no acknowledgment that the head of the monastery had just passed them on the stone path. Nor did the Abbot acknowledge the two elderly monks.

When the two monks had put a good bit of distance between them and the Abbot, Brother Hung said, "I could feel the evil emanating from him. Did you, Shen?"

"I did. We must not speak again of this, Hung, until we are certain it is safe to do so." Brother Hung bobbed his head up and down in agreement.

The two monks parted company, Brother Shen to the kitchen to bake his plum tarts and Brother Hung to the great room, where he poured himself a cup of tea. He needed the quiet and solitude of this room so he could think. And plan.

As he sipped at his sweet tea, Hung let his mind go back in time to when Wong Guotin, Jun Yu, Dishbang Deshi, and Wing Ping were students here at the monastery. He was teaching back then, and he liked all the boys except Wing Ping. The truth was that no one liked the son of the prominent Wing family. The boy was arrogant, full of himself, and had a sense of entitlement that didn't go with the teachings of the monastery. Every day there was a new problem. And it was always with Wing Ping. In the four boys' last year as students, it was finally decided by the Abbot at the time to send Wing Ping back to his family in disgrace. The reason given to the family was that Wing Ping would never master the teachings of the monastery because he had an evil heart and wanted nothing more than to hurt and maim his fellow students. The Wing family did not take their son's ouster well. They withdrew their financial support and encouraged other prominent families to do the same. And yet the monastery had survived, and over time the families other than the Wings returned to the fold. For that, all the monks and the Abbot were grateful. Serenity and tranquility once again reigned at the monastery as it went about the job of training students in its traditional teachings.

Jun Yu had been pronounced the number one kung fu expert, to Wong Guotin's dismay. Dishbang Deshi openly questioned the Abbot's decision, saying quite forthrightly that Wong Guotin's expertise exceeded Jun Yu's in the area of martial arts. He was told in no uncertain terms to keep his opinions to himself. Dishbang Deshi did as he was told because obedience was what the monastery and its teachings were all about.

Secretly, Brother Hung agreed with Dishbang Deshi but knew better than to voice an opinion. He was just grateful that the three young men, each so very different from the others, remained good friends. Given that Jun Yu was staying in China, Brother Hung could understand the Abbot's decision.

Dishbang Deshi relocated to Hong Kong to take over the Dishbang family's silk business. Wong Guotin, now Harry Wong, went to America. While Brother Hung understood it all, he wished someone had told Wong Guotin that he was the first choice, but with circumstances as they were at the time, that was impossible.

Truth be told, of the four boys, it was actually Wing Ping who was the finest gladiator of them all. It should have been Wing Ping named as the number one kung fu expert, but his early expulsion prevented him from ever being granted the title that he, along with the Wing family, so greatly coveted.

Brother Hung stared at the leaves in the bottom of his teacup, fervently wishing they would provide the answers he was searching for. He immediately recognized the wish as foolish and knew that if he wanted answers, he was going to have to ferret them out on his own, or possibly with Brother Shen's help.

Once again, he longed for his lost youth and slim body as he contemplated his next move. Whatever it was, he hoped he was up to the task.

Chapter 1

It was quiet, as it always was at three o'clock in the morning in the upstairs apartment over Harry Wong's dojo. Yoko's breathing was deep and even, barely making little puffs of sound. Harry's sleep was restless, his breathing raspy, his head full of dreams he never wanted to remember in the morning.

Outside, the wind sounded angry as it slapped at the lone, bare, arthritic maple tree, causing the gnarled old branches to slam against the multipaned windows of the living quarters. It was a sound Harry was used to, so he simply rolled over and punched at the pillow under his head. Once again, he drifted into his restless sleep.

Harry knew that he was dreaming, because the dream he'd been having continued right up to the sound of buzzing on the nightstand. Knowing that it was his cell phone, Harry snaked out his arm to silence it before the noise could wake Yoko. In his dream, he mumbled something that sounded like a greeting in Chinese. And then he listened, the hair on the back of his neck screaming a warning that he should pay attention. Someone was talking. He listened when the voice said, "Don't talk, Harry, just listen to me, as I don't have much time." So he listened to the voice rattle on about danger, and he, Harry, was the only one whom the person on the phone could trust to safeguard something he was sending him. "Guard it with your life, Harry. I am counting on you."

Harry called the voice by name then. It was Jun Yu, the number one expert in the world of martial arts. And his friend, but more than a friend—a true brother. Even though the press and the martial arts world liked to pretend that Jun Yu and Harry Wong were hated adversaries, the truth was that there existed an unbreakable spiritual bond between them, a bond that would carry into eternity. In fact, as boys they had studied together at the Shaolin Monastery under the ever-watchful guidance of the monks. They had formed a deep friendship that both men knew even then would last a lifetime and beyond. Jun Yu's son Hop and his daughter Gan were students at the monastery, as was Harry's daughter, Lily. Hop was a year ahead of Lily, while Gan had entered the monastery at the same time Lily did, leaving Jun Yu and his wife, Jun Ling, alone the way Harry and Yoko were. The departure of their daughters was truly a sad time for both families.

The voice from across the world continued, more intense, sounding fearful now. Harry tried to absorb the rapid-fire dialogue, first in Chinese, then in English, and finally back to Chinese. He tried to say something, but Jun Yu cut him off. "Do not speak, my dear friend and brother. Just listen to me. They're coming for me, Harry. I don't have much time. I thought . . . I thought I had more time. I should have contacted you sooner, but I thought I could handle it. I was wrong, Harry. I did my best, but I was only able to get Hop and Gan. Lily was nowhere to be seen. I swear to you in my own blood that I did everything I could. I pass the sword to you now. Use it wisely, my dear brother.

"One last thing, Harry. I cannot leave this world with you thinking you are number two. You were never number two. We were equal, even the Abbot said so. I don't even want to talk about Wing Ping right now. It was the elders who felt they had to pick just one of us. And I was staying in China. It was the luck of the draw, as you Americans say. I must go now, Harry. I place all my faith and trust in you. Do not fail me. Good-bye, my brother."

Harry sighed deeply and rolled over. His arm reached out to Yoko's shoulder just so he could feel a warm presence next to him, and at that very moment, a branch from the maple tree gave a loud *thwack* against the window.

Yoko woke with a start. "What was that?" she asked, her voice clogged with sleep. "Harry, what's wrong?"

"It was the tree banging against the window. Nothing is wrong, I just had a really bad dream. Go back to sleep. We'll talk in the morning."

"Okay. Nuzzle my neck, Harry. I always fall back to sleep when you do that." Harry obliged as he struggled to remember the bad dream. Eventually he, too, fell asleep as he dreamed of his boyhood at the Shaolin Monastery with his good friend and brother Jun Yu and how they and Dishbang Deshi had boyishly schemed to outwit the monks, who so often had looked the other way to allow them to be the little boys they were.

Three o'clock ticked off to four o'clock, and still Harry slept fitfully. He finally rolled over and realized it would be better to get up and start his day than spend two more hours having bad dreams. He moved cautiously, so as not to wake Yoko, and headed for the shower.

Today, he had two classes of midshipmen from Annapolis at six thirty. Jack Emery was going to help him with them.

* * *

As Harry stepped into the shower, forty miles away as the crow flies, Jack Emery was having his own dream, which was so vivid and real, his eyes snapped open as though they were spring-loaded. While it was a dream, Jack knew that the message it contained was real and that he needed to pay attention. When he dreamed about the mystical dog Cooper, he always paid attention. Maybe *mystical* wasn't the right word; maybe *ethereal* was the word he was looking for. Maybe. The word *supernatural* flitted through his brain at the speed of light. While Cooper the dog was a beautiful, gentle animal, he nonetheless scared the living hell out of Jack. And Harry, too. Even if Harry wouldn't admit it.

Cooper belonged to Julie Wyatt, who lived in Rosemont, Alabama. They had all met Julie and Cooper when Annie and Myra traveled to Rosemont to help Julie. Cooper had taken an immediate liking to Harry and stayed at his side during the entire time they and the sisters were helping Julie, and in the end, when they left to return home, Cooper came with them to take over as the guardian and protector of young Lily. Julie had been heartbroken to give up her beloved dog, but she, like the others, knew it was meant to be. No questions asked.

When young Lily left for the Shaolin Monastery, Cooper had signaled that it was time for him to return to Rosemont to do his next job, which was to take over as protector and guardian of Julie's new grandchild.

Jack headed for the shower, his head buzzing with thoughts of Cooper, who he knew was waiting to return to Harry. The question was, why?

Jack zipped through his shower and shave and was dressed within minutes, his thoughts all over the map as he made coffee, gulped it down, then headed into the District, where he was scheduled to help Harry with two classes scheduled for six thirty.

Jack made the trip from the farm in record time, managing to beat the early-morning rush-hour traffic. He wasn't the least bit surprised to see lights on in the dojo even though it was just a little past five thirty. Time he could spend with Harry playing catch-up . . . and . . . and . . . telling him all about his Cooper dream.

Using his own key, which Harry had given him years ago, a sure sign that Harry considered him a true brother, Jack let himself into the dojo. As always, the strong smell of eucalyptus and disinfectant, together with the scent of the shitty tea Harry brewed all day long, assailed his nostrils. It was not an unpleasant scent, more like a familiar one that he would miss if it were gone. He announced his arrival at the top of his lungs as he headed to the locker room to change into his training gear.

Carrying his Starbucks coffee, Jack marched into the room and sat down next to Harry. "You should dim these lights, Harry; you look like crap!"

"Eat shit, Jack," Harry snarled. "It's too early for this. It's not even six o'clock yet."

"Ooooh, and what happens at six o'clock? Something magical? Hey, listen, Harry, I had this crazy-ass dream, and that's why I'm here so early. Just so you know it isn't for your charming company." The two old friends always talked to each other this way. Nikki said it was because neither one of them wanted the other to know how much they cared for each other. Yoko agreed entirely. Everyone on the face of the earth who knew them was convinced that each of them would take a bullet meant for the other. They just wouldn't admit it.

"Yeah, something magical. I had a bad dream, too. Man, it was so real, it scared me half to death."

Jack grinned. "You tell me yours, and I'll tell you mine."

Harry sighed. "You brought it up, so you go first."

"It was about Cooper."

"Oh, shit!" Harry said.

"Yeah, yeah. Something's up. I dream about that damn dog, then something happens. I think he's coming back, Harry."

The dojo phone rang. Jack and Harry looked at each other.

"You should answer that, Harry. It might be Admiral whatever his name is, canceling the midshipmen's class this morning. Plus, this is your place, so obviously you should be the one answering the phone, not me."

Harry swiveled around and reached for the phone. He barked his name and waited. Jack didn't think Harry's eastern eyes could round out, but they did, and they filled with panic as he listened to the voice on the phone, his eyes on Jack the whole time. "Uh-huh. Yes, of course. I will. Like now. Four hours, five tops. Same place. Right? Okay."

Jack slapped at his forehead. "Let me guess. That was Julie Wyatt, and she's on her way with Cooper and will meet up with you in Atlanta."

"Wiseass," Harry shot back. "But, yes, it was Julie Wyatt."

"Did she give you any clues, any hints as to what's up?"

"No. She just said Cooper woke her around three this morning, and when she got up, all his gear was piled up by the door. That's what he does when he's ready to leave."

"That's all well and good, Harry, but how does she know Cooper wants to come *here*?" Jack's voice was so fretful that Harry winced.

"Because Cooper had Lily's sunglasses in his mouth and was dragging that feathered boa Lily used to deck him out in. Julie said the message was loud and clear."

"Okay, what's the plan here?" Jack asked.

"You take the class, and I'll hook the seat on the Ducati and go to Atlanta. Cooper likes to ride in the sidecar. We used to do it all the time with Lily."

"Not on the highway, you didn't. You just did that in Rock Creek Park. I'm going with you. We can get Yung Li to take today's class. Those navy guys are so green, they won't know the difference. He's already here; he came in right after I did. Wan Soju can spell him. I'll change, and you tell Yoko. We'll go in my car. Move, Harry!"

Fifteen minutes later, Jack drove onto the interstate. "How'd it go with Yoko?"

"She started to cry. I've seen her cry only twice, Jack. When we got married and when Lily left for China. She was still crying when I walked out. She just kept saying over and over that something bad was happening, and Cooper knows. That's why he's coming back. Do you believe that, Jack?"

"Hell, yes, I believe that. The question is, do you believe it, Harry?"

"Damn straight, I do. What could it be? That dog can't talk. How are we supposed to know what it is?"

"You know what, Harry, some way, somehow, Cooper will let us know. He's . . . He's . . . um . . . not of this world."

"Well, at least you got that right, Jack. That dog hasn't aged a day since we first saw him at Julie Wyatt's house. She sends pictures of him at least once a week. Cooper stares right into the camera as though he's sending a message. You know, like those news commentators who stare right into the camera when they're delivering some earth-shattering news no one wants to hear.

"What I don't get, Jack, is why are you the one who always has the dreams about Cooper, yet it's me that he comes to. What the hell does that even mean?"

Jack guffawed. "When we pick up Cooper, let's ask him."

"All I have to do is pinch your neck, and I can kill you. You do know that, right?"

"Yeah, and while you're *trying* to do that, what do you think I'll be doing?"

"Dying," Harry shot back immediately. Both men laughed, but it wasn't a funny ha-ha laugh; it was hysterical, verging on a total collapse.

Jack turned the heater to low as he raced down the interstate, ever mindful of speed traps and smokies out to gather their quota of speeding tickets for the month.

"So how come you were so snarly this morning, Harry? You still not sleeping well?"

"I had another of those wild-ass dreams I've been having lately. This one was a real whopper. The phone rang, and it was Jun Yu. He said he was dying or something like that. Then he said he was sending me something, and I needed to guard it with my life. Said he trusted me.

"Then he said something about his son Hop, his daughter Gan, and Lily, that he found Hop and Gan but couldn't find Lily. He kept calling me brother and said how much he loved me. And, get this, he said I wasn't really number two. We were tied, but the Abbot was pressured by the elders into picking just one, and they went with him because he was staying in China. He sounded truthful, and I've never known Jun Yu to lie. He said I was now number one. It was a crazy dream, Jack. Still, it bothered me.

"I had it in mind to call him today. I haven't talked to him in months. Figured we'd have a good chuckle over the dream. I can't tell you how real it seemed. What could he possibly be sending me, Jack, that I need to guard with my life?"

"Beats me, Harry. Why don't you call him now?"

"I didn't bring my phone. I meant to charge it last night, and I thought I had, but I guess I forgot, because when I went to get it before we left, it was dead. So I left it in the charger."

Jack was silent for a good three minutes before he said, "Harry, are you sure the phone call was a dream? What if it was a real call, and you answered the phone, then fell asleep and left the phone on. Did you think about that? You said you *think* you charged it before you went to bed. If you thought you did, then you probably did. Habits like that are hard to break. Use my phone and call Jun Yu. Like *now*, Harry. I know you know the number by heart, and even if you forgot, I know it. Now, Harry. I don't like coincidences, because I do not believe that there is really any such thing as a coincidence. The phone's right there on the console. Do it, Harry!"

Harry bit down on his lower lip as he pressed in the digits that would send his call halfway around the world. "It's ringing. One, two, crap, it's going to voice mail."

"Leave a message, Harry."

Always succinct, Harry left a message. "Call me, it's urgent." He placed the phone back in the console. Then he looked over at Jack and said, "It was real. It wasn't a dream, right?"

"That would be my guess. What's the time difference? I can't remember, twelve hours I think. Something like that. Try calling Quon Fang or Pye Min. If you can't reach them, then call the damned monastery. All three of those numbers are on my call list. Jun Yu always calls right back. Do you have Jun Yu's wife, Jun Ling's, number? I think her number is on my call list, too, though I have never had occasion to use it. Harry, are you listening to me? Why are you staring out the window? C'mon, get with the program here."

Harry licked at his lips as he stared at Jack. "I don't think in my entire life I ever experienced real fear, Jack. Whatever it is that I'm feeling right now, this minute, it has to be real fear. I know, Jack, I know, when I dial those numbers, there will be no answer. You know it, too, don't you?"

"Yeah, but do it anyway," Jack said as he steered his Beemer around an eighteen-wheeler to get into the fast lane, where traffic was less congested.

Harry's fingers moved like pistons as he dialed number after number. His agitation increased with each number pressed into Jack's smartphone. And Jack knew what his friend was going to say before the words shot out of his mouth.

"Quon Fang's and Pye Min's went straight to voice mail. So did Jun Ling's. There is no answer at the monastery, but that's not unusual. They shut down at seven o'clock. No calls in or out. The monks refuse to believe anything could be an emergency. The monastery is a place of peace and serenity. An emergency would never dare present itself, or so they think.

"It's all a dry well, Jack. I just tried Jun Yu's number again, and it went straight to voice mail this time. At least I got to leave a message earlier. What the hell is going on, Jack?"

"I don't know, Harry, but I'm thinking it's not good. Jun Ling should have answered. When was the last time you spoke to Jun Ling?"

"Quite a while back. Yoko is the one who calls her. It's a girl thing."

"Yeah, yeah, I get that. Nikki makes calls to guys' wives, too. I get it. Just keep trying. Don't you have any other numbers at the monastery, like the Abbot's?"

"Nope. The monks and their staff do not

like it when we call, and they will not put the calls through. They call us when needed. In the whole time Lily has been there, we only ever got one call, and that's because Lily came down with the mumps, and the attending physician called to assure us she was recovering nicely."

"Well, that damn well sucks, Harry," Jack growled.

"Tell me about it. Yoko and I are living with it. In the end, it was our decision, and we knew the rules going in just as my parents knew the rules. I turned out okay, so we just have to think positive."

"It bothers me, Harry, that in all these years, Jun Yu never before told you that you were equals. You thought of yourself as number two all this time, and you're not. You are as much number one as Jun Yu is. For some reason, I'm having trouble getting past that.

"I know you say I am your equal, and perhaps I am on certain levels, but I will *never* be what and who you are. I know this, and I accept it. The reason I know this and can live with it is, you were born to the art, and I had to learn it. It's not the same, Harry, and we both know it. Having said that, I appreciate your little lie." Harry simply nodded.

They were three hours into the long drive before either man spoke again. Harry broke the silence by saying, "The calls are all going straight to voice mail. I'm starting to think this is all a conspiracy of some kind."

Jack turned slightly to the right so he could better observe his friend. All he could see was the misery etched on Harry's face. He'd never seen him this worried before. On occasion, to be sure, he'd seen him concerned, antsy, bewildered, but never fearful. He wished he knew the right words to erase the distress that he was seeing on Harry's face. All he could think to say was, "Keep trying. Sooner or later, someone is bound to answer. I would think that when the monastery opens in the morning, they'll answer."

"My gut is telling me they won't, Jack. Listen, if it wasn't for your dream and our heading to Atlanta to pick up Cooper, I might agree with you. Cooper has changed all the dynamics here. Tell me I'm wrong, Jack."

"I can't tell you that, Harry, because I agree with you. Cooper is the game changer."

"It all comes down to a dog!" Harry said as he pounded out numbers on Jack's cell phone.

"That's pretty much how I see it, too. An hour to go, and maybe Cooper will give us a clue or something."

"And if he doesn't?"

"Then we fall back and regroup. I'm not a seer, Harry. Why don't you go into one of your . . . um . . . trances, zone out in your body, find your core, and see if you can see something in the future."

Harry simply ignored him as he continued to press the numbers that he now had memorized.

Jack had no other recourse but to keep his eyes on the road and drive.

There were a little less than sixty miles to go before they set eyes on the magical dog, Cooper.

Chapter 2

The GPS squawked to life, alerting Jack that he was to make a right turn fifty feet ahead in order to proceed to the appointed place. He followed the instructions, slowed down, and took the curve nicely. The robotic voice, which irritated him no end, then instructed him to drive one mile and make a left turn to arrive at his destination.

"Showtime, Harry. You having any luck?"

"No. I think I am wearing out the digits. I have to admit, I have never been this frustrated in my whole life. If that dog doesn't have answers for us, I don't know what I will do."

Jack laughed. "And you think Cooper is going to *speak* to you? Is that what you're saying?"

Harry carefully placed Jack's cell phone back

onto the console. "You know, Jack, sometimes you really are an asshole. No, Cooper is not going to speak to me. I am going to read his mind. It's called thought transference. You of all people should know that. You had a session or two with that dog, and as I remember it, he spooked the living hell out of you. Go ahead, try to deny it, and I'll lay you out cold right here."

"Testy, testy, Harry. Relax. I see the Holiday Inn up ahead. Looks like snow, doesn't it?" When there was no response, Jack said, "What's Julie driving these days, do you know?" Harry shrugged because the question to his mind was too stupid to be worthy of a response. "Okay, okay, be that way. I'll cruise the parking lot, and you keep your eyes to the right and I'll keep mine to the left.

"Hey, here's a thought, Harry. Call Julie and ask her where she is at this moment. If she's still driving, we can go into the Holiday Inn and get a cup of coffee and a sandwich. I'm starving. We could get something for Cooper to go, too. I could use a bathroom break, and I also want to call Nikki. Plus, we need to get gas for the return trip."

As Jack drove around to the back parking area, Harry was pressing in the digits to Julie Wyatt's phone. He identified himself and asked where she was. Jack could hear Cooper barking in the background. He clicked off and turned to Jack. "She's about forty minutes out. She said that she was delayed because of an accident on the interstate. That gives us time to do everything you want to do. Do you want to eat inside or do takeout and eat in the car? If you want to do either one, I can fill up the tank. Your call, Jack."

"Okay, what do you want to eat?"

Harry looked at Jack as though he'd grown a second head. "Tea and sprouts. I'm sure they have a salad bar, and it is lunchtime. I'll head over to the Shell station at the end of the parking lot and come back for you."

"Okay, okay. Don't you need a bathroom break? How silly of me, I forgot you're part camel. All right, all right already, I'm going," Jack bellowed as he sprinted from the car against the wind on a path that would take him to the entrance of the Holiday Inn.

Jack hit the men's room, washed his hands, smoothed down his hair, and was in line at the salad bar in the main dining room within minutes. He filled two Styrofoam cartons and asked for hot tea and a coffee for himself. He was back outside within eighteen minutes, just as Harry brought the Beemer to a stop in the same parking space Jack had parked in. He didn't get out, which meant from here on in Harry was in control of the Beemer. Jack shrugged as he slid into the passenger side. "Damn, it's cold out there. It wouldn't be so bad if it wasn't so windy. That wind knifes right through you. I got your sprouts and tea."

"Don't you ever shut up, Jack?" Harry said, reaching for his food.

"Sometimes," Jack said as he speared a fat shrimp from his salad with a plastic fork. "I've even been known to talk to myself from time to time. And on occasion, I answer myself. Is that what you want to hear?" He just loved baiting Harry, but all Harry did was shoot him a look that would have caused other mortals to run for cover. Not Jack. "You need to get over yourself, Harry."

"I think I will be the one who sheds the most tears when they lower you into the ground," Harry said in his most menacing tone. Jack laughed. In spite of himself, Harry laughed, too. "Cut me some slack here, Jack. I'm uptight right now."

"I know that, Harry. Accept the fact that we don't have all the answers right now, but we *will* get them. Until then, we go minute by minute, hour by hour, and hope for the best."

They ate in silence, neither man enjoying or even tasting the food they were eating, their thoughts elsewhere entirely. They both looked up when they heard the soft tap of a horn. "They're here!" Jack said, hopping out of the car, Harry on his heels.

Julie Wyatt parked her old Range Rover, which had close to two hundred thousand miles on it, one row over and got out of the car. She'd said on more than one occasion that the SUV was perfect for the dogs, and every part that could be replaced had been replaced, so why would she want to trade it in. And besides, the dogs didn't like change or the smell of a new car. Who could argue with such logic, Jack wondered.

Both Jack and Harry waited as Julie made her way across the lot to where they were standing. She looked sad, and her eyes were wet as she hugged both men. "I don't know what to tell you; he was ready to leave. He had everything piled up. I know the signs by now. He's champing at the bit to get out of the truck. He knew he was coming here about ten miles back, because he unbuckled his seat belt—you know what a whiz he is at that—and hopped into the front seat. What's going on?"

"We don't know. Jack had a dream and . . . I guess I knew subconsciously that something was up," Harry said, a catch in his voice. He went on to explain about Jun Yu and the phone call. "He's sending me something that I am to guard with my life. He said something about his son and daughter, Hop and Gan, and my daughter Lily and how he couldn't get to her even though he tried. I guess it all ties in to Cooper somehow. And Lily. That dog is . . . is . . ."

"I know, Harry. Someday we all need to sit down and talk about Cooper." Her voice lowered to a whisper. "You guys haven't . . . seen Cooper in person in a while. He . . . he's not getting older for some strange reason. He looks the same as the day he came to me after my son died. He just showed up at the door, like he was company. I can't explain it," Julie said, tears rolling down her cheeks. "Let me get him before he chews the door off."

Harry and Jack watched as Julie sprinted to the Rover and opened the door. Cooper leaped to the ground, then sat on his haunches. He barked a loud, boisterous greeting. Jack and Harry waved because they didn't know what else to do. They waited.

Jack took a step to the side so he could better see how this little reunion was going to play out. Harry dropped to his knees and waited for Cooper to come to him. Dog and man eyeballed each other before Cooper put his paws on Harry's shoulders and somehow managed to nuzzle his neck before he backed off and sat a foot away. Man and dog stared at one another—for six and a half long minutes. An eternity in Jack's mind.

Jack risked a glance at Julie, who just flapped her hands in the air, a sign that she didn't know any more than Jack about what was going on. Tears continued to slide down her cheeks. Jack felt like crying himself for some reason.

Cooper let loose with two sharp barks, then meandered over to Jack, and Jack later swore that the big dog was grinning at him. Jack leaned down and scratched Cooper's ears as a thought raced through his mind that Lily was in trouble. Cooper barked again, his signal that Jack was supposed to respond. "Yeah, yeah, I get it. I get it, Cooper." The dog trotted over to Julie, who was holding a bright purple plastic basket filled to the brim with Cooper's gear. She set it down and hugged the dog as she wailed for her loss. Cooper barked, rose on his hind legs, and licked at her tears.

Jack could hear Julie say, "Yeah, I know you're coming back at some point. I'm okay. I'm okay, Cooper."

"You getting all this, Harry?" Jack hissed.

"Yeah, you?"

"Uh-huh."

"Okay," Jack bellowed. "Let's hit the road before the snow comes." He had no idea whether it was going to snow, but it seemed like the moment called for a comment, and snow was as good as anything else he could come up with.

Harry picked up the purple basket and settled it on the backseat. "Get in the car, Cooper, and buckle up." The big dog woofed and did as instructed.

The threesome hugged one more time. Julie's eyes were dry now, but her voice was sad. "I love that dog, I really do. He literally saved my sanity. Take care of him and bring him back. I think I'm . . . I'm his home base."

"Will do. Drive carefully, Julie," Harry mumbled. Jack waved, and Cooper barked.

They were back on the interstate within minutes, the sky dark and dreary.

Cooper somehow managed to lie down even

with the seat belt on. He was sleeping peacefully, and clutched in his paws was a stuffed
rabbit that had only one ear and half a tail.

When Jack couldn't stand the silence any
longer, he blurted, "Any luck?"

"No. All the calls just go straight to voice
mail. It's Lily. Cooper confirmed it. That's
what Jun Yu was trying to tell me. Something's
happened to Lily. That's why Cooper is here.
Tell me I'm wrong, Jack."

Jack let half a second go by before he responded. "I wish I could tell you that, Harry,
but I can't. I more or less surmised that when
you said Jun Yu told you on the phone that he
got Hop and Gan out but couldn't find Lily. I
don't know anything about Buddhists, Harry,
so help me out here. You said you lived with
the monks for years and years. Jun, too. So
what could have gone wrong after all this time?
What would put those kids in danger?"

"Ask Cooper," Harry snapped. "Jeez, I'm
sorry, Jack. I don't know. I can't even begin to
imagine. You were there, you saw how wonderful it was, how peaceful and tranquil and how
all those kids, no matter their age, were happy
and thriving. Maybe it has something to do with
the new Abbot. He's into tourism and commer-
cialism.

"Several months ago, Jun Yu did tell me that
the monks were convening to discuss the Abbot's
ouster, but then he never said anything more. We

need to go there. As soon as possible." Cooper
barked vigorously at that comment.

"I thought the dog was asleep," Jack said,
looking in the rearview mirror.

"He just pretends. As far as I know, that dog
never sleeps," Harry whispered. Cooper barked
again to show he'd heard Harry's comment.
"See!"

"And by *we* I assume you mean all of us, the
girls, everyone, right?"

"How else can we do it? Annie and Dennis
are the ones with the Gulfstreams. We'll need
Jack Sparrow to clear the way for us. The paperwork alone could bog us down for months.
While yours and mine are up to date, the others
have to start from scratch. So, when we get
back, are we heading straight for Myra's or my
dojo? I only have enough juice for maybe two
more calls at the most. Unless you remembered to bring your charger. Did you?"

"Well, no, Harry, the charger wasn't exactly
on my mind when I left the house after that
dream this morning. Call Yoko and explain
things and have her call everyone to meet either at Myra's farm or at our place, which is
just next door across the field."

Harry was already pressing the number two
button that would connect him with his wife.
"Crap, she isn't answering. She's probably at
the nursery. Christmas trees were supposed to
be delivered today. I think. Then again, maybe

it's tomorrow. Yoko never carries her cell phone in her pocket, and she is notorious for leaving it someplace and not being able to find it. For some strange reason, she really hates the cell phone. Sometimes I don't pay attention to things like that when she's going on and on."

"Call Nikki. She always answers. It's the lawyer in her."

Harry pressed the number one on Jack's phone. Nikki picked up on the second ring. "Jack said to call everyone for an emergency meeting at Myra's for six o'clock . . . Shit, Jack, the phone died."

"Well, at least you got the gist of it out. Nikki will know what to do." Cooper barked to show his agreement as he continued to snuggle with his one-eared rabbit with the half tail.

Neither Harry nor Jack spoke again until Jack took the exit that would take him out to Pinewood. "Forty minutes and we're home."

"You're home. How the hell am I supposed to get back to the District?"

Jack looked at his old and dearest friend. Was Harry losing it? "Duh. With your wife, of course. Unless she hitched a ride with Alexis or Kathryn. But knowing that you and Cooper are going to be there, I assume she is savvy enough to figure it all out on her own. Don't you think, Harry?" Not bothering to wait for a response, Jack continued. "Listen, Harry, you need to look sharp here. I can't do it all. I need you to be the down-and-dirty guy you always pretend to be. You know our rule. We kick ass and take names later. Now, are you part of the problem or part of the solution?" He waited for what he was sure was going to be a surly response delivered in a way only Harry Wong could deliver it.

"I hear you, Jack. You're right. I'm just worried about my daughter."

In the backseat, Cooper let loose with a series of soft woofs.

"See, even the dog is telling you he's on it. Keep it together, Harry."

"Okay, Jack."

Jack felt his stomach muscles cramp up. He hated it when Harry was nice and agreeable, because he never knew what Harry would do next.

"Five miles out," Jack said. "See that mile marker." Cooper barked to show he saw it.

Harry laughed. "I really need to know who Cooper came back as. You know they say sometimes people die and come back as someone else or an animal. That kind of thing."

"And you know this how?" Jack asked.

"I know it because that goddamn dog is not of this world, and don't even think of trying to tell me that he is. See, you don't hear him barking, do you? That means I'm right. We are in the presence of . . . of . . . something."

"I am not going there, Harry. I am *never ever* going there, so just shut the hell up."

The moment Jack turned on his turn signal, Cooper unbuckled his seat belt. He leaned forward and nuzzled Jack's neck and ear. Jack went from relaxed to downright rigid.

"He's in a good position to sink those canines into your carotid artery or your jugular. You know that, right?" Harry said.

Cooper threw his head back and barked, then resumed the same position. Jack could feel the dog's warm, wet breath on his neck. "Rub my neck, Coop. Dig those paws into my shoulder blades. Ahhhh, that feels good. Good boy."

"You're an asshole, Jack," Harry said as he opened the car door before Jack could put the car in park. He sprinted across the courtyard to Myra's kitchen door, where she was waiting with one of Charles's jackets over her shoulders.

"Where's Yoko?"

"She couldn't make it, Harry. She called and said something came up and for you to head home as soon as you got here. She said to hurry. What's wrong? What happened?" Instead of responding, Harry ran back to the car.

"Jack, I need you to lend me your car. Yoko isn't here. She told Myra to have me come home right away. Stay, Cooper," Harry said, but he might as well have saved his breath. Cooper was already in the passenger seat and buckled up.

Jack tossed his keys to Harry. "You want me to come with you?"

"No. I'm going to speed, and I don't need you yelling at me. I'll call you. Here," he said, handing Jack his cell phone. "You need to charge this. I'll call you after I get home."

His mouth open, his eyes glazed, Jack watched Harry burn rubber as he backed out the Beemer and tore down the road to the gate, which was standing open.

"What the hell . . ."

They were all there suddenly, throwing questions at him as Nikki led him into the warm, fragrant kitchen.

"Talk to us!" Annie and Myra said at the same moment.

Chapter 3

Harry hadn't lied to Jack. He drove like a bat out of hell, Cooper growling his displeasure the entire time. Harry ignored him as he grumbled that he was in a hurry. Cooper growled louder. Twice, police cars pulled him over, but he flashed his special gold badge and was rewarded the second time around with a police escort to his dojo. He mumbled a quick word of thanks to the police officer, who simply stared at Harry and the dog while scratching his head and wondering who this off-beat character with the special shield was. The purple basket of dog toys and gear that he could see through the open car door mystified him even more. Maybe the dog was some kind of movie star. Yeah, he had heard that they were filming in town for some movie. He relished the idea that he would have something juicy to talk about when he returned to the precinct. Too bad it was a dog and not someone like Lindsay Lohan.

Minutes later, man and dog raced through the dojo to the stairs leading to the second floor. Harry shouted Yoko's name every step of the way, Cooper barking shrilly to announce their arrival.

Yoko was standing at the top of the steps, her hands out in front of her, the signal for Harry to grind to a halt. "What? What?" Harry bellowed. Cooper continued to bark. Harry was so relieved that his wife was all in one piece and okay, he flopped back against the wall to catch his breath. "What's the emergency?"

"Calm down. Take a deep breath, Harry. Then we are going to go into the kitchen. Oh, Cooper, it's good to see you. Welcome home!" Yoko said as she hugged the dog and tickled his ears. He allowed it, and when she was done, he beelined for the kitchen and started to howl.

"What the hell. . . ."

"Come along, dear. Mind your manners now," Yoko said in a voice that Harry could only describe as fierce.

Harry went through the kitchen doorway first, and his jaw dropped as he stared across the room at the tiny woman and two children huddled together. Teacups were on the table, along with rice cakes. Guests. No, not guests.

Jun Yu's family. His wife Jun Ling, daughter Gan, and son Hop. At the sight of Harry, Jun Ling burst into tears. The children huddled even closer.

"Do something, Harry," Yoko hissed. "And make Cooper stop barking. He's scaring the children."

One look from Harry, one light touch to Cooper's head, and the big dog grew silent. He sat back on his haunches, statue-still. Yoko sighed at the silence. Then Harry started talking in rapid-fire Chinese. His words shot out faster than a runaway train. Being Japanese, Yoko was only able to decipher every fifth word or so, and none of it made any sense to her. Though Jun Ling usually spoke pretty good English, as upset as she was, her English seemed to have deserted her, so Yoko continued to listen as Jun Ling, using her hands, spoke totally in Chinese just as fast as Harry had as she tried to say everything she needed to say.

It was something bad. Yoko could tell by the way Harry's head bowed and his shoulders sagged. It took a full ten minutes before the kitchen was once again silent. Yoko knew it was ten minutes because her eyes had been on the clock on the range the whole time.

"Harry, tell me, what's wrong?"

Harry turned around, his eyes wet as he stared at his wife. "This," he said, indicating Jun Ling and the children, "is what Jun Yu said he was sending me. What he wanted me to guard with my life because he told Jun Ling I was the only one he could trust. He managed to smuggle them to safety with just the clothes on their backs, Jun Ling's backpack, and the three *special* cell phones he gave them. He said they were not to use them until they were safely out of China."

"But why? What happened? Does she know?"

"No, she doesn't know. She just said Jun Yu was in trouble. Big trouble. He told her the less she knew, the safer she would be. She says she's not safe even here. She flew into New York, then from New York to here. Some of the same people on the plane from China followed her here. She thinks so, anyway. It's possible the people she's referring to had Washington, D.C., as their final destination, just as it was her final stop. As you can see, she is petrified, as are the children, and her English seems to have deserted her for the moment. Not surprising, given how upset she is."

"What are we going to do, Harry?"

"We're leaving right now. Get everything together, and we'll head out to Pinewood. I'll call Jack to alert him."

"Harry, there's nothing to get together. What you see is what there is. They arrived like this. Does she think they, whoever they are, followed her here to the dojo?"

Another rapid volley of Chinese. Harry shook his head as he punched out the number of Jack's cell phone. "She doesn't know. She said there were too many cars, and they all looked alike to her. The children are afraid of the dog."

Harry was surprised at how calm his voice suddenly became when he heard Jack say hello.

"Jesus, Harry, I've been counting the minutes till you got home. I was just going to call you when you called me. I had my finger on the send button."

"Why? Why were you calling me?"

"Because I have something to tell you, and I want you sitting down when I tell you. Tell me Yoko is there with you. Tell me that, Harry."

"Yes, Yoko is here. So is Cooper. So tell me what you have to tell me."

"You called me, so you go first. Is everything okay? What was the emergency?" Jack said, stalling for time.

"You remember that Jun Yu said he was sending me something I needed to guard with my life?"

"Yeah, yeah, I remember that. Did it get there? What is it?"

"His wife, Jun Ling, and his two kids, Hop and Gan. They're sitting here in my kitchen. They came with only the clothes on their backs and special cell phones, whatever the hell that means. Jun Ling said some of the same people who got on the plane with her in China traveled all the way with her to Washington. Asians. She came through Kennedy in New York to Dulles. She said Jun Yu managed to smuggle them out. I

want to bring them out to the farm, but first I
want you to call Jack Sparrow to have his
agents give us an escort. Then I want you to get
in touch with Pearl, so she can take this little
family to safety via her underground railroad.
Can you do that, Jack?"

"Well, yeah. I have you on speakerphone.
Annie and Myra are on it right now. Don't open
the door to anyone, Harry. Do you hear me?"

"I'm not stupid, Jack. What did you want to
tell me?"

"I don't think this is the time and the
phone . . . we can talk when you get here."

"Tell me now. Nothing can be worse than
this."

"You wanna bet? You know that old saying,
when it rains it pours? When I got here, Fergus
and Charles had C-SPAN on, and a bulletin
flashed across the screen. Just a bulletin, Harry,
with *no* details."

"Okay, I get it, a bulletin with no details. Do
I need to yank it out of you?"

"Jun Yu is dead. He was killed today. Actually, they used the word *slaughtered.*

"If I remember correctly, Jun Ling doesn't
speak English, and you said the kids are there,
so how are you going to handle this?"

"Very carefully but not here," Harry said, his
head reeling at the news and not bothering to
tell Jack that Jun Ling's English was usually
quite good. "Right now they're exhausted, and
I don't think Jun Ling can handle any more

bad news. You're sure, Jack, there's no mistake."

"Harry, I'm as sure as the bulletin I saw sliding across the screen. It's still running across. It's for real. Still no details. You okay, Harry?"

"No. How long before the agents get here?"

"Ten minutes," Harry heard Annie loudly in the background. "Be downstairs waiting. Two agents, Panellie and Dante. We'll be waiting for you to get here. And Pearl should be here by the time you and the others arrive. We have it covered, Harry."

"I'm going to China," Harry said.

"We're all going to China but not right this minute. The girls are on it, Harry. They're waiting for Yoko. You know they don't make a move until everyone is present," Jack said, coming back to the phone. "Easy does it, buddy. See ya when you get here."

Harry looked down at the phone in his hand, then over at his wife, who was staring at him, her eyes narrowed. How much to tell her? Everything, by the expression on her face. He swallowed hard as he led her from the room and whispered what Jack had told him. Yoko's hands flew to her face as she fell into Harry's arms.

"Don't tell them. Not yet. I'm so sorry, Harry. I know how much you loved Jun Yu, and he you. Proof is sitting in our kitchen. Of all the people in the whole world, he chose you to safeguard his little family. We must honor that wish."

Harry's head bobbed. "Gather them up and meet me downstairs. Do we take Cooper or leave him here?"

There was no need for Yoko to respond, because Cooper had his one-eared rabbit with its half tail in his mouth. He was ready to go. So ready, he beat Harry to the steps and the workout room. He settled himself by the steel door as a sentinel.

Harry reached down to pat Cooper's head. "This is something I never expected. I don't know if I can handle this, Cooper." Cooper whined to show he understood.

The knock when it came seemed exceptionally loud to Harry. He leaned in closer in time to hear the words, "Agents Panellie and Dante. We have orders from Director Sparrow to transport you and your family to Pinewood. Are you ready, Mr. Wong?"

Harry opened the door to admit the two agents. "Wait here, and I'll gather up the family."

Dante, the taller of the two, looked at Cooper sitting by Harry and said, "No one said anything about a dog."

Harry stopped in his tracks. "The dog goes with us. He's the reason we have to leave. What's it going to be?"

Panellie was whispering on the phone. When he ended the call, he said, "Director Sparrow said the dog goes. Can you speed this up, Mr. Wong?"

"Sure thing, Mr. Super Agent," Harry muttered as he raced through the workout room, down the hall, then up the steps, bellowing every step of the way. All he could hear was rapid-fire Chinese that sounded like curses to him, crying kids, and Yoko screeching in Japanese.

Harry whistled between his teeth, a sharp, shrill sound that created immediate silence. "That's better. Let's go. The agents are waiting for us."

"Is it safe, Harry?" Yoko whispered.

"As safe as two special agents of the FBI can make it be is my guess. Plus, we have Cooper."

Outside, everyone piled into a dark-colored van that said MONGELLO HEATING & AIR on the side panels in stark white lettering. The doors slid open. Yoko went in first, then helped the kids and Jun Ling. Next, Cooper hopped in, his rabbit between his teeth. Harry climbed in last and yanked at the door. He immediately set the lock before he settled back in his seat for the forty-five-minute ride to Pinewood.

"Crap! I forgot my phone again. Yoko, did you bring yours?"

"No. It's on the kitchen counter charging right next to yours."

Harry closed his eyes and leaned back as he tried to come to terms with what was happening all around him. He refused to allow thoughts of his daughter to enter his head. Maybe Jack was right, and he was losing his edge.

Forty minutes later, Harry found himself standing in Myra and Charles's kitchen. Explanations happened quick and fast, with everyone offering an opinion. He moved off to the side of the kitchen, out of the way. The others could handle things now. He'd gotten everyone here in one piece. He needed to do something right now.

Find your center, Harry, he warned himself. *Work outward. Find your center. Clear your mind.* He moved then from one plane to the next, his breathing evening out until he was at peace with his body and his soul.

Yoko watched her husband and knew exactly what he was doing. She sighed with relief as she stared at the family across from her. How lost they were, how sad. She knew they would all be devastated when Harry told them about Jun Yu. She was devastated, and she barely knew the man, but Harry always said he was a brother to him.

Annie looked around Myra's overflowing kitchen. "I think we need to relocate to the family room. Harry can stay here as long as need be. Hustle, people," she said as she watched Myra herd Jun Ling and the two children forward.

The youngsters were clinging to their mother's legs, their eyes filled with terror at the gaggle of people all talking at once.

"Where the hell is Pearl?" Kathryn bellowed.

"Five minutes out," Nikki shouted back.

All seven dogs, not knowing what to do either, followed Cooper's silent orders and lined up in front of the fireplace, then sat back on their haunches to await further orders.

Ted Robinson scribbled notes in a ratty notebook he kept in his back pocket as he muttered to Maggie, who just looked befuddled at what was going on. Espinosa discreetly snapped pictures of the mother and her children.

"I'm going outside to wait for Pearl. I don't want her coming through the kitchen door and disturbing Harry. I'll bring her through the front," Jack said.

Charles stepped forward to where Jun Ling was cowering and held out his cell phone and asked for hers. She shook her head no. Charles nodded yes and held out his hand. Jun Ling started to cry and speak in Chinese. The children wailed at the top of their lungs. The dogs howled but did not move out of position. In the end, Charles had the three special phones in his hand.

Fergus looked at Annie and shrugged. "If the phones were the last thing her husband gave her, then that's why she's unwilling to part with hers and the ones the children were clutching in their hands. I understand that. We need Harry to speak to her but not until he's ready."

"This is not going to go well," Kathryn muttered as she remembered the last dustup she had had with Pearl and her rules of secrecy.

"No, dear, it isn't," Myra agreed as she finally gave up trying to appease the children. "They are frightened out of their wits. We need to keep that in mind."

"Yeah, well, I'm thinking that mother does understand *some* English and is playing stupid. Harry told us all back when Lily entered the monastery that she would be learning Chinese and those children from China would be learning English. So there is a good chance the boy Hop knows some English, as do his mother and sister. For all we know, the father might have told them to pretend they don't understand. The way things are going now just does not work for me."

"You want to bring it to a test?" Isabelle asked. "If so, corner Pearl when she gets here and threaten to separate the children from the mother. That should give you your answer."

"That sounds . . . cruel," Alexis said.

"Do you have a better idea?" Kathryn snapped.

Alexis was saved from replying by Jack and Pearl's appearance in the family room. Once again, everyone started talking at once. The dogs remained in place, with Cooper growling low in his throat. But he didn't advance or make any other move.

Jack whistled sharply. The room went silent to give Pearl the floor. "One person, talk. Everyone else, keep quiet," Pearl said as she eyed the three newcomers.

Myra explained the situation right down to Kathryn's opinion. Everyone in the room knew that Pearl and Kathryn were not bosom buddies and that Kathryn had brought Pearl to her knees twice when she refused to divulge information the sisters needed. To those keeping score it was Kathryn 2 and Pearl 0. Pearl kept nodding to show she understood what was needed and expected.

"I admit we came up with this scenario on the fly, Pearl, but we thought if we could spirit them across the field to our farmhouse, you could take it from there just in case anyone followed them out here. The agents said there were no tails, but those Chinese are a slippery group," Nikki said. "If we can get them to our house, can you take it from there?"

"I will need to make some calls first, but I think it's doable."

"And we need to know where they are at all times," Kathryn said. "That is not negotiable, Pearl."

Pearl sighed. She didn't have the stamina to go up against Kathryn yet again, so she simply nodded.

Harry took that moment to enter the kitchen. Jack looked at him sharply. Okaaay, this was the old Harry, bright-eyed and bushy-tailed. Jack brought him up to speed within minutes. Harry nodded. He nodded again when Jack told him Kathryn's opinion and surprised Jack even more when Harry said that Jun Ling had a fair command of English. He did not, however, think she was faking an inability to understand but that, as upset as she was by what was going on, her English had pretty much deserted her.

"What's our plan?" Charles asked.

"I think we should do it Nikki's way. Turn all the floodlights off outside. We will take them across the field to Jack and Nikki's by way of the pickup truck with a tarp spread over the passengers in the back. We can drive without lights since there is no traffic to take into account."

"That should work," Jack said, his eyes on Pearl, who was talking quietly on her cell, her head bobbing as she listened to the voice on the other end of the line. She hung up and nodded to Jack.

"How much time do we have?" Nikki asked.

"Forty minutes," Pearl said flatly.

Jack looked at Harry. "The floor is all yours."

Harry looked across the room at Cooper, who was at his side in a nanosecond.

The sisters looked from one to the other as Harry rattled on at the speed of light. He was rewarded with moans, groans, tears, and sobs. Harry remained steely-eyed as he gathered up Jun Ling and carried her over to Pearl. He stood her upright and rattled off a string of Chinese. He went back and grabbed the children and carried them under his arms.

"Go!"

Annie looked at Yoko. "Did he tell them Jun Yu is dead?"

"Yes. That's why they gave up the fight. What happens now?"

"I guess the boys will come back here once Pearl's people take over. You do all understand that there is no way we could leave that mother and her children on the loose while we go to China," Annie said.

"Of course we all understand that," Fergus said. "It was the perfect solution. Actually, if you stop to think about it, it was the *only* solution. When we leave, we'll be knowing they are safe. Starting a mission with something like that hanging over our heads simply would not work."

They all agreed. Even Kathryn.

Myra looked over at her husband. "I think we could all use something to drink, and possibly something to eat, Charles. This has been a very hectic evening, and I see it getting still more hectic."

"It will be my pleasure. Come along, Fergus, let's leave the ladies to whatever it is they want to do or say that they don't want us to hear."

Chapter 4

Charles Martin risked a glance at the sisters and brothers over the top of the bank of computers he and Fergus Duffy were working on. He took a step back and looked over at Fergus, his right hand. "I don't think I've ever seen them look so . . . so . . ."

"*Pissed off* is the term you're looking for, mate. Can't say as how you're wrong since I agree. From this vantage point, all I can see is snapping, snarling, angry men and women. It would appear to me that not a single one of them is in the mood to listen to anything we might have to say. They're used to dealing in action. They want to *DO* something. And they want to *DO* it now. As in *now*, Charles."

"I know, I know. But the simple truth is that that is not going to happen. Not until we come up with a plan that is foolproof. We can't just send them into China willy-nilly and not expect repercussions. We don't even really know what we're dealing with here. Oh dear, now they're all stomping their feet."

"That means they're tired of waiting for you to . . . um . . . get on the stick and advise them. Tread carefully, my friend. Very carefully. Time to blow that whistle you have hanging around your neck."

Charles took a deep breath and exhaled slowly before he clicked the remote device that turned the switch on the huge monitor that hung from the top of the dais that would reveal Lady Justice in all her glory. He was rewarded with instant silence and surly looks. But there was always respect for the scales of justice.

"You're not scaring me, ladies and gentlemen, so get rid of those surly looks and focus on what I'm going to tell you. That's an order unless you vote to impeach me, and if you do that, then Fergus goes with me. Just so you know. Ah, that's better," Charles said when he saw a small smile work its way to Myra's lips.

"For starters Ms. Jun Ling and her children are on their way to safety via Pearl's underground railroad. That means they are no longer a cause of worry for any of us. Second, Jun Yu is dead. We will mourn his passing later on. For now there is nothing we can do since he has passed to the land of his ancestors. Our imme-

diate concern is the child, Lily Wong, Harry
and Yoko's daughter, because we cannot account for her presence at this moment in time.

"Having said that, we need to form a plan. A
plan that will work for all of us. I want to repeat
the 'all of us' part again. Harry and Yoko, you
are to sit on the side. We cannot have you in-
terfering with the plan, because you are both
too emotional right now. You have to trust us,
your friends, all of us here in this room, to do
the right thing. You also want to avenge Jun
Yu, whom you consider a brother. We will help
you to achieve vengeance for your brother,
too. But only when we come up with a plan
that benefits us all.

"Last but not least, we all know, though perhaps Myra, Annie, and I know more than any
of you, that there is nothing worse in the whole
world than losing a child. We will find Lily or
die trying. Do you understand me?"

Harry chewed on his lower lip, his eyes like
angry storm clouds. He nodded, as Yoko wept
on his shoulder.

"One last question. Are all your calls still going
straight to voice mail?" Harry nodded again.

"Do you have a plan, Charles?" Jack asked.

"Not yet, but I'm working on it. Fergus and I
need another few hours to gather all our information. I am also waiting to hear from Avery
Snowden in regard to what Jun Ling referred
to as the *special* phones that her husband gave
her and the children when he arranged to have

them smuggled out of China to the United States. We're hoping Jun Yu somehow provided us with clues that he felt Harry would be able to figure out. Since time is of the essence, I suggest you all catch a bit of a nap and return here to the war room in two hours. Annie, you can alert the pilot of your Gulfstream. Have him and his crew on standby. Myra, call Jack Sparrow at the FBI and clue him in. Have him expedite all the passports and whatever else we need to get into China. Ask him if he would like to make the trip with us. He will probably decline, saying he can be more help here on the ground, but ask him anyway. Any questions?"

In a scratchy-sounding voice, Dennis West asked if he needed shots or a visa.

"Myra will help with all that. No visa is required. We have a doctor on call who can come out to the farmhouse at an hour's notice and take care of whatever needs to be done. The truth is we all need a physical of sorts before we leave, so someone arrange that ASAP."

"Are we all going?" Maggie asked.

"I assume so. Since the flight time from Dulles to China is about fourteen and a half hours, it is questionable for Abner with his ear problems. He will have to make that decision himself after his physical. All right, then, if there are no other questions, you can all return to the house, and Fergus and I will do what has to be done down here. Two hours tops, ladies and gentlemen."

When the door closed behind the chattering group, Charles threw his hands in the air and stomped his way down into the main part of the war room, where he plopped down in Myra's chair. Fergus joined him, sitting in Annie's chair.

"This is not going to be a walk in the park, Fergus. China is . . . is . . ."

"The last place anyone in their right mind wants to travel to. We need to be ever mindful that Harry might try to take matters into his own hands and try to go on his own. If that were to happen, I can almost guarantee that he will be red-flagged. He'll never get into China on his own."

"I know, I know. At this moment in time, we are totally dependent on FBI director Sparrow and Avery Snowden. Snowden has the contacts and the people. He should have gotten back to us about those special phones by now.

"Fergus, what about your old contacts at Scotland Yard?"

"I've contacted all of them. No one has gotten back to me as yet. We need time, Charles. I sense a certain impatience in you, and that's not who you are. I've always thought of you as a slow-and-steady, leave-no-stone-unturned kind of operative. This is just another case for the boys and girls. So, mate, tell me what's really eating at you?"

"The child—Lily. I think you and I both know she's being held hostage with the other children. Jun Yu told Harry he tried to get her out but was unsuccessful. And yet he got his son and daughter out. That's bothering me."

"Perhaps the children from outside China are separated from those inside, and he didn't know where or how to locate her. I'm inclined to believe him, Charles."

"Yes, yes. But I don't think Harry believes him, for some reason. It's just a gut feeling, nothing more. All he sees is that Jun Yu got his boy out and girl out but left Lily behind. And, of course, any resentment he holds for Jun for not telling him that he was Jun Yu's equal in the martial arts and was equally deserving of being named the number one martial-arts expert in the world. Yes, he denies it, but even so.

"Anyway, right now Harry is not thinking too clearly. His daughter is foremost on his mind; Yoko's, too. And that is as it should be. Any parent would feel the same way, helpless. Then there is the death of a man Harry considered a brother. Add the arrival of that brother's family, which the dead man sent to him for safekeeping, and Harry Wong's plate is filled to overflowing.

"The only positive thing right now is that Jun Yu's family is safe, thanks to Pearl and her underground railroad. At least that worry is not hanging over our heads as we move forward."

Charles stared up at Lady Justice. "I don't have a good feeling about this mission, Fergus. This one is different. If it were any country but

China, I might not be so worried. The Chinese do not play by our rules, we all know that."

Fergus struggled to find words that he hoped would portray confidence. "Having said that, Charles, the Chinese have never come up against the Sisterhood. Look lively here, mate, and tell me. If you were a betting man, where would you place your bet?"

Charles knew what he was supposed to answer, but the words stuck in his throat. "The special gold shields won't work in China. Do you know anything about Chinese prisons, Fergus?"

"A thing or two. I don't exactly live in a cocoon, Charles. I know more about Chinese prisons than I care to, thanks to all my years in service at Scotland Yard. I assume you have no intention of notifying the State Department that we will be visiting China."

Charles gave off a snappy salute to Lady Justice before he climbed the three steps that would take him to his workstation, where Fergus was waiting for him. "In a manner of speaking. Tell me what you think of this . . . plan? Subject to change, of course."

"I'm all ears, mate."

"We go in as a tour group. Crescent China Tours. We have Lizzie Fox backstop us, set up a dummy company that's been in business for like twenty-five or thirty years. She knows how to do all that. She can have CCT incorporated within an hour, and up and running in two hours. She can come up with everything we will need, and if she requires Avery's help, he will be available. Jack Sparrow can help, and he has sources we can only dream about. Then there's Annie. As she is fond of saying, money talks and bullshit walks. If she's willing to spend, and people are willing to buy what she's selling, I think we can make it all come together to make it work for us."

Fergus's jaw dropped. His eyes were round as saucers as he stared at Charles in admiration. "I guess that's why they pay you the big bucks. In a million years, I never would have thought of something like that. It's pure genius, Charles. Absolutely pure genius. One small question. Who is going to plot out the tour?"

"You are! Avery just sent a text. He should be here in about fifteen minutes. He has news. With all the information Harry gave you, and using Google, you can map out something that will pass muster. In the end, it won't matter because that's just a tour on paper for anyone who needs to check it on the Chinese end. Once we arrive on Chinese soil, we will be going in an entirely different direction. Get cracking, Fergus. I'll call Lizzie now and have her get on it right away. Make sure when you do your bogus itinerary that you do not put the tour group anywhere near Song Mountain. I also think we should go via Hong Kong, as that's where Jun Yu sent his wife and children to get them to Harry in Washington, D.C. Hong Kong must have been important to Jun Yu for some reason. I think those special phones are going to give us the answers we're looking for."

"I'm on it, Charles."

While Fergus went about his assigned tasks, Charles dialed Lizzie's personal cell phone number in Las Vegas from memory. He let loose with a huge sigh of relief when she picked up on the second ring. Sensing the urgency in Charles's voice, she got right to the point. "Tell me what you need, when you need it, and I'll take it from there."

Ten minutes later, Charles clicked off. Fergus raised his head from the computer keyboard he was working at to see his partner raise his clenched fist to indicate done and done. He grinned, knowing that Lizzie Fox could outmaneuver anyone, and that included the Chinese government. Suddenly, his heart felt lighter.

He went back to work with a new intensity and didn't look up again until he sensed another presence in the war room. Avery Snowden had arrived. Charles continued to work, knowing that if he was needed, someone would call his name.

Charles once again descended the steps to join Snowden at the conference table so as not to distract Fergus. "I hope you are bringing some good news. I don't mind telling you, Avery, this little caper has my undies in a bit of a twist. *China* is a foul word these days."

"I hear you, Sir Charles. I do have a bit of news. It will be up to you to decide if it's good or bad. I daresay I have to agree with you about China."

Charles clucked his tongue. "Are you ever going to stop calling me Sir Charles? We're in America now, and titles mean nothing. I'm just plain old Charles Martin. You know I no longer go by Sir Malcolm Sutcliff. That was another world ago. I mean it, old chap, from here on in it is simply Charles and Avery. Or Martin and Snowden, if you prefer. Now, tell me what you have for me."

Snowden shrugged as he stared at the man who had once controlled his life while working for the Queen. It was a hard habit to break, and he wasn't sure he could ever show a lack of respect for the man who had saved his young life on too many occasions to count by calling him Charles. "Those phones. Your man Jun Yu must know some very powerful Americans because those *special* phones are used only by the CIA. You can't go into a Radio Shack and pick one up, nor can you buy them on the black market. I have it on good authority that only a certain number were made and, apparently, according to my source, all of them are accounted for, which I find remarkable. And, of course, that is manifestly untrue since I have three of them sitting in my pocket right now. My source asked countless questions on how I even knew about them. I kept mum, just said

I'd heard a rumor. That means someone is lying, but right now we don't have to worry about that."

"All right. Now, tell me what all that means."

"I don't know what it means, Si—, um, Charles. All three phones are programmed with one name and one phone number. In Hong Kong. Am I right in saying Jun Ling and the children came through Hong Kong?"

"Yes. What's the name?" Charles asked.

Snowden grinned. "Dishbang Deshi. It means protect the country. I don't think its meaning is of any importance to us—perhaps not to anyone else, for that matter. The phone number is in Hong Kong. I did some research, and Dishbang Deshi lives in Kowloon and owns an export company. He has a showroom on Silk Road in Hong Kong. He specializes in silks. He's quite wealthy. He's married, with seven daughters. But, Charles, here is the kicker. He was a student at the monastery with Jun Yu and Harry Wong. I guess the three of them hung out together or whatever it is kids do who go to a monastery. In other words, they have been friends for ages. So that means Jun Yu was comfortable sending his family to Dishbang Deshi to make sure they made it to America and Harry Wong.

"Oh, before you can ask, no, I did not try to call the number. I thought that would be something you or the ladies would want to do, or maybe Harry. But somebody had better call

that number, and soon, would be my advice.
For all we know, the guy could be waiting on
pins and needles to help us and also to know if
Jun Ling and the kids arrived safely."

Charles nodded. "My thoughts exactly. I assume you saw everyone upstairs when you came
through. We'll be reconvening in"—Charles
looked down at his watch—"about an hour.
We'll discuss it then. You're welcome to stay unless you have something you need to do."

"I need to get my team ready. Three days,
four? What's our timetable for departure, and
do I go with the crew or do we go separately?
Right, right, too early to make that decision.
Shoot me a text when you have something
concrete."

Avery reached behind to pull out a sheaf of
papers from the backpack he was never without.
He tossed it to Charles. "This is all the research
on Dishbang Deshi. By the way, Dishbang Deshi
did not, I say did *not*, send any of his daughters
to the monastery like Harry and Jun Yu did.
He married an American woman, and she would
not allow it. That information might come in
handy when you present it to Harry."

Once the door closed behind Avery, Charles
sat for a few moments as he tried to digest
everything Avery had just told him. There was
a monkey in the woodpile somewhere. He was
sure of it. He flipped through the stack of papers and glanced at the highlighted areas. His

eyes narrowed more than once. He didn't know why, but he felt like he was missing something. Something that in another place, another time, would have jumped out at him and bitten him on the nose. Maybe he was getting too old to play in the big leagues. Maybe he was losing his edge. The thought scared him half to death, because the sisters depended on him to get it right. The thought of any one of them languishing in a Chinese prison was enough to bring on a head rush, the likes of which he'd never felt before. "Not on my bloody watch!" he bellowed.

Fergus poked his head around the corner of the computer he was working on. "Did you say something, Charles?"

"Not really. I was talking to myself. You know how I like to do that when I'm working on a problem that I can't solve in an instant. I'll figure it out. How are you doing with the tour?"

"It's coming along. Two days in Hong Kong for starters. I don't know why but I think, and Charles, it's just a feeling, but Hong Kong is somehow crucial to all of this. I can't be more specific—just a gut feeling and more than forty years at Scotland Yard is the best I can come up with by way of an explanation."

Charles nodded in agreement. How well he understood that vague, uneasy feeling that could only be traced back to years at MI6 and his childhood friend, Lizzie, the reigning Queen of

England. Before this was all over, he just might have to enlist her aid. Just the thought that he could made him feel better immediately.

"All right then, Fergus, you show me what you have, and I'll show you what I have."

Fergus laughed out loud. "So that's how it's going to be, eh, mate?"

Charles barked a laugh, then his shoulders shook. The tension left his body and he was back in the groove. A bit of levity worked every time.

Well, almost every time.

Chapter 5

Myra's kitchen was like a hive, with everyone buzzing like furious bees. Food prepared by Dennis West was being served and gobbled down helter-skelter by the sisters and the boys. Ted Robinson was adding logs to the fireplace in the kitchen, which was big enough to roast an ox. A monster *swoosh* of flame shot upward, sending the dogs scurrying, except for Cooper, who sat and stared into the flames as though mesmerized.

Myra toyed with her tuna sandwich and the pickles on her plate. Annie watched her, wondering why she wasn't fingering the pearls that adorned her neck and she was never without. "What has you worried, my friend?" Annie leaned closer to ask.

"Harry and Yoko. I've never seen either one of them this quiet. That's probably not quite true. Harry rarely says much. I've never seen Yoko so . . . so . . . weepy. Sometimes, I think she's stronger than Harry. And, Annie, as hard as I try, I can't get our last trip to China out of my mind. I'm talking about my . . ."

"Don't say it, Myra. I know what you're thinking. While I wasn't here at the time for that little caper, I heard every single detail, so I know it by heart. You made that heartless bastard with diplomatic immunity pay for killing your daughter. Don't go there, Myra, please. Let that go. We made a pact not to live in the past, and that's what you're doing, and you need to stop right now. We need to all be on the same page for Harry and Yoko's sake. We *will* save Lily. And then we will wreak whatever vengeance we need to wreak in the process. Tell me you're with me, Myra."

Myra's shoulders straightened imperceptibly. Her right hand went to her pearls while her left hand picked up her sandwich. She took a huge bite and looked across the room at Dennis, who was waiting for a compliment. She nodded, and he smiled.

All was good.

The old-fashioned wall phone took that moment to ring. Kathryn was the closest, so she picked it up, and they all heard her say, "Okay."

"What?" Nikki demanded.

"Our fearless leader is ready for us in the war room."

Harry was off his seat like he'd been shot out of a cannon and was on his way out of the kitchen when he turned around as he remembered his wife. She ran after him.

The dogs decided to voice an opinion, but their barking was cut short when Cooper started to herd them all into the family room. The sudden silence was almost deafening.

"That dog scares the living hell out of me," Alexis whispered to Isabelle. "I think he . . . I think he isn't . . . *real.* He looks real, acts real, but I think he's . . . a *spirit* or something. What do you think, Isabelle?" Her voice was so fretful, Isabelle shivered.

"Let's just, you know, pretend he's real, okay? That way we won't have to worry about . . . whatever it is we're worrying about."

"That doesn't make any sense," Alexis said.

"I know. Move, Alexis, or they'll close the door on us, and we'll be stuck up here with the dogs and . . . and Cooper." That's all Alexis had to hear. She picked up her feet and ran to the opening that would take them down the old, moss-covered stone steps to the war room.

Once inside, no one spoke as they took their seats. To the naked eye, nothing had changed except that Charles's sparse hair was a little more askew and Fergus seemed more agitated, but nobody dared to mention it. The only sound to be heard was the clatter of the computer keys and the whirring of the fax machine. They waited, each busy with his or her thoughts, their eyes on Lady Justice.

Harry kept his eyes on the oversize watch on his wrist, his breathing slow and shallow. When the minute hand turned over for the tenth time, he rose from his chair just as Charles and Fergus descended the steps into the major part of the war room. He sat down immediately, his eyes narrow and speculative. Yoko reached for his hand and squeezed it. Harry squeezed back.

Charles spoke bullet fast to make up for lost time. "Lizzie is incorporating Crescent China Tours and backstopping everything. We need three days. Actually, five days would be ideal, but we all know time is of the essence here. I'm sorry, Harry, it's the best we can do to ensure safety for everyone. As much as you don't like it, you will have to accept it. If there were a way to speed this up, you know we would do it.

"We, Fergus and I, have come up with what we think is the perfect entry into China, via Hong Kong using Crescent China Tours. A gambling junket for us all. Annie's owning Babylon in Vegas gives the whole trip credibility. Our story is she is considering building a casino in Macau. Two days in Hong Kong, time to get some clothing and shoes made to order, buy some jade, and have high tea at the Peninsula Hotel. From there it's an hour-long ferry ride to Macau, where all the gambling is done. Everything legitimate and aboveboard. If I'm not mistaken, there are several Vegas casinos already in Macau. Gambling is a very, very big business in China. Actually, it's one of their major industries as far as I can tell. No one will give us all a second thought or look. You only go to Macau to gamble. It will be as legitimate as we can make it. A day or so to set the wheels in motion, then we take off for Song Mountain. I don't exactly know how we're going to do that. Yet. We're working on it."

Annie jumped up off her chair. "Good Lord, do you know how absolutely perfect that is, Charles?" Without waiting for a response, she prattled on, excitement ringing in her voice. "Bert and I have been having discussions this whole past year on whether we want to take our business to Macau. He's made two trips already to scout it out and lay the groundwork. We've had dozens of meetings with our lawyers, who think it's a great idea. I've been dragging my feet for some reason, and I don't know why. Wynn has a casino there, and the Sands also. Bert was in talks with both owners just last week. Did you know that, Charles? Of course you didn't, because I never told you," Annie said, answering her own question. "I think we should call Bert and alert him and take him with us. He's going to need some time to arrange things in his absence. Oh, oh, this is just so perfect. Now, I'm feeling a whole lot better about this junket to China."

"Well, I'm not. We're talking five days here on American soil, then another four or so once we hit China. That's practically ten whole days!" Harry exploded. "Do you know what could happen to my daughter in *ten* days? Already with this plan of yours, we're into next week. This is not going to work for me."

"It has to work, Harry. Right now, you're dealing emotionally while the rest of us are dealing with the reality of a trip into China to do a rescue. First of all, no one with half a brain would try that without proper government sponsorship. But . . . we're going to do it, so that means we have to make sure our plan is foolproof. I am as sure as I can be that your daughter is safe. She might be a hostage with the other children, but they're also safe. If you need further proof, just ask yourself why Cooper isn't sitting by the door or crawling up your leg to get this show on the road. That damn dog knows Lily is safe, and he knows we're working it. Get with the program here, Harry," Jack said firmly but not unkindly.

"Or?" Harry snarled.

"Don't go there," Jack snarled in return.

"We're good here, Jack," Yoko said softly. "We understand."

"All right then, moving along here," Charles said, his tone indicating relief that things were back on an even keel. "Avery Snowden tells us the special phones Jun Ling and her children had on them are one of a kind. As in CIA special. Where Jun Yu got them is a mystery, which means we will probably never know. Avery tells us that the same name and phone number are programmed into each phone. No, he did not call the number. On the off chance, I'm sure, that they might self-destruct. As in *Mission Impossible*. That kind of thing. There is just no way of knowing, since none of us has ever seen such a phone."

"Whose number is it? What is the name?" Yoko asked. "Is it anyone we know?"

Charles looked at Harry. "We do know that much. The number belongs to someone named Dishbang Deshi. Avery said the man runs an import-export business in Hong Kong. His showroom is on Silk Road. He imports and exports raw silk. He's quite wealthy, is married, and has seven daughters, none of whom go to the Shaolin Monastery because Dishbang Deshi's American wife will not allow it. I understand that you know this man, Harry."

Harry's face registered pure shock. "Very well, as a matter of fact. The three of us were at the Shaolin Monastery as boys. We're the same age. We were like brothers without the bloodline. We palled around together as much as it was allowed. You could say we bonded out of necessity back then. We swore our lives to each other. Dishbang Deshi was every bit as good at martial arts as Jun Yu and I. But he didn't take it as seriously as the two of us did. He wanted to have fun, and having fun was not something the monks approved of. In many ways, I think Jun and I would have cut and run during the early years but for Dishbang Deshi. He kept us level, if you know what I mean. In his own way, he taught us not to take ourselves so seriously. He wanted us to know there was a life outside the monastery, and we needed to know that so we could survive once we left the monks. He had a different upbringing than Jun Yu and I. Dishbang Deshi came from wealth. The Jun family and the Wongs were simple farmers. Neither of our families or we knew anything of the world outside the farm and the monastery. Dishbang Deshi educated us. To the monks' chagrin, I might add.

"I talk to Dishbang Deshi perhaps twice a year. If there is a trial, a contest, or an exhibition, then I see both of them more often. None of us ever missed an event. Jun Yu and Dishbang Deshi saw each other more often because they both still lived in China. Jun Yu used to go to Hong Kong on a regular basis, mini-vacations if you will. He was always granted special privileges because of his status. Now it's starting to make sense to me that Jun Yu would smuggle his family to Hong Kong and trust Dishbang Deshi to get them to me here in America. Why haven't you called the number? What are you all waiting for?"

"We want *you* to call. Your friend will talk openly to you as opposed to someone he doesn't know. At least I'm hoping he will. There is no speaker feature on these phones. We want you to call the number, and we want you to speak English. Dishbang Deshi does speak English, doesn't he?"

"Fluently. He has to because of the business he runs. Give me the phone, and I'll call him. What's the time now?"

"We're good timewise. I'm thinking it wouldn't matter if it were the middle of the night, if he's expecting you to call him."

Jack wondered if he was the only one to notice the tremor in Harry's hands as he reached for the phone. In all the years he'd known Harry, this was the first time he'd ever seen Harry anything but rock solid. Seeing what he was seeing set his stomach into turmoil. He felt rather than saw Nikki's hand on his arm. She had noticed it, too. Her touch calmed him right away, much the way Yoko's touch could calm Harry.

The room was deathly quiet as Harry hit the programmed number on the strange-looking cell phone. Jack didn't realize that he'd been holding his breath until he heard Harry say, "It's Harry, Dishbang Deshi. Talk to me." He listened for a full two minutes before he said, "The three of them are safe. Even the triads can't find them." He listened again, longer this time, four minutes, Jack thought as he stared at his watch. It felt like an eternity.

Harry spoke again. "What do you mean *you* aren't safe? You sent your family back to the States yesterday. Why are you so worried? You need to tell me right now what is going on if you want my help. I don't want any bullshit, either, Dishbang Deshi. Stop beating around the bush and tell me straight out what's going on. Not what you *think* is going on, what is actually going on. Jun Ling said she knows nothing, only that Jun Yu said he was in trouble. How's that possible, that she doesn't know what kind of trouble her husband was in? Don't go giving me that crap that this is America, and we do things differently here. Pillow talk is the same the world over." Harry listened again, this time for five minutes, according to Jack's watch. An eternity.

"Three days, four at the most. I can't tell you that. You'll see me when you see me is the best I can offer you right now. I have one question, Dishbang Deshi. Why didn't you help Jun Yu?" Harry listened, his mouth a grim, tight line in his face. Two minutes this time, Jack thought. Back among the living. That was good.

"I want to know about my daughter. I don't care about your sorry ass or how many excuses you come up with. Nor do I care about the two tons of silk you need to ship. You should have been there for him. You should have *sensed* he was in trouble, Dishbang Deshi. Didn't you learn anything at the monastery? Now tell me again why Jun Yu couldn't get my daughter when he snatched his son Hop and daughter Gan." Harry's shoulders sagged as he listened to the voice on the other end of the line. Then he shrugged and tossed the phone to Charles. "It's dead."

"Talk to us, Harry," Myra said gently.

"Dishbang Deshi did a lot of talking, but he really doesn't know anything. He said when Jun Yu called him he was vague and wouldn't confide in him. He said Jun Yu told him the less he knew, the less he could be blamed for if things turned dicey. That's how Jun Yu was. He did, however, scare Dishbang Deshi enough that he sent his family to the States. Mississippi, to be precise. He said the watchers, that's what he called them, which translates to the triads, would be no match for the bubbas in Mississippi. He got word a short while ago that his entire family is safe and in the bosom of his wife's family. He said he knows he himself is being watched. He's scared. No, that's wrong; Dishbang Deshi is petrified."

"But why?" Annie demanded.

"He doesn't know. He thinks it has something to do with gambling. The monks are a peaceful lot and not into deviousness. There's a new Abbot at the monastery, and he's not exactly in favor. He said he's heard rumors over the past year, since the new Abbot took over, that there is a faction that wants to commer-

cialize the whole province. He has no proof.
He thinks Jun Yu had the proof, but he isn't
sure. Dishbang Deshi is living at his place of
business now that his family is gone. He says
there are a lot of people around him to protect
him and also to warn him if they sense trouble.
He is anxious for me to get there. He doesn't
want to end up like Jun Yu.

"He said, the day Jun Yu went to get his son
Hop and daughter Gan, he didn't know the
foreign students had been moved several days
before. His son told him that men came, a lot
of men, who walked with the Abbot and took
all the foreigners away. And some of the older
Chinese. Hop did not know where they were
taken so he couldn't advise his father. Dishbang Deshi said Jun Yu wanted to stay to try to
find Lily, but the people with him said it was
too dangerous and that they had to leave. I believe him. For whatever it's worth," Harry said
sadly.

Maggie Spritzer let loose with a very unladylike sound. "So where does all this leave us?"

Charles looked up at the bank of clocks on
the back wall that told the time all over the
world. They hung directly behind Lady Justice.
"Where that leaves us right at this precise moment is where we are. It's late. I suggest you all
try to catch some sleep, and we'll reconvene in
the morning. Fergus and I will be working here
throughout the night. By morning, we should

have something significant to report. All of you, stop looking at me like I'm some kind of ogre. Fergus and I are just two people. We do have other people working with us, but they also need time to gather information and get it to us, at which point we'll know better how things will work." Charles's voice took on an edge of steel when he said, "If any of you think you can do a better job, have at it. If not, skedaddle and let us do what we do best."

Skedaddle? Now that's a word I haven't heard in at least a hundred years, Jack thought. He risked a glance at Harry, who looked like he was ready to explode any second.

Topside, which meant the kitchen, Jack took Harry aside, and said, "Let's take all the dogs for a run. Across the field. You need it more than they do, Harry, so let's do it. You need to lighten up, or this whole thing is going to come crashing down around all of us. You know in your gut that Charles is doing all he can. He loves Lily just the way we all do. We're gonna make it work. You need to believe that. If you don't, I'm going to kick that scrawny ass of yours all the way to the Canadian border. Now, what's it going to be?"

Harry was saved from responding when Cooper appeared out of nowhere and nudged his leg. Harry shrugged as he reached for his jacket and opened the door. Cooper raced off into the dark night.

Harry whirled around. "You really believe all that, Jack?"

"I do, Harry."

"Okay, then. What are we racing toward?"

"Nothing. Just running till we can't run anymore. You okay with that?"

Harry thought about it for a minute. "Yeah."

Chapter 6

Bert Navarro stared at the monitor above his desk. The floor of the casino was a throbbing mass of human flesh making enough noise to rock the casino. Nine o'clock at night, and the place was juking and jiving as it did every weekend night. He sighed as he continued to watch for his right-hand man, Dixson Kelly, as he approached his private office.

He felt good about leaving Dix in charge. They were old buddies from back in the day when Bert ran the FBI. Dix was his counterpart at the CIA. The spook business didn't pay anywhere near what the casino paid him, and Dix liked Anna de Silva and the weird way she did business, so he had been an easy recruit. He liked and respected Bert, so it was a no-brainer when Bert asked him if he wanted the job as his right-hand man. He'd snapped it up, hopped into his RV and headed west, set up shop, and the rest was history.

Bert watched Dix as he strode down the long hallway that was off-limits to everyone except key personnel. Dix would be the perfect person to head up a casino in Macau if that's the way things ended up. He had no baggage, no wife, no children, a few brothers he saw once every other year or so. His downfall, if you could call it that, was that he liked the showgirls. Maybe a little too much, but that was the private side of his life, and as long as it didn't interfere with the job he had to do, Bert was okay with it.

Bert grinned as he watched his associate approach. He was everything Hollywood and the big screen depicted when featuring a CIA operative. Tall, six-four, weight around 210 depending if he ate pasta the day of the weigh-in. He was buff and ripped or whatever the saying was these days. The thing about Dix was his eyes, piercing blue, and they commanded truth. He could spot a cheat a mile away on a foggy day. It was said up and down the strip that Bert and Dix ran the tightest ship in all of Vegas, something both men were proud of.

Right this moment, Bert's dilemma was how much to tell Dix. Certainly nothing about the sisters or the guys. Best to keep it strictly to the business at hand. Dix had stood in for him on the two occasions when he'd gone to China to get the lay of the land, so he was privy to all of that. This third trip fell right into that plan, so maybe the ex-spook wouldn't ask too many questions.

Three sharp knocks on the door—Dix's announcement of his presence. Bert pressed a button, and the hydraulic door hissed open.

The piercing blue eyes took everything in at one glance, Bert's casual attire of jeans, Izod pullover, Nike running shoes, the duffel bag by the door. "Nothing like waiting for the last minute to tell me you were leaving," Dix said lazily as he flopped down on one of the three ergonomic chairs in the office. That was another thing about Dix—he was like a bendable Gumby, loose as a goose.

"Cut the shit, Dix. You knew I was making the trip the minute I got off the phone with the boss. And that was twenty-three hours ago. Gossip leaks like a sieve in this place. Plus, I know you saw the car waiting for me out front. Right or wrong?"

"On the money, boss, on the money." Dix grinned, revealing a magnificent array of pearly whites. "I was just making conversation. Any special instructions while you're gone? And how long do you plan to be away?"

"Just run the place like I do. It's up in the air. Those guys like to mess around and stall and make you sweat. I'm thinking three days. If I don't make any progress, I'll take my marbles and come home. I'm meeting up with Todd from the Wynn and Big Al from the

Sands first. I think it's a go. Clinching the deal is step two. In other words, it all depends how bad they piss me off.

"We talked about this already, Dix. Tell me now if you are having any second thoughts. You sure you want to run the Macau casino? Life will be quite different over there, as you well know. I'm not signing on any dotted line until I have your full commitment."

Dix laughed. It was a deep rumble of sound. "Told you I'd give it five years as long as I got a piece of the action, and Annie and you both agreed to that. That's a piece *plus* my salary. Just so we're clear on that. At the end of the five years, I want the option of bugging out so I can buy an island somewhere and live off my dividends while I'm being catered to twenty-four seven. That's the deal."

"Okay. When I get back, we'll put it together if it's a go, and then you can take up residence in Hong Kong until the casino in Macau is completed. Then it becomes your headache."

His blue eyes locked on Bert. "Why don't you tell me now why you're *really* going over there? Yeah, yeah, I heard everything you said, but there's another reason, isn't there?"

The guy was good, he had to give him that. "NTK, pal."

"Need to know, my ass, Bert. Come on, level with me. This is me you're talking to, pal. I thought we were best buds."

"Can't, Dix. Boss's orders. You know how

that goes. Hold the fort. You have my number. Call me if anything goes awry. Gotta run."

Dix was up and out of the chair he'd been sitting on. The piercing blue eyes narrowed to slits. "This isn't shits and giggles, is it, Bert? This isn't even really *all* about the casino, either, is it?"

"No, Dix, it is not shits and giggles."

"Okay, you need some guys, let me know. I know quite a few in the Orient who would jump at the chance to help if need be." Bert nodded as he slapped Dix on the back.

"I'll be in touch. Make sure those four weddings in the chapel go off smoothly." Bert laughed out loud at the look on Dix's face. He hated chapel duty. Especially when the preacher was an Elvis stand-in.

Ten minutes later, Bert hunkered down into the backseat of the casino car and closed his eyes. What the hell was he getting himself into? His least favorite people in the whole world were the Chinese. There was no trust there, no code of honor. At least that he could see.

He hated Hong Kong. Almost as much as he hated Macau. But he had gotten five pretty snappy custom-made suits the last time he was in Hong Kong. Maybe he'd get a couple more this time around since Kathryn said he looked sexy in them. Yeah, yeah, maybe some shirts, too. The monogrammed ones she liked so much. God, how he loved that woman.

His eyes closed as his mind took him from

thoughts of Kathryn, the sisters, Dix, and other stray thoughts, to Lily Wong, Harry's daughter. His heart skipped a beat at the thought of the little girl being in any kind of danger. That thought took him back to Kathryn and the fierce tone of her voice when she'd called to tell him what was going on. He shivered.

With an hour to kill before boarding, Bert sent off texts to Todd and Big Al in Macau, apprising them of his arrival and the wish to set up a meeting ASAP. Within minutes, he had a meeting, lodging at the Wynn, and a luncheon all scheduled. The third text he sent off was to Annie, informing her of the latest developments.

Satisfied that every last detail had been taken care of, Bert leaned back and watched the travelers as they scurried about. His FBI training served him well as he looked for oddities. Seeing nothing that seemed out of the ordinary, he let his mind take him to other places that were more pleasing at this hour of the night, but in the end his thoughts always took him back to a little dark-eyed girl named Lily Wong. When he could no longer bear the thought of the little girl's being in trouble, he shifted his thoughts to Lily's father, Harry Wong.

Harry Wong. He liked Harry Wong. But . . . in the deepest part of his heart and soul, he admitted to himself that he feared him like no other man walking the earth. Harry Wong was a one-man army. A man of few words. Very few. And yet in some strange, unexplained something or other, Harry had bonded with Jack Emery, of all people. While they constantly baited one another, everyone close to the two men knew that either one would, quite literally, die for the other—that was the nature of their bond. No amount of questioning or searching could reveal the why of it. It simply was.

Bert could feel his insides start to curdle when he thought about both Harry and Jack in China. Harry wouldn't just be Harry Wong, the number two martial-arts expert in the world, with his sidekick at his side. He would be entering China as the number one martial-arts expert in the world now that Jun Yu was deceased. While that in itself was scary as hell, it was who Harry and Jack really were that made his blood run cold.

Harry Wong, the father of Lily Wong.

Jack Emery, godfather to Lily Wong.

At this point in time, probably the deadliest duo ever to enter China.

Bert's eyes snapped open when he heard the announcement that first-class passengers were to begin boarding. He switched his mental gears and once again tried to concentrate on the little girl named Lily Wong.

Bert adjusted his seat belt and reached for the glass of wine the stewardess held out to him. Where are you, Lily Wong? Are you safe, little Lily? Your dad and Jack are coming for you. Nothing on this earth will stop them from getting to you. Stay strong, little one, stay strong.

Her name was Yuke Lok, and she was seventeen years old. She had been singled out to be what Americans would call Lily Wong's big sister on the little girl's arrival. It was her job to oversee and protect the little girl, a job she took seriously. She excelled at following orders and never questioned the monks when a task was given to her. And she liked Lily and considered her a true little sister since she had no blood sisters, only brothers.

She loved her little sister, loved when Lily told her what life in America was like. They shared their limited life experiences sometimes with laughter and sometimes with sadness. Yuke Lok especially loved hearing tales of Cooper and what Lily called his mystical powers. It was understood among the monks that sometimes Lily embellished her tales, but they just hid their smiles because, wise men that they were, they knew a four-legged creature couldn't possibly know and do the things the mystical dog was credited with. They were even more amused when Lily would just smile knowingly and stare off into space.

The moment Brother Hung waddled, as fast as his plump body would allow, over to where

Yuke Lok was teaching six young girls, of which Lily Wong was one, about the different species of butterflies, Yuke Lok came to attention. She listened as Brother Hung told her to take Lily and head into the forest. He drew a map on Yuke Lok's open palm and admonished her to speak only English from that point on. "Yuke Lok, you must keep young Lily safe. She is your responsibility now. Do you understand? You must go now before the parade of men come here." He handed over a sack of food and bottles of water, explaining that there would be more when she stopped at the various points marked on the palm of her hand.

Always inquisitive, sometimes more than she should be, Lily listened but did not question anything Brother Hung said. She smiled when he bent low to kiss the top of her head. Lily had looked up at him, and whispered, "I know. Cooper told me. I will see you again, Brother Hung, when my daddy comes here with Cooper. Please do not fret about my safety."

The fat little monk shook his head to try to clear away the words, but they stayed firmly planted in his mind. A mystical dog, along with Harry Wong, was coming to the monastery. He didn't know why, but he believed the child implicitly.

"Go, my children!"

Brother Hung trundled his way to the center

courtyard and rang the bell. Monks came from everywhere, children from all directions in a blur of orange and yellow. He spoke quickly, breathlessly, his gaze on the terrain of his beloved Song Mountain, where the parade of men were advancing on the monastery. His message to the gathering was simple. Erase the life of Lily Wong. She was never here. Quickly, my brothers.

There was no need to repeat his order. Instant, unequivocal obedience was the order of the Shaolin Monastery. Only once did he turn his gaze in the other direction, praying that the two girls would remain safe.

Brother Hung had known the moment Jun Yu came for his son and daughter what would happen, and he had been right. He just wished he'd had more time to prepare, more time for Yuke Lok and Lily Wong to get farther away. He wished then that the mystical dog Cooper was sitting at his feet even if he didn't believe in such things. And yet Lily Wong believed, and her eyes had been clear and unafraid. He shuddered at the thought of her father's making an appearance along with the mystical dog.

Would life here at the Shaolin Monastery on Song Mountain ever be the same? Would the peace and tranquility that had survived for hundreds of years be able to survive the onslaught of whatever the men in boots intended?

Then Brother Hung had the first uncharitable thought of his life. He wished he weren't so fat, so that he could run.

"Be safe, my little ones."

The two girls were three hours into their trek when Yuke Lok called a halt for a rest period. "Are you tired, Lily? Do you want something to eat or drink?"

"A drink would be nice, but I am not hungry. Are you?"

"No. We still have an hour or so to go before we can stop for the night. Are you sure you are not too tired?"

"My legs are strong, Yuke Lok. Even you said so when we work out. I can walk as long as you can. I need to be safe, so Daddy and Cooper can find me. I will do whatever we have to do. Do you know why this is happening?"

"I do not. Today was the first time I ever saw Brother Hung so . . . what is the word in English, Lily?"

Lily laughed. "Rattled. My mother gets rattled sometimes, then Daddy tells her to cool her jets. That means calm down." She laughed again, but it was a sad sound.

Yuke Lok laughed. "I just love to hear your American slang. When I leave here next year, I doubt I will ever find an occasion to use such words. Then I guess I will forget them."

"Will you come back to visit me?"

"I don't think so, Lily. I live too far away. I won't forget you, though, because you are my little sister. I will think of you all the time. You will miss me at first, but then my memory will fade. You will be given another big sister to watch over you until it is your turn to become the big sister. We should go now. Are you ready?"

"Yes. But you are wrong, Yuke Lok, I will never forget you. Maybe someday you can come to America, and you and I will be like Daddy and Uncle Jack. Wouldn't that be wonderful?"

"That won't happen, Lily. Life here in China is not easy. You need a lot of money to travel. My parents are not rich. I must find employment when I leave here. I think I will teach. I must be here to help my parents when they get old. Maybe you can come and visit me. We can write letters to each other. Or we might be lucky and get computers. Then we can e-mail and do that thing where we can see each other. Sometimes I wish the brothers were more modern in their thinking, don't you?"

"Yes, but I understand why it has to be like this. Daddy explained it all to me."

"Tell me more about all your aunts and uncles back in America. How did they get to be so rich? What is it like to be rich, Lily?"

"I don't know, Yuke Lok, because my daddy is not rich. The others are, I guess. They have cars and boats and big houses. We live at the dojo. We always have food and nice clothes, but so do most people in America, and they are not considered rich. I need to study up more on that. I know Grandma Annie and Grandma Myra are rich, because Daddy said so. They aren't really my grandmas, but I have to show respect and give them that title. I love them very much. I don't know much about money. Do you?"

Yuke Lok laughed. "Enough to know I don't have any. I'd like to have money someday, so I could go shopping and buy . . . *something*. Just buy something that's all mine."

"Like what?" Lily asked, curiosity ringing in her voice.

"A pretty red or yellow hair ribbon or maybe one of those shiny hair clips. In the shape of a butterfly. And some *lipstick*! Bright red to go with the hair ribbon." Yuke Lok giggled, and so did Lily. "Brother Hung would punish me for such wishful thoughts if he knew."

Lily laughed out loud. "He's never going to know, and I will keep your secret."

The girls trudged on, giggling and laughing over this and that until the sun started to set. "We're almost there, Lily. I'm tired now, are you?"

"Yes, I am tired, and I am also hungry. We're safe, aren't we?"

"Yes, Lily, we are safe," she said aloud. Then Yuke Lok muttered, "For now."

Chapter 7

Jack Emery looked around Myra's empty kitchen. Just an hour ago, it was teeming with chattering women and silent, observant men who were now down in the war room with Charles and Fergus. He'd remained topside, to accept the UPS and Federal Express packages that were due shortly.

Jack leaned against the kitchen counter as he sipped at his coffee. He admitted to himself that he was a little nervous about the upcoming trip to China. Not nervous for himself but for Harry, who was like a scalded cat. But who could blame him. He and Yoko were both worried sick about their daughter, Lily, and rightly so. Somewhere deep inside him, he knew that the little girl was safe. He didn't know how he knew, he just knew. And as hard as he tried, he could not convey that confidence to Harry and Yoko. He knew in his gut they were focused on the worst-case scenario. If he were walking in their shoes, he might be out of his mind, too, but he didn't think so. He had been an optimist all his life. No reason to switch up now.

Jack let his gaze wander to the Wolf range and clock that said Federal Express was late. He shrugged. He moved then, closer to the kitchen window to stare out at the last of the autumn leaves swirling about in a brisk wind. They were colorful, he had to admit. He loved autumn, always had, as did Nikki. Nikki loved Halloween, her favorite holiday of the whole year. She said it brought back the kid in her, when she believed in spooks and goblins. The thing he loved about autumn was the pumpkin pie, the pumpkin fritters, the pumpkin pudding, the pumpkin bread, the pumpkin *everything*.

Jack turned to look at the clock again. Harry and Yoko should have arrived by now. Harry was always on time. And more often than not, he was early. What was keeping him? Maybe he should call. Then again, maybe he shouldn't. Harry would take the phone call all wrong, immediately assume that Jack was worried, and that was the one emotion he did not want to convey to Harry, who was antsy enough for all of them. Better to wait, he decided. Still, the thought wouldn't go away. He started to pace as his mind raced with possibilities. What the hell was going on? Something not good, he was sure of it.

What was going on was that Harry was pulling out his hair as he tried to grapple with what Cooper was doing. Yoko threw her hands in the air, moaning that something was wrong, and Cooper was trying to tell them, but they just weren't *getting it.*

"Enough, Yoko!" Harry roared. Yoko's eyes widened. She went silent in mid-moan because she had never heard that tone in her husband's voice. As in never *ever.*

Harry eyed Cooper, who was dancing around in circles, something he'd been doing for close to an hour. He would stop intermittently, run to Lily's room, and then run back out. He'd jumped on her bed, trying to reach the shelves overhead. Then he'd run to Harry and Yoko's bathroom and do the same thing. Clearly, he wanted something, but Harry had no clue what it was. His barking was incessant now, bordering on hysteria.

Harry dropped to his knees and cupped the dog's head in his hand. His thoughts were as frenzied as Cooper's as he tried to understand what the dog wanted. Something important to Lily. That was a certainty.

"I get it, I get it," Harry whispered. "You want something from both rooms, but you can't get to it. Help me out here, pal. You need to show me."

Cooper stopped barking long enough to

raise his paw and place it on Harry's shoulder. His head bobbed before he trotted to Lily's room, where he jumped up on the bed. He threw back his head and howled.

Harry's eyes scanned the shelf above Lily's bed. Books, a play cash register, a stuffed bear, a cone covered in glitter that Lily had made in kindergarten, a jewelry box.

"Obviously, it's something on the shelf. Take it all down, Harry, and see which one he wants."

One by one, Harry took the items off the shelf and laid them on the bed. Cooper didn't make a move until Harry placed the ballerina jewelry box on the bed. He raised the cover and watched as the tiny figure did a pirouette to a tinny tune. Cooper wasn't the least bit interested in the ballerina. He used his paw to poke among the trinkets. Finally, he found what he was looking for, a gold-plated butterfly barrette that Lily used to pull her hair back. Cooper clamped it between his teeth and ran to the door, where he looked around for his basket, which was out at the farm. Yoko knew instinctively he wanted a basket. She ran to her room and dumped out some trinkets she kept in a straw basket by her chair. She raced back to the door and placed it on the floor. Cooper dropped the hair clip in the basket, then sprinted for the bathroom, where he again threw back his head and howled.

"He wants something on the vanity. What?" Yoko wailed.

Harry scooped everything off the vanity and laid it on the floor. He and Yoko watched as Cooper pawed through everything until he came to several tubes of lipstick.

"Oh, God, I bet he wants a special color. Open them up, Harry, and tell him what each one is. What does this mean? Why does this dog want my lipstick?"

Harry's tone was sharper than he meant it to be. "Like I know, Yoko! This says Sunset Pink." He showed it to Cooper, who looked away. "Okay, wrong color. Let's try this one, Coral Reef." Cooper again looked away. "Third time is the charm. We have here . . . Cherry Orchard." Cooper barked. Harry capped the tube and placed it on the bathroom carpet. Cooper had it between his teeth in a nanosecond. He trotted to the door and dropped it in the basket with the hair clip. Then he sat back on his haunches and barked.

"Okay, he's ready to go," Harry said, relief ringing in his voice.

"What does all of this mean, Harry?" Yoko whispered.

"Yoko, my dear, sweet wife, I do not have a clue. If you want a guess off the top of my head, then I would have to say he was somehow, some way in touch with our daughter, and she requested these things. Why is a whole other story. If you don't like my version, make up one that makes you happy. Let's not talk about this anymore."

"We need to talk about it, Harry. I'm taking this all as a positive sign that Lily is okay, and Cooper has . . . um . . . been in touch with her. For whatever reason, she wants my lipstick and her butterfly hair clip. Lily and Cooper have always had a special bond that none of us understood, yet we accepted it. This is Cooper letting us know that our daughter is all right in the only way he knows how. We need to be grateful for this strange dog, Harry. I will never understand how it all came to be, but I will be forever grateful to this four-legged creature. I know you feel the same way, but for some odd reason, you find it hard to talk about. Give it up, Harry. Join us and believe in this mystical dog and his powers."

"I do believe, Yoko. I just feel like I need to know the how and the why of it. Why us?"

"I don't think we're ever going to know. And, Harry, I'm okay with that as long as Cooper is in our lives, especially Lily's. I feel so much better now. I really do. Cooper is telling us our daughter is safe, and that's all that matters.

"One last thing, Harry." In a voice ringing with pure steel, Yoko said, "And when I wrap my arms around my daughter, I am never letting go until we are back here in this dojo. Make sure you understand that. *Lily is coming home.*"

Cooper barked, a joyous sound.

Harry Wong was a wise man. He knew when he was beaten even before he stepped on the high road, knowing all along that this was going to be Yoko's position. He nodded.

And that was the end of that.

Jack was on his third cup of coffee, his nerves twanging all over the place, when he finally heard the UPS driver sound off on his horn. He reached up and released the gate to allow the big brown truck to roll through. He watched in amazement as the driver and his helper hopped out to unload box after box onto the dolly that would transport it all to the kitchen. Lady and her pups stood in the kitchen, eyeballing all that was going on. Finally, satisfied that her help wasn't needed, she herded her brood back to the family room and the warmth of the fireplace.

What did those women order, Alexis in particular, Jack wondered as the driver neatly stacked the boxes at the far end of the kitchen. "Eighteen boxes. Sign here, sir." Jack scribbled his signature and tipped the driver. Okay, one delivery down, one to go, plus Harry's arrival, and Jack's world would be right side up.

The Federal Express driver sounded his horn fifteen minutes later and offered up an apology, saying he'd gotten a flat tire along the way. Compensation would be shown on the next bill. Jack nodded as he, like the UPS driver, dollied in eleven boxes and stacked them next to those left by the UPS driver.

Thirteen minutes after the gate closed behind the Federal Express truck, Harry Wong tapped his horn, pressed in the code, and roared through the gate.

Jack's sigh and moan of relief were so loud that Lady appeared in the doorway to check things out. Satisfied that all was right in the kitchen, she returned to the family room to munch on her chew bone.

Harry, Yoko, and the mystical dog blew in with the wind, Cooper racing to where his basket of treasures rested. He dropped his two new treasures into the basket and ran off to find Lady and her pups.

"In a million years, you are never going to believe what I am about to tell you," Harry said in the strangest voice Jack had ever heard. Yoko's bobbing head scared him.

"If I'm not going to believe it, then don't waste your time telling me," Jack said, hedging as he tried to figure out Harry's strange tone and the blank look on Yoko's face. "Okay, okay, tell me before you explode."

They told him, their words tripping over each other. "Go ahead, Jack, check Cooper's basket, and you'll find one butterfly hair clip and a tube of, what was the color of that lipstick, Yoko?"

"Cherry Orchard. He didn't want the pink

or the coral, he wanted the Cherry Orchard. It was like he knew the color he was looking for. Stop looking at me like that, Jack. It's all true."

Jack's head reeled at Yoko's fretful tone, which sounded as if she was on the verge of tears.

"Uh-huh. Okay." He wondered if Harry and Yoko thought he was as stupid as he felt. He shrugged. In the end, it was what it was, and nothing was going to change. A tube of Cherry Orchard lipstick and a butterfly hair clip were not going to change the world as he knew it. He shrugged again.

"Guess we should go down to the war room and let them know that all of Alexis's and Charles's purchases arrived."

The war room was quiet, with Lady Justice holding court on the wide screen that hung suspended from a giant rafter. Jack looked around at the thick files covering the special table Isabelle had designed to accommodate everyone. The only sounds to be heard were pages being turned, the soft hum of the heating unit, and the constant pinging of the fax machine. In spite of himself, Jack grinned at the show of reading glasses in colorful designs that everyone was wearing. He particularly liked Nikki's purple polka-dotted ones. He had a pair of black polka-dot glasses, a gift from Nikki. She said no one would laugh at him because they were manly. All the guys laughed.

He waved and took his seat at the table, as

did Harry and Yoko. Jack tried not to see the
way Harry's eyes bugged out at the thickness of
the report at his seat. Like Harry was really
going to plow through all those pages. Not.

The silence came to a screeching halt when
Charles blew the whistle hanging around his
neck. The whistle was proof that he was in
charge. The moment he had everyone's attention, Charles honed in on Jack. "Did everything arrive?"

"It did, and it's all stacked up in the kitchen."
Hoping to ease Harry's misery, Jack looked up
at Charles, and said, "Do we really need to read
all of this right now?"

"No, of course not. You'll have ample time to
read all of it on the plane to Hong Kong. Just a
few minutes ago I received confirmation from
Annie's and Dennis's pilots that the planes are
being readied. Our ETD is tomorrow at nine in
the morning. Just to make sure everyone is
clear here, Avery Snowden and his people will
be flying on the Welmed Gulfstream, courtesy
of our young friend Dennis. The rest of us will
be on Annie's plane. Look at the screen, ladies
and gentlemen!"

The wide screen showed two magnificent
planes back to back. Charles clicked the button on his remote. Annie laughed when she
saw the bright red-and-gold lettering that said
CRESCENT CHINA TOURS and underneath the
blocked Chinese letters that said the same
thing. The Welmed plane had the same iden-

tical lettering, but there was a bright sky-blue number two next to the letters. "It was Lizzie's idea to make Crescent China Tours look solvent should anyone inquire. She backstopped everything beautifully, as she always does. I will be the one carrying all the legal papers, just so you know."

Charles looked down at Myra. "All physicals are done, passports in order. Are we a go?"

"We are good to go, dear."

"Do any of you have any questions?"

Dennis's hand shot in the air. "Who is staying behind?"

"Just me," Abner said. "You guys are going to need me here. I'll just be a click away, as will Lizzie just in case things turn sticky."

Dennis had another question. It was the reporter in him. "Are you staying here at the farm or going back to your loft?"

"I'm camping out here and will be in charge of all of the dogs except for Cooper, who is going with you. I don't know how Lizzie did it, but she got clearance to take Cooper into the country. I've got it buttoned down here, so relax." Isabelle winked at him, then smiled. Abner turned bright pink as Dennis sighed with relief.

"Anything else?" Charles asked.

All eyes turned to Harry and Yoko. Yoko shook her head to indicate she was okay with everything. Harry simply waved his hand in the air, indicating the same thing. As one, the room relaxed.

"Okay then, let's go topside and start opening those boxes. We have a lot of packing to do and quite a bit of preparing." Espinosa was on his feet in a nanosecond to escort his ladylove topside. There was a brief scramble as everyone gathered up their papers and files and jammed them into their respective folders.

"It's happening, isn't it?" Myra whispered to Annie.

"It is, Myra, it truly is. Are you having second thoughts?" Annie whispered in return.

"Good Lord, no. I am heartsick over that little girl, and I want Harry and Yoko to have her in their arms again. It's just been a long few days with so much preparation. I worry that maybe one of us missed something crucial along the way that might come back to bite us at some point."

Annie watched as Myra fingered the pearls around her neck. "You have to leave those behind, you know. I'm referring to the pearls, Myra."

"I know what you meant. I will be sure to leave them in my jewelry box. By the way, Annie, I made an important decision last evening."

"Oh. Care to share that important decision?"

"I'm leaving my pearls to Lily in my will."

Whatever Annie was expecting to hear, that

wasn't it. Suddenly, she was at a loss for words. Next to Nikki, Myra's adopted daughter, and Charles, the most important thing in the world to Myra was her pearls. All she could think to do was bob her head.

"It was a big decision, and I didn't make it lightly, Annie."

"Hmmnnn. Why are we having this discussion, Myra?"

"I was trying to get you to relax. You're strung too tight, Annie. Not only can I see it, but I can feel it. Things will be okay."

"China is a scary place these days," Annie said.

"I have an idea, Annie. While we're over there, why don't you see if you can go straight to the horse's mouth and find out why all those Chinese stocks you talked me into buying are falling so rapidly."

"No one likes a smart-ass, Myra," Annie snapped.

"Takes one to know one, but I would like an answer on those stocks."

"I'll see what I can do," Annie snapped again.

Myra giggled all the way up the moss-covered stone steps that would take them to the chaos that was going on in the kitchen.

Chapter 8

The morning was exceptionally cool, with a brisk wind ripping across the tarmac. The caravan of cars came to an organized stop at the private airfield where Annie's private plane and Dennis's corporate plane were housed. They were out on the runway, the Welmed plane behind Annie's Gulfstream, poised for takeoff.

Nikki was first out of the car. She stared at the weak winter sun shining on the skin of the sleek jets, making them look like sheets of glistening silver. She smiled when she saw the logo on both: CRESCENT CHINA TOURS. She almost believed it for a minute.

She felt rather than saw Kathryn Lucas step up behind her. "What do you think, Nikki?"

"What I think is, we're all going to China to

rescue a little girl. What are you thinking? Is something wrong, Kathryn? You don't seem like yourself. Are you worried about us, Lily, or Bert?"

Kathryn raised her hand to shield her eyes from the sun that was getting brighter by the moment. She tensed as she struggled to find the words she wanted. "It's Bert. We had an understanding, but he's stepped off the grid and is pressuring me. He does this every so often— we fight, we make up, then it happens all over again. I can't take it anymore."

Alarm registered on Nikki's face. "And yet, here you are. You should have recused yourself this time around. Your thought processes are not one hundred percent on the mission. One little slip and you could put us all in jeopardy. You realize that, don't you?"

"Of course I do, and it's not true, Nikki. I can do my job. You don't have to worry about me. Bert didn't have to go to Macau. The person who should have gone is Dixson Kelly. Bert chose to go because of me. I resent it. I really do."

"That's what I'm talking about, Kathryn. You're dealing with emotion here. This is not good. I'm going to have to tell the others. Sometimes I simply don't understand you, Kathryn. What is it you really want? What can't you come to terms with? We've gone over this so many times that I've lost count."

Kathryn's facial features went taut. "Let me assure you that the one thing you do not have to worry about is me. Listen to me. I'm going to tell you something in confidence, friend to friend, girl to girl. Bert and I parted company. We're done. We've had a very long, contentious relationship, but it no longer works for me. I'm not sure why he was so insistent on doing this China thing, which, as I said, in my opinion is a mistake. And before you can ask, Nikki, all I feel is a sense of relief. Like a thousand pounds have been taken off my shoulders. I'm good here, I really am. Just so you know, I moved all my stuff out of Bert's place. I'm back at my home space in Virginia with Murphy, who, by the way, is at doggie camp until I get back. If you want me to sum this up, it's that I need to be free to be me. Right now I actually feel as if I could fly to China with my own wings. Look, Bert wants to get married and have a family. That's not in the cards for me. I care about him enough to want him to have those things. Just not with me."

Nikki stared into Kathryn's eyes, and whatever she saw there satisfied her. She smiled. "I think you are good. I understand. Your word is good enough for me. I do have a question, though. What happens if you come face-to-face with Bert in Macau?"

"Two old friends meeting up on the other side of the world. Nothing more, Nikki. Please, you need to believe me."

And, Nikki realized, she did believe the long, lanky truck driver. Kathryn might be many things—outspoken, bombastic at times—but she never lied. The two women eyeballed each other one last time. Kathryn spoke first: "I know, I know, if I screw up I go to the sidelines. It ain't gonna happen, Nikki. For the first time in a good many years, I finally feel as if I'm my own person again. I like the feeling, and I intend to keep it that way."

"Okay. Come on, we have a plane to catch."

"Ah . . . Nikki . . ."

"This conversation never happened. You're back in your own ballpark again."

Kathryn laughed, a sound of pure mirth. Nikki felt stunned for just a bare moment as she tried to remember the last time that she'd heard Kathryn laugh like that. Probably never, was her best guess. She ran then to keep up with Kathryn's long-legged stride.

Ten minutes later, the two private planes were airborne and climbing steadily to their cruising altitude of thirty thousand feet. The occupants settled back for the long, twenty-hour and thirty-minute flight that would bring them to their destination.

"First," Annie said, "we're going to have some breakfast. Eggs Benedict. Mimosas. Fresh Hawaiian coffee from Kona. Then we can get down to business and work on our plans." The announcement was met with hoots of approval. They laughed outright when Annie said lunch would be shrimp scampi and beef medallions in a red wine sauce, basil risotto, and a fresh garden salad. Dinner, she went on to say, was going to be a surprise because the caterer had not told her what it was before boarding. "I'm sure it will meet with our approval. In the meantime, the coffee and wine are at your disposal." More hoots of pleasure.

The group paired off. Alexis and Isabelle went to the back of the plane to start separating the outfits they would all don before disembarking in Hong Kong. Maggie and Ted had their heads together as Crescent China Tours tour leaders. Dennis settled himself next to Espinosa to talk about what he called the snatch and grab. "I hope those guys over there buy our cover that we're doing a pictorial for the paper," he fretted. Espinosa assured him they were pros, and neither one had a thing to worry about. "Listen, kid, everyone likes to have their picture taken and nice things written about them. That's what we're going to do. But first we're going to have breakfast. And then we'll map out our strategy."

Harry and Yoko were huddled together whispering to each other. Cooper snoozed at their feet, happy and content.

Nikki and Kathryn sat side by side, speaking softly about the upcoming Christmas season, shopping, and decorating, while Myra, Annie, Charles, Fergus, and Jack shared what each knew about Buddhism and the monks at the monastery at Song Mountain in China—which wasn't all that much, and more than anything was just a bunch of words to pass the time.

"I'm tired of talking about monks. Let's decide what we're going to buy when we get to Hong Kong. I think we girls should have some gowns made for our New Year's Eve party," Myra said.

"What party?" Charles and Fergus asked in unison.

Myra laughed. "Actually, it was Annie's idea, and it is such a good idea, I immediately agreed. We want to have a party at the farm for all the people we've helped these past years. To see how they're doing, to see if they need our special brand of help. Basically, to show them all we're still here should they ever require our services in the future."

"That's a great idea, Annie. Count me in," Jack said enthusiastically. "Are you sure you can fit everyone at the farm? It's a very long list."

"It may be a little crowded, but I don't think anyone will mind. I'm going to bring it up after breakfast to see if everyone approves. If so, then Annie and I will get on it when we get back to the farm," Myra said, glee ringing in her voice.

Further conversation came to a halt when the hostess appeared with the food trays.

Cooper bounded down the aisle and took up his position next to Jack as he waited for his plate. Jack leaned toward the dog just long enough for a thought to work its way through his head. "I think the dog wants six slices of bacon, three sausage links, and one scrambled egg."

The hostess blinked. "The food came already prepared. I don't think anyone requested that kind of meal."

"Maybe you should check again," Jack said. Cooper barked to show he was in agreement with Jack's suggestion.

The hostess served the plates from the cart, then scurried back to the galley to return, carrying a dish with a cover on top. Even from where he was sitting, Jack could read the note on the cover: SPECIAL FOOD. He didn't need to lift the cover to know the plate held six slices of bacon, three sausage links, and one scrambled egg. He looked down at Cooper and grinned. The dog barked twice, sharp and shrill.

"I don't want to know how that happened, do you, Annie?"

"I absolutely do not. Eat your eggs, Myra." Annie giggled.

Myra dug into her eggs Benedict with gusto.

How the hell does he do that? Jack wondered as he watched Cooper devour his breakfast. Realizing he wasn't going to get an answer, he attacked his breakfast like a starving man.

An hour later, when all the breakfast trays had been gathered, the group settled down to review the materials they'd carried with them. One eye on the written pages and the other on Harry, Jack did his best to absorb what he was reading. He'd always wanted to visit Hong Kong with Nikki but not under the current circumstances. He wondered after this mission if he would still feel that way. Probably not, he decided.

Satisfied that Harry was dozing or pretending to, Jack forced himself to concentrate on the papers in front of him. They would be staying at the Peninsula Hotel, the flagship property of the Peninsula Hotels group. It was known for its fleet of Rolls-Royces painted the distinctive Peninsula green. He wondered what it would be like to ride in one.

Visitors were encouraged to have high tea at four in the afternoon. Because . . . he read on, Prince Charles always made a point of having high tea there when he visited. Jack knew that Charles would be over the moon at the thought.

The hotel had a helipad. Great in case they needed a quick getaway. He hoped Charles knew about it. He hoped they had time to dine in one of the famous restaurants. Even though he'd just finished his breakfast, he drooled at the thought of dining at Gaddi's or Felix. Maybe lunch at Spring Moon or Imasa because they specialized in Cantonese, Japanese, and Swiss cuisine. He did love good food.

He knew that the girls would be thrilled with the oldest arcade in Hong Kong, which housed the shops of Chanel, Dior, Hermès, Gucci, Prada, Shiatzy Chen, Louis Vuitton, and Cartier.

Jack set his folder aside and closed his eyes. He hadn't had a good night's sleep in over a week. A little nap might be just the thing. His eyes snapped open to take one last look around the cabin. Everyone was doing their thing. Cooper was sleeping peacefully at his feet. He sighed, closed his eyes, and was asleep within minutes, his dreams invaded by a little girl with big dark eyes and shining black hair. "We're coming, Lily, we're coming," he mumbled in his sleep. The only one who heard his mumblings was Cooper, who cracked one eye, then closed it

The path Yuke Lok and Lily were following spread out to make for easier walking. It was cold, and both young girls were shivering despite their quilted outerwear. "I know you're tired, Lily—so am I—but it is not much farther. I can see smoke straight ahead. That means the little temple where I will be leaving you is near. Can you make it, little one, or do you want me to carry you?"

"I am not a baby, Yuke Lok, I can walk." Always truthful, the little girl added, "But I am getting tired. And hungry."

"There will be food at the temple and a nice warm bed. And, best of all, a nice hot bath."

"Will whoever is there tell us why I have to stay there? I want to know."

"I don't know, Lily. I hope so. Look, Lily, there it is! We have arrived safely," Yuke Lok said, relief ringing in her voice. "They are coming to greet us." She pointed to four monks swaddled in bright yellow robes who were advancing, their arms outstretched.

"Welcome! Welcome, my children," a giant said, scooping Lily up in his arms. She laughed.

"Come, come, we have food for you and a warm bed. We can talk later. Now it is a time to relax from your journey."

Yuke Lok fell into line. She looked up at the giant carrying Lily and boldly asked in English, "Then, when we talk, will you tell us why we are here and what is going on in this child's life that she is to be kept safe?"

"We will converse when it is time," the giant said in Mandarin Chinese.

Yuke Lok's facial features hardened. "Brother Hung said we were to speak English only. Lily's Chinese is not as fluent as ours is. Do you not speak English, Brother?"

"I do, of course. We all speak English. We will, of course, obey Brother Hung's orders.

"It is only natural that I speak my native language. My apologies. We must hurry, the temperature is dropping, and it will snow this night. Not much, but it will turn very, very cold here where we are situated."

Both girls almost swooned when the parade of brothers led them through a heavy wooden door, down a long hallway, and into a toasty kitchen full of fragrant scents. A long table with benches took up the center of the floor. The room sparkled with cleanliness.

The girls were shown into a small bathroom, where they could wash the weariness away and brush their teeth.

"That felt good, didn't it, Yuke Lok? I was starting to itch. I can't wait to take a nice warm bath. Did you ever take a bubble bath?"

"No. What is a bubble bath?" Lily explained. Yuke Lok giggled. Lily went on to describe that one time she had dumped the entire bottle of Mr. Bubble into the tub and the bubbles filled up the room, and she couldn't see Cooper. Yuke Lok giggled again. She loved hearing her little sister tell her tales of her other life in America.

"Come, I am starving. Did you smell the fresh bread? I hope they have jam. I wish for something sweet. Do you?" Lily nodded. She went on to explain about Hershey's Kisses. Both girls were still giggling when they sat down on one of the benches and waited to be served. But first there was a prayer of thanks for their safe arrival, then a prayer of thanks for the food they were about to eat. Then there was another prayer of thanks for the hot bath that awaited them. Under her breath, Lily prayed for an end of the prayers so she could eat.

Mindful of her manners, Lily tried not to gobble her food, but gobble she did, to the amusement of the monks standing by. When her bowl of stew was finished, she sighed, then smiled when she saw a wedge of pie with clotted cream placed in front of her. "Brother Sune made this pie from apples in our orchard. It is very good," the giant, Brother Lok, said.

Lily took a bite and closed her eyes. "You are right, Brother Lok, this pie is splendiferous."

"I do not know that word."

"It just means 'very good.' We use that word sometimes in America to say something is very special. Do you want me to spell it for you?"

"Later, little one. Finish up so you can bathe and go to sleep. We will speak again in the morning, and at that time you can give me a spelling lesson."

"That sounds like a good plan. I am finished, Brother Lok. Can we save the rest of this splendiferous pie for when I wake up?"

"But of course," Brother Lok replied, smiling with pleasure at the little girl's obvious delight.

The bathroom was warm and scented with incense, a pleasant smell. Fresh clothing, many sizes too big, rested on a small stool. Yuke Lok stood watch while Lily bathed, because she was afraid the little girl would nod off in the water. When she finally had her tucked into the bed, she bent over to kiss the top of her head. "Go to sleep now, Lily. You had a very busy few days."

"I have to say good night to Cooper. We talk every night. I need him to know that I am all right. He worries about me."

Yuke Lok watched, fascinated as Lily stared off into space, oblivious to everything around her. Finally, she focused again on her surroundings, smiled, and snuggled deeper into the covers.

"What . . . what . . . did you talk about to Cooper, Lily?"

"He told me he's on the way with my family. They are coming to get me. He said he knows the way. He told me not to worry. I love Cooper," she said sleepily.

Yuke Lok stared at the little girl for a long time, wondering if what she was saying was true or just a fantasy on Lily's part. In the end, she decided it was easier to believe than disbelieve. She hoped to meet Cooper someday. The thought brought a smile to her face as she filled the tub a second time.

As she lowered herself into the steaming water, she couldn't help but wonder what life had in store for Lily and her.

Surely it would be something wonderful.

Chapter 9

The moment that Annie's pilot's voice came over the intercom, announcing they were starting their descent to Hong Kong International Airport, the occupants became busier than beavers as they prepared for their landing.

Maggie took center stage as she started to bellow what would happen the minute they set foot on Chinese soil. "You follow my and Ted's lead in all things. We are, as you know, Crescent China Tours tour guides. Remember that there will be eyes and ears everywhere. Also remember that the Chinese do not like Americans. They tolerate us. Never forget that. The one thing we have going for us is all the demonstrations going on with the students. The authorities are going to be concentrating on that and not so much on new arrivals from America. Still, two private planes with American travelers will not go unnoticed. Stay alert. Any questions?"

No one had a question, not even Dennis West, who was Mr. Question himself when it came to a mission.

Maggie looked around and marveled as she always did at what Alexis had done with her red magic bag of tricks. Annie now looked like an aging Shirley Temple. Snowden had warned that even the Chinese knew who Countess Anna de Silva was. As far as Maggie was concerned no one, not even Fergus, would have recognized his ladylove had he met her on the street. Her new passport said her name was Alice Sylvester, a retired schoolteacher from Fargo, North Dakota. Myra, just as recognizable, according to Snowden, now looked like a watered-down version of Cher. The name on her passport said she was Elsa Miller, a librarian from New York.

Harry was the biggest challenge, Snowden warned. Alexis had stewed and fretted until she came up with what she thought was the perfect disguise. Latex to fill out his cheeks, a little filler to his lips, and a fat pigtail secured with a special hair glue along with a second hairpiece of unruly curls that sat smack on the middle of his head. Huge window-glass eyeglasses completed his facial features. A little spare padding around his middle took away his lanky, sinewy frame. His passport said his name was Chi Chung, the owner of six Oriental markets that sold all things Chinese from clothing to food in Omaha, Nebraska.

Yoko was now an awkward twelve-year-old student dressed in a plaid skirt, matching blazer, white knee socks, and lace-tied shoes. She sported a Buster Brown haircut, full bangs, and a short bob. Artificial braces adorned her teeth. Wire-rim glasses perched on her nose. Her passport said her name was Lee Ann Sylvester, the granddaughter of Alice Sylvester, a.k.a. Annie.

The others, including herself and Ted, had only minimal alterations to their appearance. As Snowden put it, just enough that you couldn't be sure who was who.

"We're good to go, people," Alexis said as she packed up her red bag of magic tricks and stowed it in a cavity at the back of the plane.

Charles stepped forward to open the overhead bin to remove his duffel bag and Myra's. Everyone had one duffel bag, and that was it. All were red and gold, China's favorite colors, emblazoned with CRESCENT CHINA TOURS on both sides. The name tags also bore the name of Crescent China Tours.

The attire they would be wearing when they disembarked was khaki slacks and lightweight matching Windbreakers, again with the name Crescent China Tours spread across the backs of each jacket. Baseball caps for the men with the same logo on the brim, and floppy fishing caps for the ladies also, as Maggie said, logoed out the kazoo.

The red light overhead turned on. The hostess's voice could be heard ordering all passengers to take their seats and buckle up. Everyone obeyed immediately.

In just minutes, they would be standing on Chinese soil.

Jack looked around. Everyone seemed calm, even he and Cooper. Harry, however, looked to Jack like a ticking time bomb. And as far as he could tell, there was no way to defuse Harry. He childishly crossed his fingers and hoped for the best. Harry was not stupid—he knew what was at stake. Mentally, Jack ordered Harry to take deep breaths and relax. Much to his surprise, he saw his best friend in the whole world do just that. And then he winked at Jack. Son of a bitch! Harry did have it going on. Cooper barked to show he got it, too.

Jack leaned back in the luxurious seat and closed his eyes. He didn't open them again until he felt the wheels of the Gulfstream hit the runway. He steeled himself for the pullback, then let loose with a long sigh. On land again. Jack really did hate flying.

As planned, the moment the cabin door opened, Maggie and Ted were the first two people off the plane. They skipped down the steps, duffels on their shoulders, and took up their positions at the base of the steps. When everyone was gathered in a circle, Maggie, with Ted's help, went into her spiel. "All right, people, we are here! Here meaning Hong Kong, China. Also known as the Pearl of the Orient. We have some time before our host hotel's, the Peninsula's, fleet of Rolls-Royces arrives to take us there, where we will spend the next two days. I'm told the vehicles are Peninsula green. Keep your eyes peeled for them.

"Does everyone have their gear? Are you sure you didn't leave anything on the planes? Raise your hand if you're good to go." Every hand shot in the air, even Snowden and his people, who had somehow arrived ten minutes before the rest of them did.

"All right, then, a short lesson on Hong Kong, but first, see the hats my partner and I are wearing? Notice the huge plumed feather. That's so you can spot us easily as we make our way around. If you lag behind or get lost, just look for the feather. Raise your hand if you understand," Maggie said in what she hoped was tour-guide dialogue. Hands shot in the air. The feather, they got it.

"Is this a warm cookie moment?" Isabelle grinned.

"Not yet," Ted snapped.

"Some facts, people. Pay attention. For starters, Hong Kong is located on China's south coast. It is a mere thirty-seven miles from Macau, which we will be visiting while we're here. As you know,

Macau is the gambling Mecca of the Orient. You might possibly win, but the odds are you will lose, so gamble accordingly. Do not lose more than you can afford to lose. Please. Crescent China Tours wants you to have enough left after this trip to come again.

"While we're here, we'll be visiting, if time permits, the Kowloon Peninsula and New Territories, with over two hundred offshore islands, the largest being Lantau Island. But only if time permits.

"Another fact is that Hong Kong averages 1,948 hours of sunshine per year. That's if you can see it with all the smog. The air in Hong Kong is very polluted. We've issued paper-filtered masks to you, and I urge you all to use them. I can guarantee that you will not like the diesel-scented air."

Maggie looked around to see if the Peninsula Rolls-Royces were anywhere near, so she could cut short her spiel, which was boring everyone to tears.

Ted decided to take over. "For those of you who don't know this, Hong Kong has the seventh largest stock exchange in the world, with a capitalization of US $2.3 trillion. That was back in 2009, so we can assume it is much more by now.

"Hong Kong is the eighth most expensive city for expatriates. Hong Kong is also rated fourth in terms of the highest percentage of millionaire households, behind Switzerland,

Qatar, and Singapore, with 8.5 percent of all households owning at least one million US dollars."

"Like we really care about this," Kathryn grumbled. "Someone should be paying attention to those four guys over by the gate. They haven't taken their eyes off us since we got off the plane."

"Thank God, here come our rides!" Nikki shouted.

Maggie blew her whistle for silence. "Orderly fashion, everyone, and yes, I have been watching those four guys myself. Pile in. We need to go through customs. And then we're on our own. Don't look obvious, people. Some pictures of our observers would be nice if someone can manage that little feat without drawing attention to ourselves. If successful, we can upload them and send them on to Abner to check out for us."

Dennis was happily snapping away, his phone pointing everywhere but at the four men standing at the gate. In his haste, he pretended to stumble, giving him just enough time to aim and click before righting himself. "Done and so done," he chortled as he quickly pressed more buttons. "Abner will have it in five seconds."

"Good work, kid," Ted said.

Finally, the tour group was settled in the luxurious limousines and headed to customs, where they were whizzed in and out in under thirty minutes.

And then they were finally on their way to the Peninsula Hotel. The drive was made in virtual silence as the people in the various cars tried to make sense out of the congestion, the smell, the demonstrations, and Hong Kong in general.

The time was late afternoon.

On their arrival, the group waited while Maggie and Ted as the tour leaders checked the group in. Lizzie Fox had requested the entire eighth floor even though they wouldn't be using all the rooms. There had been no problem once she agreed to wire the money from a hastily set-up corporate account. Armed with all the paperwork, they found that it took just minutes for everyone to locate their rooms and settle in. They all agreed to meet in the lobby in ninety minutes, enough time to shower and change. No one was upset that the time for high tea had come and gone, nor were they upset to see that it was fully dark outside. So much could be accomplished once the sun had set.

Snowden and his people took off on their own, the agreed-on plan.

The gang asked for and got a hotel van with no windows that would accommodate all of them to Dishbang Deshi's showroom on Nathan Road, where the plan was to order bolts and bolts of silks to be shipped back to the States. Harry sat in front with Ted, who was doing the driving.

While the ride wasn't as pleasant as the ride to the hotel in the Rolls-Royces, it met their needs, and no one complained. Not even Dennis, who had to hold Cooper on his lap because of the lack of room.

Ted turned on the radio and instructed Harry to tell them what was going on in regard to the demonstrations taking place. "Are we going to run into any trouble? Are we even near the area where it's all taking place? And while you're at it, tell us what the hell they're demonstrating for. This would not be a good time for a van full of Americans with bogus passports to get arrested. And just for the record, this map looks like a three-year-old drew it up with some bad crayons."

Harry leaned forward to hear better. He listened for a full five minutes before he told Ted to turn down the sound. "They're saying there are over nine thousand demonstrators, and they're using umbrellas to confuse the issue. It seems last night they took back part of the Mong Kok District that they'd ceded the day before. Talks failed. The university president, Leonard Cheng, was the moderator.

"It's a pro-democracy demonstration. Beijing is not happy with what's going on. We're okay the way we're traveling. We'll skirt the troubled areas. Just be alert and always cede to the other guy, and you won't get in trouble.

"They're saying two hundred and forty people were injured and taken to hospitals in the last twenty-four hours. Eighteen police officers were also injured. They arrested thirty-three people for property damage, disorderly conduct, weapons possession, and resisting arrest. This took place in a residential area of Kowloon. Another area that is close, but we'll skirt it, too. It's the area they call the main section of downtown."

"Turn here, Ted! Jeez, you almost missed it. Damn, I never saw such congestion. Where the hell are we supposed to park? Harry?" Jack bellowed

"Like I'm supposed to know? Wherever you can see a spot," Harry shot back.

"I've never seen so many people in my life. It looks like the seven million people who live here are out and about. The air is so putrid, you can barely breathe. How do these people live here with this pollution?" Jack asked. "It just seeps into this van."

"It's not like they have a choice, Jack. They live here. They also die young," Harry said ominously.

"I see a spot! Hurry, Ted, snag it, and let's get this show on the road. If this crazy-ass map is even half right, then the showroom we want is about a block up on the right.

"You called your buddy Dishbang Deshi, right, Harry?" Jack said, making it more of a statement than a question.

"I did, but he wasn't taking calls. I had to leave a message. Entrance to the showroom is by appointment only. In my message, I left the key word that Dishbang Deshi and I agreed upon, which was *Jun.* Don't worry, he'll be here. He's just playing it careful because he's scared out of his wits."

Ted managed to squeeze the hotel van into a space so small, he was sweating profusely when he climbed out. He immediately started to gag, as did the others. They quickly put on their filtered masks, then formed a straight line like a mother duck and her ducklings as they followed Maggie and Ted to make their way to the Bang Import and Export showroom, with those behind keeping Ted's and Maggie's plumed feathers in sight. Cooper barked the entire way.

It was a modern showroom, with plate-glass windows decorated in red-and-gold Chinese symbols. The waiting room was a comfortable area with bamboo chairs, colorful cushions, and a proliferation of luscious green plants. Colorful art hung on the wall, models wearing presumably silk gowns with the silk purchased at Bang Import and Export. A bell tinkled somewhere, then a buzzer sounded from the back of the showroom. A slim man nattily dressed in a custom-made silk suit, of course, walked toward them. He looked around, puzzled at the group of people standing clustered together. He stood on his tiptoes to see the taller men in the back—Ted, Jack, Espinosa, and Dennis.

The nattily dressed man frowned, his eyes worried. "Can I help you?"

Harry stepped forward. "Cut the crap, Dishbang Deshi, it's me, Harry. We're in these getups to protect you. Start showing me bolts of silk and talk like you've never talked before."

Dishbang Deshi fought a smile. He nodded and gestured for Harry to follow him to the far wall, where long bolts of colorful silk were stacked one on top of the other. He started to gesture with his hands at the various bolts just as the doorbell tinkled from the front of the shop.

Nikki and Kathryn were the closest to the door. They watched as five men pushed against the door just as the little lady at the desk pressed the buzzer to try to lock it. Her job done, she picked up her purse and a light stole and left the showroom, a look of fear on her face. "So much for by appointment only," Nikki whispered. "Don't take your eyes off them. They are trouble with a capital T."

Isabelle looked at Kathryn and Nikki and said, "Now I ask you, do those guys look like they're here to buy silk?"

Yoko, sensing trouble, turned around and

ran to Nikki and grabbed her around the waist the way a child would if frightened. She hissed, "They do not belong here."

"You're right about that, too. The question is, did they make us or are they here for that guy we came to see? Kathryn whispered. "We can take them, Nikki."

Jack sidled up to Nikki and said, "They look like gangbangers. They're spreading out. Classic maneuver. Also a big mistake."

Nikki looked at Ted and said, "Make sure the door is locked, then turn the sign around to say that the showroom is closed. Then lower the blinds."

Dennis jumped up to help. If the five men noticed, they gave no sign that anything had changed since they had entered the shop as they perused the many bolts of colored silk.

Out of the corner of his eye, Harry watched the way the men spread out. "You in shape, Dishbang Deshi, or do I have to take these guys out on my own?"

Harry's longtime friend tried for a nonchalant smile, but it came out as more of a frightened grimace. "I think I can hold my own."

"Maybe you should sit this one out, pal. Between me and the ladies, we can take these guys with our eyes closed."

"You're jesting of course," Dishbang Deshi said in a jittery voice. In the same jittery voice that was lower, he whispered, "In case you haven't noticed, Harry, those women are *old*. Except for the child. I don't think either one of us should expect any help from a gaggle of old women and one child."

"Look at me, Dishbang Deshi. Do I look like I'm jesting? Do you think I came halfway around the world to let five scrawny guys who haven't shaved yet take me? For your information, those old women could take us both out and never break a sweat."

While Harry and Dishbang Deshi argued back and forth, Annie and Myra were trying to take it all in. "This is exciting, isn't it, Myra?" Annie said as she fingered a bolt of sky-blue silk. "Those men do not have a clue. Look how the boys are positioning themselves. Definitely third-string. I think you and I could take them, but from the looks of things, you and I are sitting this one out."

"Hit it, honey," Harry bellowed.

Her eyes dancing, Yoko started to skip across the room to come to a stop in front of one of the five scraggly-looking men. It happened so fast, the others barely had time to blink. Yoko dropped down slightly, bringing her clenched fists directly up into the man's groin before she straightened, whirled, and kicked out, sending the gangbanger across the room, where Kathryn caught him under his arms. Nikki grabbed one leg, Isabelle the other, and they had him trussed like a Thanksgiving turkey within seconds.

"One down and four to go," Nikki grunted as she dragged the man to a small alcove, where she shoved him between two bolts of champagne-colored silk. When she turned around, she saw that the other four men were similarly bound.

"Now what?" Charles demanded.

All eyes turned to Dishbang Deshi. He shrugged. "As much as I hate to lose all this silk, I think we should simply stuff them inside the cores. Each bolt can hold two men. But first, don't we want them to talk? They must have cell phones. Shouldn't we be checking on that?"

"Maybe you aren't so dumb after all, Dishbang Deshi. Good thinking. Annie, Myra, call Snowden, explain we need to get rid of some silk. Tell him time is of the essence."

"Okay, Harry, you have the floor. Talk to these guys and see what you can get out of them. If they speak English, go with that. If not, translate as you go along. Ah, five cell phones. This is good. No other ID. Not good," Jack said. "I guess in a way we should be flattered that whoever is behind this thought these five could take us. My, oh my, now, aren't they going to be surprised," Jack said.

One by one, he tossed the phones to the girls. "See who they called last and who called them."

Fergus ran to the door the moment he heard the bell. He peeked between the slats of the door covering before he opened the door to reveal Avery Snowden and six of his men.

"I have to say I did not expect this much action this fast. It goes without saying I'm going to need a delivery truck," Snowden said happily.

"It's out back," Dishbang Deshi said.

Cooper took that moment to get up from his position behind a bolt of scarlet silk. He walked into the room and circled it before he came to a stop next to Harry, who was getting nowhere fast with his interrogation. He let out a soft yip, then another, as he encouraged Harry to step back. Satisfied at the distance, Cooper moved forward, growled, and snarled, his teeth glowing brightly as he lunged at the man Harry had been questioning. The man, his eyes wild with terror, started to scream as he let loose with a string of Chinese that made Harry laugh out loud.

"Good job, Coop. Good job. You can go back to sleep now." Cooper strutted back to his bolt of scarlet silk and lay down.

"Okay, everyone, listen up. This is what this scumbag just volunteered."

Chapter 10

"Spit it out, Harry! What did that weasel just say?" Jack demanded after ten long minutes of hysterical Chinese dialogue.

Harry grinned. "Well, for starters this particular weasel said he's more afraid of *the kid* than the dog. Kudos, honey," he said to Yoko, who beamed in delight.

"What else?" Jack said, quickly losing his patience.

"Actually, nothing. These guys are thugs for hire. They got their orders over the phone. Money is left at a noodle shop after they call in the results. I have the address of the noodle shop. None of them have ever seen their employer. You were right; they're the third string. They don't even know who the second or first string is. I guess we should take that to mean when these guys don't report in, the second string takes over. That's just a guess on my part. This guy doesn't know what the next step is."

"Did they come here for us or for your friend Dishbang Deshi?" Charles asked.

"For Dishbang Deshi. He said the five of them have been staking out his offices, but Dishbang Deshi has some good security and hasn't left the premises since he spirited his family out of China. Today was the first time he's left since then. They tried to get to him on the way here, but as I said, Dishbang Deshi's security is tight."

Another volley of Chinese reverberated about the room, this time coming from Dishbang Deshi.

"English only!" Kathryn bellowed. "How are we supposed to know what's going on if you babble in Chinese. English!" she thundered again. The others started to mumble and mutter among themselves. Dishbang Deshi drew back in horror, his eyes on Harry.

"He wants Snowden to smuggle him out, to get him to the airport. He also wants to know why these women have such authority. He says right now he doesn't trust his own security if these guys were able to make it here to the showroom. He knows the second string will be . . . should we say, more dangerous if not lethal."

Annie stepped forward. "Well, now, I'd say

that all depends on what Mr. Dishbang has to tell us. About your friend Jun Yu and what went down," she drawled.

Harry looked at Annie, then at Dishbang Deshi, and shrugged. "She's the boss. What she says goes. Don't even think about telling me you don't know anything. Just for the record, Dishbang Deshi, you're going to hate Mud Flats, Mississippi. You sure you don't want to stay and fight?" Harry waved his arms about. "What happens to all of this, the business, your money, if you leave?"

"I have to think about my family. I'm not a coward, if that's what you're implying. I have loyal people who are capable of running my business." Seeing the disbelief on Harry's face, Dishbang Deshi cringed. "I'll have to take my chances. I have money in the States in various banks. I'm not a complete fool, Harry, even if you think I am."

"Where's the duct tape?" Snowden barked.

Startled, Dishbang Deshi pointed to a cabinet under the window.

"Cut the bullshit, Dishbang Deshi. Right now, all you're worried about is your own skin. Which, by the way, means squat to me and the rest of this group. So before my friend makes the decision to take you or leave you here, start talking."

"I thought you were my friend, Harry."

Harry's jaw dropped. "I'm taking that to mean you think I should put you and your safety ahead of my daughter. If that's what you mean, then no, I am not your friend. Now start talking. I want to know everything, and only speak English."

"I told you on the phone, Harry. Jun Yu did not tell me anything. He said the less I knew, the less I could tell. Rumors have been rife this whole past year. I'm repeating rumors, so treat what I say as such." Dishbang Deshi threw his hands in the air to make his point, and muttered, "I don't believe this is happening.

"All right, all right!" he shouted at the menacing look he was seeing on Harry's face. "Remember, all I'm saying now is rumor. You must know that China is the number two film market in the world. You must also know that having the convenience of an online subscription streaming service is a natural fit for Alibaba's e-commerce network. You must have heard about that company. The whole world knows about Alibaba and that guy Jack Ma. China, you should be aware, is not a straightforward place to do business. Just recently, Chinese regulators announced that they would cap the amount of foreign TV programs local providers could stream to online subscribers. Billions are in the offing. Not yen, Harry. US billions with a capital B. I bought Alibaba stock. I hope you and your people did, too. It's going to skyrocket. Take my word for it.

"You must also know that there is a new temporary Abbot at the monastery. There are those who say he isn't even an Abbot but an imposter. His name is Chi Xongin. The Chinese media refer to him as the CEO monk. He and whomever he represents want to commercialize the Shaolin Monastery. He's rented out the monastery as well as its name for films, reality television shows, and computer games. What was once sacred has now become a sick joke. The man believed to be an imposter even went so far as to approve an online store selling Shaolin kung fu manuals for 9,999 yen or $1,600 US. Many are saying he leads too lavish a lifestyle for a holy man. To Jun Yu that meant he is not a holy man but a shill of some kind. I heard that Jun Yu was planning on exposing him, but that was just a rumor. I want to stress that Jun Yu did not tell me any of this, so let's be clear on the facts as I know them.

"About a month ago, I heard that an exhibition was being planned with Jun Yu, you, me, and Wing Ping. You remember Wing Ping, don't you, Harry?" Dishbang Deshi said, a look of revulsion on his face. When he saw Harry clench his fists and his jaw tighten, he rushed on. "I called Jun Yu, and he said there was no truth to the rumor. You do remember how Wing Ping was expelled, so that they crowned Jun Yu the number one martial-arts expert. And all those threats he made. How his family lost face. Then it got worse; Wing Ping joined the triads and became a contract killer. At least that was the scuttlebutt. I asked Jun Yu if it was true, and he said he didn't know. But he also said that, in his opinion, it was a route Wing Ping would take.

"Wing Ping hated us, Harry. We were everything he wanted to be and for some reason could not. We were never able to figure out what his problems were aside from the fact that he was in love with himself. You know that. What I don't understand is why he would wait all these years for payback if that's what this is. If we're being honest here, then we have to agree that Wing Ping is the one who should have been number one. He was born to the art. We had to learn it. He was better than all of us put together, and you know it, I know it, and Jun Yu knew it. We spoke of it many times.

"Then, during our last year, the Abbot kicked him out before the decision was made. The Wing family, one of the oldest families in all of China, lost face. Wing Ping dropped off the face of the earth. As far as I know, the Wing family never recovered. I do know for sure that both of Wing Ping's parents are dead. Wing Ping has only a brother and three sisters. All three have families, many children among them. All are older, and all of them went to the monastery and left honorably. Wing Ping was the outcast, the black sheep of the family. The sisters and the brother cut all ties to Wing Ping. Again, Harry, this is all rumor. There is nothing I can pin down as pure fact.

"You know as well as I do that the monks

never kick anyone out. They work you tirelessly and themselves as well, but in the end, when you leave the monastery, you leave honorably. You do not leave in disgrace. Wing Ping was the first to be cast out at the Shaolin Monastery. It has been said the elder Wings died in disgrace and that Wing Ping is finally trying to reverse all of that."

"That's bullshit!" The words exploded from Harry's mouth like gunshots.

"What do you want from me, Harry? I told you it was all rumor. I don't know anything. Once I left the monastery, I took over my family's business. I'm a businessman. I got married, started a family, and I mind my own business. Yes, I saw Jun Yu from time to time for a dinner or a lunch when he would come to Hong Kong. He stayed at my house. My children played with his children. My wife and Jun Yu's wife shopped and had tea together. Jun Yu and I talked. I stayed in touch with you because that is what friends do, they stay in touch. It was your decision, Harry, to send your daughter to the monastery, not mine. Had you asked me, I would have told you not to do that, but you did not ask me. You can't blame me for any of this. I did what Jun Yu asked of me. As I would do for you. I would hope that you would do the same for me."

"So you're going to cut and run, is that the bottom line?" Harry barked.

"Yes, Harry, that was my original intention. However, in these last minutes I am thinking I need to stay here, or you're going to get yourself killed. I think you are going to need me. And, as you pointed out, I probably won't like living in Mud Flats, Mississippi. So where does that leave us?"

Harry looked around at the group to see their reaction to Dishbang Deshi's little speech.

Charles stepped forward. "I personally think Mr. Dishbang will be an asset. Poll the others for their opinion."

Avery Snowden spoke up. "Can you hold up on your voting here and give me the go-ahead. By now, whoever these guys work for are going to be expecting some kind of progress report."

Dishbang Deshi moved then, quickly like a panther stalking his query. He headed for the back of the showroom and threw open the huge metal doors to reveal a service truck used to haul the huge bolts of silk. In the blink of an eye he had the truck's rear doors open. He stepped back as Snowden and his men loaded the bolts of silk containing the five men inside the tubes. They were not gentle.

"Where are you taking them? There are eyes everywhere. You will be marked before you reach the main road."

Snowden rolled his eyes at the little Chinese for a moment before he turned away. "I'll call you or Harry to let you know where you can pick up your truck," was his response. Dishbang Deshi shrugged. He closed and locked the showroom doors with not one lock but three. He was back in the main part of the showroom within seconds.

"Now what?" Nikki asked. She pointed to Dishbang Deshi and asked if he was going with them or where else he was going.

"What's it gonna be, Dishbang Deshi? You travel with us, they'll know we made them. Whoever *they* are. Or you take your security you aren't too comfortable with at the moment and head back to your offices, where you aren't sure whether you'll be safe. It has to be your decision. They're onto you as it is, and there is strength in numbers, and we have quite a few numbers right here," Harry said, waving his arm about. "If you plan on going with us, you need to get rid of that snappy custom jacket you're wearing. Dennis, give him your Windbreaker and ball cap."

A smile tugged at the corner of Dishbang Deshi's lips. He raised his hand to stop Dennis. "Well said, Harry, my good, old dear friend, since you put it like that, I think I will, as they say, join up. I just told you that. A no-brainer, no? That's a favorite expression of my oldest daughter. She loves American slang."

"We need to get out of here right now. We've been here too long as it is. Those guys are probably past due in checking in with whoever," Isabelle said as she nervously looked around.

Harry quickly explained about the van they'd hired and where it was parked.

"How do you lock up here?" Charles asked.

"It's a spring-loaded latch, the door is steel, and it will automatically lock behind us. It's dark out, which is a good thing. Move quickly once the door closes."

Cooper sat back on his haunches and howled. Then he did his circle dance to get everyone's attention, still howling. Everyone stopped in their tracks.

"What?" Jack bellowed. "What's up with Cooper, Harry?"

"Someone is on the loading dock out back. The dog senses or smells them, and that is why he is barking," Dishbang Deshi said. "What do you want to do, Harry? Invite them in?" This last was said with a cocky grin that made Harry laugh out loud.

"Jack, Dennis, Yoko, and I will stay with Dishbang Deshi. Take Cooper and head for the van. Go back to the hotel. Be quick about it. If anyone is in front, take them out," Harry barked.

Dennis grew light-headed at the prospect of Harry's thinking his martial-arts expertise was good enough to be part of whatever was going to go down. His stomach churned like a windmill in a wild hurricane.

"With pleasure," Kathryn said, saluting Harry

as Charles ushered everyone, including Cooper, out the front door.

"Do you want to open the bay doors, or should we wait for them to kick them in?" Jack asked as he bounced on his toes to flex the muscles in the calves of his legs.

"Let's make them work for it." Dishbang Deshi grinned. Harry agreed. Yoko just laughed. Dennis fought to keep all the snacks he'd eaten on the plane in his stomach.

"Hey, Harry, these guys any good?" Dishbang Deshi jerked his head in Dennis and Jack's direction.

Harry laughed, an evil sound. "I trained them both. Jack is a black belt, the kid is third-degree brown. You saw my lovely lotus flower in action. Any more questions?"

Dishbang Deshi grinned. "Nope. Like old times, eh, Harry?"

"Sounds like they're using a sledgehammer on the doors," Dennis said in a jittery voice.

"It does sound like that, doesn't it," Yoko agreed. She sounded as if she was discussing whether it was going to rain.

"What do you think, Harry, ten minutes? Five? This must be a mind-your-own-business neighborhood since no one is coming to your friend's aid with all that racket," Jack observed.

"It's live and let live," Dishbang Deshi said. "No one wants to get involved."

"The door is weakening," Harry said, peering at the hinges that held the massive double doors in place. "But to answer your question, Jack, I'll go with five minutes. Want to guess how many guys are out there?"

"Sounds like a dozen or more," Dennis said.

"Four would be my guess. I read somewhere, or possibly I saw it in a movie, but I think the triads send out groups of four. They take no prisoners." Dennis shivered at Yoko's ominous tone.

"Yes, that's how it works. They're well trained, and they work in sync. I love to gamble and go to Macau at least once a month. Want to place a wager, anyone?"

"On what?" Jack asked.

"Them. Us. Who takes who out. There's always a winner and a loser. I have never been a loser. Well, once when the Abbot picked Jun Yu over Harry and me. But right now, that doesn't count. Oh, one last thing. These guys fight to the death. That's what taking no prisoners means. You all need to know that."

Jack looked at his watch when another earth-thundering blow hit the double doors. Two and a half minutes to go. He rolled his neck on his shoulders in an effort to loosen his cramped muscles. While he wasn't loose as a goose, he nonetheless felt confident that he could hold his own and not let Harry and Dishbang Deshi down. He sighed. Why did life always have to get so complicated?

BOOM!

"One more good hit and the doors will cave

in," Dishbang Deshi said as he held his hands up, his fingers moving like pistons. Jack knew those stiff fingers could kill if they hit the right targets.

"I think we should all sit in a circle and pretend we're meditating. That will throw them off for a few seconds, just enough time for us to spring up in surprise," Dennis said as he flopped down and assumed the lotus position.

"Good thinking, kid," Harry said as he dropped to the floor, Yoko at his side. Dishbang Deshi did likewise. Jack was the last to drop, his eyes never leaving the heavy metal doors, which were slowly caving in.

"Does he shave yet?" Dishbang Deshi hissed in Harry's ear.

"Once a month," Harry hissed in return.

Dennis heard the question and laughed. "Actually, it's twice a month these days."

BOOM! The hinges on the heavy metal doors gave way and the doors sagged. Four men, all dressed in loose black clothing, advanced into the room. Dennis was right—for the barest seconds, the scary-looking men stood rooted to the floor as they stared at the small circle of people.

"On the count of three, guys," Harry whispered.

"One."

"Two."

"Three."

Chapter 11

The moment the five Americans heard Harry hiss *three*, their legs were spring-loaded pistons, and they were airborne, arms windmilling in all directions, leaving the four black-clad figures spinning in shock and dismay. It was over in less than five minutes. It took an additional two minutes to use up the rest of the duct tape Snowden had used on the first group of thugs and left behind.

"Good job!" Dishbang Deshi said as he eyed the four bound men. He watched as Yoko searched their baggy pants for cell phones.

"Burners," she announced. "These look just like the others, one number programmed in. My first thought is these phones were used to call the first guys. I guess that when they didn't report in, this group knew something was up. What's next?"

Jack was already on the phone with Snowden, telling him he needed to return to the showroom to pick up another delivery. He held the phone away from his ear so the others could appreciate the man's rich vocabulary. "He said if nothing goes wrong, he should be here in thirty minutes."

Dennis found himself giggling and didn't know why. It rubbed off on Yoko, who also started to giggle. Harry glared at both of them until Yoko flipped him the bird.

"We need to get out of here, and we need to do it quickly," Dishbang Deshi said. "Timing is everything with these goons. The first string will be within striking distance. Your friend driving my truck might not be so lucky this time around. Let's take another crack at the one with the pigtail. He looks to me like he knows something. Just a gut feeling, Harry."

Yoko held up her hands and said, "Allow me to do the interrogation, my dutiful husband. Unless you think you can do it better."

Harry wasn't going there. He simply stepped back and watched his petite wife hitch up her white knee socks, scuff her ballet slippers on the carpet, then adjust the wire-rim glasses on the bridge of her nose. "Does he have a name, my dutiful husband?" Yoko singsonged.

"Um . . . he said it was Shen, but they all said their name was Shen. Obviously, they're all lying."

"Do you think any of them understand English? This one in particular?" she asked.

"Not sure."

"It doesn't really matter. I think I can get my point across in English. It's all in the expression, in the eyes, the flare of the nostril. Stand back. Allow me to proceed," Yoko said in the same lilting tone.

The others watched, mesmerized, as Yoko made her way over to the man Harry and Dishbang Deshi thought might be the ringleader. She dropped to her knees and studied the man for a full minute before she removed her wire-rim glasses. She made a slow-motion production of prying off the cap that cushioned the back of the ear and was left with a slender, sharp wire in her hand. Slowly and deliberately, she leaned over and whispered, "I am going to stick this wire in your right ear until it comes out your left ear." She gave a brief demonstration. "Then I am going to shove it up your nose and wiggle it around inside your brain." She tickled the end of the man's nose to demonstrate what the wire could do. He recoiled in fear, his eyes wild as he started to jabber hysterically in Chinese.

"If that doesn't kill you, I will stick it in each eye, and after that, it will go into your . . .

penis. That is, if you haven't bled out by then."
The wire moved in all directions, the man's
eyes filling with tears. "Just so you know, the
pain will be unbearable." To make her point,
she dug her clenched fist into the man's groin.
"That was a love tap." The man howled in pain.

"What's she saying?" Dennis demanded.
"She's just trying to scare him, right?"

"Trust me, kid, you do *not* want to know.
The reason you don't want to know is, she will
do everything she's telling him she'll do. From
the look on his face, the guy knows it, too. Just
watch and . . . *learn*."

Dennis wasn't sure he wanted to learn, so he
squeezed his eyes shut.

The man thrashed about as he tried to move
his head as far away from Yoko as he could get.
"See, my wonderful husband, he does understand English. How astute of you and your
friend to figure out he is the one. I say that
only because he looks so stupid.

"Speak!" Yoko shrieked.

"I know nothing. I follow orders. I know
nothing."

Yoko looked up at Harry with an adoring
look. "What is the Chinese word for bullshit,
my wonderful husband? When you say it to
him, say it forcefully, to make sure he understands."

Harry barked out the appropriate word in
Chinese.

"Then tell us everything you *don't* know," Yoko said. She put the wire right up to his ear. The man tried to pull away, but Yoko held his shoulder to the floor with amazing strength. The man stared up at Harry, his eyes pleading for mercy as he tried to struggle free to no avail.

In Chinese, Harry warned the man that his little lotus flower had no patience and loved the sight of blood. The man started to babble. When he wound down, spittle oozing out of the corners of his mouth, Harry said, "What he said is all the English he knows. I think he's telling the truth," he said in disgust.

"He's lying," Yoko said. "I can see it in his eyes. I changed my mind, I'm going to start at the bottom and work my way to the top. Tell him that in Chinese, Harry."

Harry laughed out loud when the bound man rolled over onto his stomach. "So much for my insight. I was wrong and you were right, my precious flower petal."

"Pull his pants down, Harry." Harry happily obliged, but he had to keep his foot on the man's back to hold him in place.

Yoko crept closer. "This is going to *really* hurt!" She wiggled the wire to make her point. Her arm was raised and then lowered to plunge the wire into its target when with a Herculean effort the man rolled away from under Harry's foot, screaming at the top of his lungs.

"I know nothing. Maybe one little bit. Not much. I hear . . . maybe something."

"What?" Jack exploded.

"Fix my pants. Not good exposed. Is cold here. Not like you look."

"It's cold here because of the silk, you weasel," Dishbang Deshi bellowed at the top of his lungs.

"I like the view. Makes me laugh. See me laugh, ha-ha," Yoko said.

"Oh, jeez," Dennis muttered.

Dishbang Deshi's face was a study in confusion.

Harry turned away so his earsplitting grin with Jack couldn't be seen by the bound, half-naked man.

"What time is it?" the man asked.

"What difference does it matter? You aren't going anywhere," Dishbang Deshi said.

"More men come if I no call. I miss call. They kill me and you and all in room. You see. Soon they come."

"Yeah, right! Them and what army? We took you guys without breaking a sweat," Dennis said bravely, his eyes now open wide so he wouldn't miss anything.

"The bastard is stalling us. I know a stall when I see one," Jack said as he craned his neck to listen to any strange sounds that might be coming from the loading dock. "Dishbang Deshi, turn off the lights! Let's not make it easy on them. If that jerk is telling the truth, no sense giving them an edge. Snowden can find his way in the dark."

The room turned dark, only a faint yellowish light coming through the loading dock's open doors. Then a bright light appeared. It was Dishbang Deshi's delivery truck, being driven by Snowden and his people.

"We need to go in the truck, too. Your man can drop us off away from here. We can make our own way back to your hotel. They won't bother us there. Hurry!" Dishbang Deshi said.

"What about these doors? Won't someone rob you?" Dennis asked.

"Without a doubt. It is only silk. My life, your lives, are more important than bolts of silk. Hurry! The phones. Who has the phones?"

"I do," Yoko chirped. "Oooh, one is ringing now."

"Don't answer it," Harry bellowed.

"Bring the duct tape!" Jack ordered. "These guys might try screaming. At this hour of the night, that is not what we need." Dennis picked up the tape and slid his hand through the opening to wear it like a bracelet.

"Let's go! Let's go!" Dishbang Deshi shouted as the last man was dumped into the back of the van. He stood watch until all the others were safely inside before he climbed in and pulled the doors shut. "Go!"

The big truck trundled out of the narrow alley and onto a congested thoroughfare.

"We're going to be a target. My shop does

not make night deliveries, so we have to get rid of this truck as soon as possible. Go straight, make the next two rights, then a left, go maybe half a mile, and let us out. Then go wherever you plan on going and ditch this truck. Slash the tires, pull out the battery if you have time, and be sure to take the keys."

"You got all that, Snowden?" Jack bellowed.

"I got it! I got it! Like the countess says, this isn't my first rodeo. I've been here in Hong Kong so many times, I've lost count. I got it! We'll meet for breakfast, so put my order in for coffee, bacon, and eggs. I do not do tea. None of us do tea."

"Okay. Okay. I got it, too."

The big truck ground to a stop. Pedestrians scurried to get out of the way, and the five Americans and Dishbang Deshi exited through the back of the truck. The big truck lumbered off.

"Follow me, people. We're going to a pastry shop for tea and rice cakes. Just a normal stop before heading to the hotel. Try to look . . . like tourists. I will pretend to be your guide. Harry and I will speak Chinese. Just keep quiet and smile. Be sure to drink the tea and eat the cakes. If you don't, it will raise suspicion. Eyes are everywhere just waiting to report something to someone for a few yen."

Within minutes, the small group of six was seated at a round table. The shop was crowded, even at this late hour, with customers eating rice cakes and drinking tea or slurping noodle soup. It was a noisy crowd, all speaking Chinese. Harry more or less paired off with Dishbang Deshi, while Jack and Dennis sat next to each other. Yoko sat in the middle, still pretending to be a child. Her glasses, minus one arm, were still perched on her nose.

While Harry and Dishbang Deshi jabbered away in Chinese, Dennis leaned closer to Jack and whispered, "She wouldn't have . . . you know . . . *done that*, would she, Jack?"

Jack smiled as he bit into one of the sticky rice cakes sitting in front of him. "That and more, and she wouldn't have missed a beat, kid. All those women march to a different drummer. I thought you knew and accepted that."

"I did, I do, it's just that it was so real, so in my face. Hearing about things like that and actually seeing it going down is something else. I'm not being a wimp here."

"Yeah, you are, kid. Otherwise, we wouldn't be having this conversation. Let me ask you this, Dennis. Let's say Yoko faltered, tripped . . . whatever, and she dropped the wire, and the rest of us were preoccupied, could you have picked up that wire and did what Yoko intended?"

Dennis thought about the question for a moment. To lie or not to lie. "Probably not," he said honestly.

A grin split Jack's face. "Me either, kid. I

would have just smashed his nose up into his brain. Women just have a different take on . . . what works and what doesn't. And they've been at it longer than we have. In short, they don't mess around."

"I get it," Dennis said, gulping at the tea in his tiny cup. "What do you think Harry and that guy Dishbang Deshi are talking about?"

"No clue, kid."

What Dishbang Deshi and Harry were talking about had nothing to do with their present circumstances. While the conversation was the news of the day, their ever-watchful expressions were not.

"Everyone in Hong Kong is talking about the Brit who worked for the Bank of America who was arrested today in Wan Chai for a double murder. It's where you go for a special kind of nightlife." Dishbang Deshi lowered his voice to a whisper. "Just listen, Harry, that's all the people are talking about. We need to do and act like them, or we'll come under suspicion."

"I don't give a good rat's ass about some dumb-ass banker getting arrested. So that means you'll have to do the talking, and I'll ask questions," Harry said.

"The guy was twenty-nine, a British banker. They found one body stuffed in a suitcase and left on his balcony. The other one was inside the apartment."

"Prostitutes?" Harry asked.

"According to the press and TV coverage, yes.

The truth is, Hong Kong has a very low murder rate. The last big one was one of your Merrill Lynch bankers who was clubbed to death in 2003 by his wife, who drugged him beforehand by serving him a milkshake full of sleeping pills. Since he was one of yours, Harry, I thought you might remember." Dishbang Deshi lowered his voice and hissed. "Look like you're interested and say something, for hell's sake. People are watching us. And they're listening."

Harry cleared his throat. "Ah, yes, the milk-shake murder. It had a big run back in the States at the time. What's the Brit's name? Anyone you know, Dishbang Deshi?"

"No, but I use that bank here. The guy supposedly liked the high and good life. At twenty-nine, that's all guys think about around here. The British consulate is involved but not saying much. He was what you Americans call a mover and a shaker. He worked at Barclays. Attended Cambridge—Peterhouse, the oldest college—and was president of the Cambridge University History Society. Prior to Cambridge, he went to Winchester College, one of Britain's most famous and oldest public schools. He was also a cross-country runner and rower.

"You, of course, know what Facebook is, eh? He made a post that said, 'Money does buy happiness,' and twenty-nine is the perfect age."

"And I need to know all this crap, why?"

"You aren't listening to a thing I say, Harry. I told you to tune in the other patrons here and listen. Mr. Rurik George Caton Jutting is the sole topic of conversation. When in Rome . . ."

"Yeah, yeah, yeah! Can we leave now?"

"I don't see why not." Dishbang Deshi dug in his pocket and withdrew a fistful of yen notes and placed them under the teapot. "Slow and easy, everyone, smiles, little waves. A few bows to the waitstaff, and we can go. Walk very slowly, and do not draw attention to yourselves." No sooner were the words out of Dishbang Deshi's mouth than Dennis tripped over his own feet and fell forward. A portly little man at the next table acted quickly and stiff-armed him, breaking his fall. Jack pulled him back and upright. Dishbang Deshi stepped forward and let loose with a long string of dialogue that made the round little man smile and nod, then laugh out loud. Dennis winced, knowing he was the butt of some secret Chinese joke, but at the moment he simply did not care. He just wanted to get out of here.

"What did you say to that guy?" Dennis demanded the moment they were back out on the street.

"I said you were a tourist and in need of dancing lessons. Step lively now. We're almost to the hotel. Did anyone alert those in the hotel as to what happened at the showroom this evening?"

"I did," Yoko chirped. "Everyone is excited that things are moving so quickly. They're waiting for us in Myra's suite. We're to go straight up. We rented the entire floor, so there is plenty of room for you."

Dishbang Deshi nodded. "Ah, I see the lights, the Peninsula is just ahead. Step lively, act like you actually belong, and no one will stop you. Walk straight to the elevator and don't look at anyone."

The group followed Dishbang Deshi's directions. As Jack said later, it didn't look to him like anyone was paying undue attention to them. Yoko agreed. Dennis said he thought the majordomo looked at them a little too long as they made their way to the elevators. They all heaved a sigh of relief when they reached the partially open door to Myra's suite. They breezed in like a brisk wind. Jack had the presence of mind to turn and lock the door behind him.

Then everyone was talking at once. Alarmed, Dishbang Deshi stepped away from the others as he stared at them, then at Harry. "Who are these people, Harry? All these women! What do you think this is, a garden party?"

"Oh, dear, did that man just say what I think he said?" Annie asked.

"I think he did, dear," Myra cooed.

Kathryn took a step forward, and when her face was a bare inch from Dishbang Deshi's, she said, "I think the question should be, who are *YOU*?"

In a nanosecond, Dishbang Deshi was surrounded by women. "How nice. Now we can
play ring-around-the-rosy," Nikki said.

"You might want to stand over there by Ted,
kid. This could get real ugly, real fast." Dennis
scurried across the room, where a buffet of
food was set up. He was hungry, wanted to eat;
but more important, he wanted to know what
was going to happen to Harry's friend Dishbang Deshi. He popped a plump pink shrimp
into his mouth and crunched down. Kathryn
was a hothead. Nikki could kill with a look. Isabelle looked like she could chew nails and
spit rust. Alexis was toying with a long silken
cord, stretching it back and forth. Like a gar-
rote. Myra and Annie simply smiled as they
closed the circle tighter.

"Harry!" It was a desperate, high-pitched
squeal that made Harry laugh out loud. "I
warned you back in the showroom, Bang.
These women are not your average women.
They do not come from Mud Flats, Mississippi. They are . . . um . . . worldly."

"Are you . . . are you . . . saying they're . . .
killers? My God, what are you mixed up in,
Harry? First Jun Yu and now you and these . . .
these people."

"They're extraordinary women, Dishbang
Deshi. I know that even here in China you
must have heard about the American Vigilantes."

"Oh, my esteemed husband, such kind words

for our little group." Yoko giggled. "I will reward you later, my precious little dove." Harry turned five shades of red, pink, and reddish pink and purple pink and pale pink.

Dishbang Deshi took his time, letting his eyes lock on first one woman, then the other, until he completed the circle. He moved slightly to see Harry better before he passed out cold.

The women laughed in delight.

Chapter 12

Dishbang Deshi came to with a start, his eyes glazed as he stared up at the circle of women peering down at him. His heart hammered in his chest as he moved his head to seek out his friend Harry. He struggled to sit up but realized there was a heavy foot on his chest. Kathryn's foot. He held out his hands, palms facing outward in open surrender.

Harry stepped forward until he was between Yoko and Isabelle. He leaned down, stretched out his hand, and pulled his old friend to his feet. Dishbang Deshi started to babble in Chinese. In a nanosecond, Nikki was in his face demanding he speak English. In a voice that could have frozen a leg of lamb, she said, "Let's hear the magic words. You *will* respect us, women or not. Or"—her voice turned sweeter than honey—"we will take you out right here. If for some ridiculous reason you don't think that is possible, just ask your friend Harry here what we are capable of."

"That won't be necessary." In a voice that was so fearful, so jittery-sounding, Dishbang Deshi could hardly believe the words coming out of his own mouth. "I'm getting the picture here. You have my apologies, ladies."

"It's a wise man who knows when to step up to the plate, Mr. Dishbang. Your apology is accepted," Myra said smartly. "Now, can we get on with the business at hand?"

"I don't see why not," Maggie said as she moved away to stand next to Ted. "Let's make our plans for the morning, then I really need to get some sleep. This jet lag is doing me in."

Two hours later, the group had a plan formulated and were about to separate for the night when there was a knock on the door. As one, the group tensed but when a rat-a-tat-tat knock sounded again, Jack knew it was Avery Snowden. He threw the door open wide and stood back.

"Just so you know, the first string is out there. My people are on it, and I'm posting two operatives on this floor, one right outside the elevator and the other one at the stairwell. I can't be sure, but I think it's your friend Dishbang Deshi they're after, not the rest of you. Seeing as how they must have followed you all here, at the very least they are suspicious of the Americans. I spotted them immediately. Surveillance-wise, they are amateurs.

"Any orders, ladies and gentlemen? If not, I'm going to retire for the rest of the night. I'll be up and ready to go by five o'clock. We'll convene in the lobby at seven."

Dennis danced around, first on one foot, then the other. He desperately wanted to ask Snowden if he thought they were safe in going to sleep but didn't want to appear like a wimp, so he just chewed down on his lower lip and let his stomach curdle at the thought of being murdered in a bed halfway around the world.

He risked a glance at the others. But no one seemed unduly worried, not even Harry, his idol.

The others gathered up their gear and followed Snowden out the door, hotel room card readers in hand. They all agreed to meet in the lobby for breakfast at seven the next morning.

When the door finally closed behind the others, Annie made sure the double lock and chain were in place. Only she, Fergus, Myra, and Charles remained in the suite. Annie's suite could be accessed through a short hallway off Myra's suite. There was no need for them to go out into the hallway at all.

"Well, the ball is in motion," Annie said. "I have to admit, I didn't think things would

move this fast. I always more or less thought of
China as being slow for some reason."

"I think what you mean is sneaky slow, dear,"
Myra said. "I will admit I do have a worry, however. What happens to Harry's friend Dishbang Deshi when we leave in the morning to
go on our shopping expedition? No one said
whether he's staying behind or going with
Avery. Obviously, if we want to keep our cover
intact as far as being tourists, then we cannot be
seen with Dishbang Deshi. Which then brings
up another question. Was Dishbang Deshi seen
with Harry, Jack, Yoko, and Dennis at the café?
If he was, then our cover is blown."

Charles could feel the start of a full-blown
migraine coming on. "We have to assume our
cover is blown if Snowden is right and the first
string is already outside. If that's the case, then
those men have already notified whomever
they report to that this is all a plot against
China. I'm not liking this one little bit."

Fergus massaged his temples. Charles was
right. "Call Snowden now, Charles. I do not
plan to close my eyes until I know *exactly* what's
going on. For all we know, when we wake up,
there could be a hundred police down there in
the lobby waiting to toss us into one of their
stinky prisons. Now, Charles!"

Myra held up her hand to stop Charles.
"This might just be a guess on my part, dear,
but I rather think Alexis has the matter under

control. She did bring her red magic bag of tricks with her. I saw it on the plane. I think in the morning, Mr. Dishbang, also known as Dishbang Deshi to the rest of us, will be someone else entirely. Just another member of the Crescent China Tours group. Annie, do you agree?"

"Of course! Of course! That's exactly how it will go down. Never mind, Charles. And, Fergus, my darling, do not fret. We ladies have it in hand. I think we'll say good night now." Annie gave Fergus such a shove, he literally sailed across the room to the open door that separated the two suites.

"Well then, my dear, I suggest we follow suit and hit the sack," Charles said as he felt the tension in his neck abate. Perhaps there would be no migraine after all. Unless Myra had other . . . *Don't go there, Charles,* he warned himself. Then again, Myra did look like she was in a playful mood. . . .

Pegasus had nothing on Charles Martin as he galloped toward the bedroom.

As was inevitable, morning came to Hong Kong as it always did. To everyone's dismay, early on the atmosphere was gray with the effects of the heavy pollution that poisoned the air. Doom and gloom in her voice, Maggie announced that things would get brighter when they partook of some good old-fashioned shopping. The others wholeheartedly agreed. They were all down in the lobby well before the appointed hour of seven o'clock.

"We do breakfast just like all tours do," Maggie announced in her best tourist-guide voice. "I suggest we all do the buffet so we can move along at a good pace. Then we can depart the hotel and head for Nathan Road, where we will shop till noon, have lunch, then shop some more until three thirty, at which point we will head back here to the hotel, partake of high tea, then settle down and discuss the day. Raise your hand if you are in agreement. And by the way, we need to welcome a new member to our group, Mr. Bik Bo. Mr. Bo is from San Francisco. He got stranded somehow, and his tour company shuttled him over to us. So, everyone, a big welcome to Mr. Bik Bo."

The gang waved with gusto. Mr. Bo grinned, showing twice as many teeth as he had when he was Dishbang Deshi. Mr. Bo also had twice as much hair, a new eye color, and ruddy cheeks, along with ten extra pounds plus two inches more in height. All thanks to Alexis and her red magic bag of tricks.

"Mr. Bo will stay as close to Alexis as possible during our shopping trip. We don't want him pairing off with any of the guys, so if someone is following us as a group, nothing will cause suspicion. If we're all good here, then let's get some breakfast so we have enough energy for all the shopping we're going to be doing. Ah, I see Mr. Snowden heading our way. Okay, everybody, showtime. Act just like the stupid tourists we're supposed to be."

"Nice talk, girl." Nikki giggled as she walked alongside Maggie, her gaze sweeping the exquisite dining room for anything that appeared out of the ordinary.

"I'm thinking I missed my calling. Maybe I was meant to be a tour guide in my other life." Maggie lowered her voice, and said, "I'm not seeing anything to cause concern, are you, Nikki?"

"No. But we are inside the hotel. I'm sure things will change once we get outside into the street."

The quick meal was accompanied by a lot of girl talk and a bit of nibbling while the guys mostly remained silent while stoking down a heavy-duty breakfast. While they chewed and swallowed, their eyes and ears were tuned to anyone who looked like they didn't belong in the elegant hotel and whatever conversations they could overhear. Surprisingly, most of the conversations they could overhear were spoken in English by tourists like what they were supposed to be.

"No cause for alarm," was Charles's assessment. Snowden agreed. "Yet." Charles followed up with a roguish wink.

And then they were outside waiting for the transportation that would take them to Nathan Road for their shopping excursion. The group separated and climbed into three white hotel vans much like the one that had been assigned to them the night before.

Maggie and Ted plopped on their hats with the huge colored feathers; gave one last, mercifully short speech; and they were on their way.

"Anything, Snowden?" Charles asked as he took his seat next to his chief operative.

"My people are out there. Nothing happened during the night. I just this minute got a text saying our departure was noted, but nothing was done. So that tells me they did not make out Dishbang Deshi, and so far as they are concerned, we're just a tourist group. At least for now. None of them followed us. I can't say with any assurance that things won't change in ten minutes or an hour from now."

The ride to Nathan Road passed quickly. When the vans stopped to park, Maggie and Ted were the first ones out and waiting, clipboards in hand, the feathers in their hats moving briskly in the foggy breeze.

Even at this early hour, the street was teeming with human flesh. The garish banners in red, gold, and sky blue; the yellow neon signs; the babble of humanity was unlike anything the group had ever seen. It was wall-to-wall people, going wherever they were going. "Keep your eyes on the feathers," Maggie screamed, to be heard above the prattle.

"This is unbelievable," Myra said as she was

jostled to and fro, her hand tightly grasped in Annie's.

"I could never live in Hong Kong, much less anywhere else in China," Annie muttered. "I bet they don't even know what a hot dog with the works is over here." Hot dogs were Annie's favorite food. "I don't much like rice unless it's covered in some kind of sauce, and I can take noodles or leave them alone. Fish heads are out, absolutely out, and I could never eat soup with one of them staring up at me."

"I think I'm getting the picture, Annie. Maybe you should think about opening a restaurant over here."

Annie, her eyes on the two feathers ahead, gave Myra a poke in the arm. "You don't like it any more than I do. I'm not seeing anything that looks suspicious, are you?"

"No. Mr. Snowden is bringing up the rear. As they say in all those spy movies you watch, he has our six."

"Our first stop, people!" Maggie bellowed as she stood on her tiptoes so everyone could see the dancing feather better. "Follow me!" And they did.

Upon entering the rickety-looking work-room that was lined with bolts of cloth stacked to the ceiling, the members of the "tour" group fanned out immediately. There was a single narrow path that led to a measuring room where, by quick count, thirty or so peo-ple were working sewing machines while others measured customers. Within seconds, they were surrounded by little men with tape measures hanging from their necks.

There was much bowing and many smiles as Harry rattled off their needs in rapid-fire Chinese. One by one, each of them was paired off with two assistants, who would measure each of them from top to bottom. One man who appeared to be in charge held out his hand. After all, money was the name of the game. Maggie opened her Crescent China Tours bag and withdrew a wad of American money. She looked to Harry to tell her how much she needed to count out.

"It's just a deposit. One thousand for starters. He's seeing this group as buying *BIG*. Just so you know, this guy says he creates, that's the word he is using, for Armani. Spread the word down the line. He said he can even sew a label in whatever he makes that says the designer's name."

"Isn't that illegal?" Maggie asked suspiciously.

"Well, yeah, but this is China. Who are you going to report him to? The police chief is probably his brother or a dear, dear cousin. Take the damn label and be happy about it," Harry snapped.

From that moment on, it was Christmas morning, the Easter Parade, and the Academy Awards gala until Charles called a halt at the noon hour. "We're done here, people. Mr. Hua Bo has assured me that all garments will be labeled and sent to the Peninsula no later than ten o'clock tomorrow morning." He looked over at Maggie and instructed her to pay another three thousand dollars to the man with the glassy eyes. Glassy because he had never had such a successful business day.

Cooper, who had been sitting by the door, reared up and ran to Harry. Time to go.

More bows, more smiles, and the group was once again outside on the main thoroughfare. The air quality, according to Nikki, was even worse than it had been at eight in the morning. They donned their paper face masks and followed Maggie and Ted to a sidewalk restaurant, where they asked for tables inside. A quick lunch of shrimp and dumplings, along with spring rolls and tea, was set before them within minutes.

"Next stop the shoe palace. We get measured, pick out the leather, then we can head back to the hotel."

The next two hours passed quickly. Money changed hands, and a promise was given to have all the shoes, boots, and slippers delivered to the hotel by ten o'clock the following morning. Another eighteen hundred dollars changed hands.

"The good thing is, the hotel will package everything up and send it out to the farm for us. We won't have to carry it with us to Macau and on to . . . to our final destination. Abner can sign for it since it will probably get there before we make it home," Jack said.

When the three vans stopped at the hotel, Avery gave the sign to Charles that nothing had changed. His operatives were still in place. The bad guys or the first string hadn't moved.

The moment the group assembled in Myra and Annie's suite, she called room service and ordered coffee, tea, Kentucky bourbon, Chinese beer, and soda pop.

Dennis worked his way over to where Jack and Harry were standing. "I thought the girls would be talking nonstop about all the shopping they did. Instead they're . . . they're working on a plan to take out those guys out there, the ones Mr. Snowden's people are watching. What's up with that? What if they get caught?"

"That's a negative, Dennis," Harry said quietly. "The women don't know the meaning of that particular word. We need to leave here tomorrow morning, free and clear. That means no one can be tailing us. We want to hit Macau clean and move on from there. Are you having a problem with any of this, Dennis? By the way, what did you order back on Nathan Road?"

"No, I am not having a problem. I ordered two suits with the Armani label. Two sport jackets, two pairs of boots, and one pair of dress shoes. Why?"

"I was just making conversation, kid. You need to relax, have a beer or something. We're

all good here. Just look at Cooper. If things
weren't right, he'd let us know."

"Yeah, yeah, you're right, Harry. I guess I
feel like this because I don't like China. I don't
care how cheap it is to get custom-made attire,
and I don't care about how ritzy this hotel is or
how many royals have stayed here; give me a
Holiday Inn or Best Western, and I'm a happy
camper. I guess that I'm a poor excuse for a
one-percenter, aren't I? And the air here is so
foul, we'll probably all have emphysema by the
time we get home to the good old USA."

"Take a nap for God's sakes, Dennis!" Espinosa snarled. Dennis blinked. Then he
shrugged. Everyone was on edge. He could
understand that easily enough.

Drinks in hand, Annie stood front and center. "I vote we pass on the high tea and avail
ourselves of these wondrous drinks I just ordered from room service. Midnight works for
me, people. Our trackers will be feeling the
lack of activity. Twenty-four hours is a long
time to spend in one spot with no action. The
witching hour has always worked for us. I seriously doubt that that bunch of hoodlums, first-
stringers or not, will think twice about a group
of American women going for a stroll at midnight. We move in, take them out, Avery cleans
up after us. Simple. Everyone on board?"

Every hand in the room shot upward, even
Dennis's, which he waved to make sure it was
noticed. Cooper let loose with a happy bark.

Harry looked over at Yoko. "One more day closer to finding our daughter. One day closer. I'm going to kill someone, Yoko. I don't want you to stop me either."

Yoko smiled up at her husband. "I would never stop you. I will help you. No rules this time, my husband." She shook her head. "No rules."

Chapter 13

The group managed to while away the hours till midnight by talking about their shopping expedition, having a room service buffet dinner, watching some local television that made no sense to any of them, then strategizing.

Kathryn held up her hand, and said, "I have an idea. I know it's dark outside right now since it's after ten o'clock, but this place is lit up like Yankee Stadium. I think Espinosa and Dennis should take a little night stroll and take some pictures. We know approximately where our stalkers are, from what Snowden told us, but that isn't going to be good enough. We need to know precisely where each stalker is. This takedown has to be quick and dirty. Espinosa can take the pictures, upload them to us here in the room, and we make out where each of the little men are, hand out assignments, and we're good to go. Unless any of you have a better idea?"

Espinosa was already sliding his arms into his Windbreaker. Dennis followed suit.

He felt brave enough to ask, "Who takes pictures at night? Won't we stand out like sore thumbs? I mean, hey, I'm okay with it. I just don't want to arouse suspicion."

"Stupid Americans, that's who. It's brighter than daylight out there, in case you haven't noticed," Kathryn shot back.

And, as usual with one of Dennis's questions, that was the end of that discussion.

Avery Snowden started pacing the elegant suite of rooms, muttering to himself until he finally exploded. "I can't believe you people sent those two"—he was going to say "idiots" but changed his mind—"puppies out there to take pictures at midnight. What are you people thinking?" He zeroed in on Charles before he threw his hands high in the air, then started his frantic pacing again.

"I think, Avery, the ladies know what they're doing. Young Dennis may still be wet behind the ears, but the boy has heart, and according to Harry and Jack, he can definitely hold his own. He'll protect Espinosa if it comes to that. Let's not worry about something that might never come to pass. Besides, Avery, your people are out there, so if things get out of hand, they can jump in. Ah, the first pictures are coming in."

Fergus and Charles both raced to the desk, where, courtesy of the hotel, their laptops were set up. The others crowded around to view the pictures appearing at the speed of light.

"Lightweights," Jack said. He hoped he was right even though he knew that he wasn't.

"Deadly," Harry said. He looked over at Jack, disgust written all over his features. He knew for certain that he was right.

The women cackled with glee.

Fergus looked at Charles, his eyes full of panic as Harry's assessment of the men outside the hotel ricocheted inside his brain.

"Easy, Ferg, look at who we have. They were born to this. Isn't it obvious?" Charles hissed. "There are eight of them if you count Maggie. There are only five men. And Snowden's people can step in should it be necessary. Stop worrying."

"Maybe you should take a look at Harry, Charles. Tell me that isn't worry and possibly fear you see on his face."

"Maybe you should look at Yoko and the rest of the ladies, then make up your mind, Ferg. Start with Annie. She's so hyped up, nothing could stop her now. The same goes for my beloved."

More pictures appeared. Comments flowed,

feet shuffled. Everything came to a halt when Cooper stirred and made a production of untangling himself. Before he headed toward Harry, he tucked his one-eared half-tailed rabbit into the blanket he'd been sleeping on. Harry simply waited. They all watched, fascinated, as Cooper did his stretches, yawned, and stopped for a drink from a bowl of water near his gear before letting loose with three sharp yips and heading for the door.

Leash in hand, Jack waited. Cooper reached up, snatched the leash, walked it over to Myra, and held it out for her to take.

Jack let loose with a nasty sound deep in his throat. "That damn dog is reminding us that we are sitting this one out. You need to do something about him, Harry."

"Me! You want me to do something! Like what? Like what, Jack?" Harry screeched, stopping everyone in their tracks.

"Well, for one thing, isn't he being disloyal right now?"

"Shut up, Jack. I can't deal with stupid right now," Harry responded, his voice now sounding normal.

Because he didn't know what else to do, Jack clamped his lips shut, his gaze never leaving Cooper, who glared right back at him.

"That's the last picture," Charles said, pointing to the final picture on the screen. "Young Dennis just sent a text saying they are on the way back in." The printer, again, compliments of the hotel, whirred to life as picture after picture shot out. Fergus passed them around for everyone to see. Ted was already working on a handmade map of the driveway, the shrubbery, and the road that led to the hotel. The hidey-holes where the stalkers and Snowden's men were located were secure with luscious, pruned shrubbery. Perfect for hiding even in the bright light.

Dishbang Deshi watched the proceedings with a jaundiced eye. Like this gaggle of women could really take out the group of thugs bent on killing him. It was obvious to him that Harry was living in a dream world these days. And his people, too, were living in that same dream world. He amplified his thinking to include the strange dog at their side. All these people had traveled halfway around the globe to rescue one little girl. And he knew in his heart, in his gut, in his mind, that if it were he in trouble, there would be no one to come to his aid. Never mind traveling halfway around the world. If nothing else, he had to respect the women's dedication. The thought was so bitter, so repugnant, Dishbang Deshi gagged.

Dishbang Deshi continued to watch as the women stared at the rough map the pretend tour guide was showing them. He could hear soft murmurs but couldn't make out what they were saying. What he did understand was how

the room he was sitting in had suddenly become electrified. Any moment, he expected to
see bolts of lightning ricochet across the room.
When nothing like that happened, he realized
he was actually disappointed.

Then they were at the door, Myra in the lead
with the strange dog. This wasn't right. It should
be the men going through the door, the women
staying behind because that was their place instead of the way it was. He risked a glance
around the room. None of the men seemed to
be having a problem with the women's going
out to slay the dragons who awaited. Obviously,
this was the way they did things in America.
The women were the dominant force. How in
the world had it ever come to this? He shuddered when he thought of what he might find
when he made it to Mud Flats, Mississippi, to
see his wife and daughters. He wanted to say
something, to make his feelings known that
this wasn't right, but he wisely held his tongue.
He needed these people, especially Harry, to
get him away safely to his family.

Dishbang Deshi leaned back in his chair and
closed his eyes as the minutes ticked by. He'd
give the women thirty minutes before they
called on their male counterparts for help.
Maybe sooner. He opened his eyes and looked
around. The others were talking, their voices so
low he couldn't make out the words. The two
older men seemed to be the only ones con-

cerned with what was going on. How could that be, he wondered. He thought about his wife then, in Mud Flats. She would never, as in never, do what these women were planning on doing outside the hotel. She'd run the other way so fast, she'd leave burn marks on the road. Somewhere deep inside his body he rather thought that was not a good thing. What were those women doing right now? Were they being hurled to the ground and stomped on? Were their necks being snapped like twigs? Were they being bound and gagged and transported to some junk, where they would be sold off to some white slave ring? Was the dog still alive? What would the occupants of this room, especially Harry, do when the hotel staff came knocking on the door with the bad news, followed by the police? More to the point, what would he himself do?

As Dishbang Deshi was thinking of all the disasters taking place outside the hotel, down below, the women strolled along the driveway, chattering like magpies about their shopping experience. They laughed, joked, poked at each other, and stopped to light cigarettes they didn't want because none of them had the filthy habit. It had been Ted's idea to bring the cigarettes to create a diversion so as to get a read on the shrubbery and their surroundings. As he said, almost all Chinese appeared to be smokers, so they would blend right in.

"I'm thinking this is pretty close to a warm-cookie moment," Isabelle said.

"How about a Jimmy Choo half-price sale on the shoes you've lusted after for months?" Nikki giggled.

"Oh no! This is like holding a new, sweet-smelling puppy that will love you forever for taking care of him," Kathryn said.

The others agreed with the three moments of bliss. Cooper let out a series of sharp yips at the mention of the newborn-puppy moment.

The women continued their leisurely stroll, chatting about everything and nothing, their eyes alert, their senses tuned to even the minuscule rustling of the leaves.

It was a cool evening, with a bit of a gentle breeze that was not strong enough to ruffle the plants or the branches on the trees. The evil-smelling smog was almost gone, the air a bit more clear, especially under the bright lights that seemed to be everywhere.

Kathryn giggled. "My four o'clock is good for you, Izzy. Nikki, I'll take your seven o'clock. Alexis, update please."

"I'm coming up to my two o'clock and can simply step to the side and take him down."

"Annie? Myra?"

"I can see the whites of our guy's eyes from where I am at the moment. I'm going to bend down to check Cooper's leash, and Myra will strike the first blow. On the count of three we

move, not one second before. Maggie, keep
your eyes peeled for trouble."

"One!"

"Two!"

"Three!"

The air moved as the women went into action.

Barely breaking a sweat, Myra had her
quarry's head between her two hands. She
gave it one good bounce to the ground before Annie's foot clamped down on the man's
throat. "Sneak attack! I like that! What do you
think, Myra, should I crush his Adam's apple
or stomp on his privates?"

"Wuss! Why are you being so shy, Annie? Go
for both," Myra shot back, pleased with Annie's
praise.

"Well, okay then, here we go! You rock, old
girl!" Annie crunched down with one foot
while the other traveled farther south. Myra,
in the nick of time, dropped to the ground
and clamped both her hands over the stalker's
mouth so he couldn't give an alert.

"Done! And really done!" Annie grinned.
"Let's see if the others are in need of our help.
This piece of human garbage is not going any-
where, and Cooper can stand guard."

Annie and Myra did their best to stay in the
shadows as they made their way back the way
they had come. There was no noise, nothing
out of the ordinary, only the sigh of the light
wind.

"Silence can be deadly sometimes," Myra whispered.

"Tell me about it." Annie stopped to step into the lush shrubbery where Nikki was using her shoelaces from her sneakers to tie her quarry's hands behind his back. He looked bruised and battered, and a slow stream of blood oozed down his chin. One leg stuck out at an awkward angle. "Looks like you snapped his kneecap, dear!"

"I was going for the other one when he gave up," Nikki said, straightening up. She blew a wisp of blond hair out of her eyes. "Is this two down?"

"It is, darling girl. Oh, dear, in all the excitement I forgot to get the man's cell phone. I'll be right back." Myra was off like the wind. She looked down at the man Annie had rendered harmless. She bent over to search the man's pockets. There was nothing else to be found. She slipped what she knew was a burner phone into her own pocket. "You really are a low-life bottom-feeding bag of scum for trying to harm a precious little girl." To show she meant business, she gave the man a vicious kick to the ribs. She was delighted to hear the sound of his ribs snapping and to see his eyes roll back in his head. "Like Annie says, done and done." She scampered off, her heart lighter, truly believing they were getting closer and closer to rescuing little Lily.

Nikki burst out into a soft giggle when she saw Yoko sitting on her assignment's chest. She was yanking at his ears, demanding he speak English. "Give it up, Yoko. He has no clue. Knock him out. Cold. Take his phone." She whistled softly, the sound that of one of the night birds nestled in the trees. Alexis and Isabelle stepped onto the driveway. "Status report?" she continued to giggle.

"One crushed windpipe, three broken legs, one broken shoulder, two smashed noses. One lost significant hair. We're good here. No English," Alexis said cheerfully.

"We have their phones. Nothing else in their pockets," Isabelle said.

Kathryn appeared out of the darkness. "My little pissant understands English. How much, I don't know. When I told him I was going to pull his tongue out through his nose, he begged me to stop. In English. Of course I didn't. I broke all his toes and all his fingers. He put up a hell of a fight, I have to give him that. Oh, yeah, one of his ears is . . . you know . . . kind of . . . sort of . . . just hanging there."

"Well then, I think our work here is done. Avery's people can take over. If those lowlifes know anything of value, he'll pass it on to us." Annie whistled softly. Cooper appeared as if by magic.

"The café in the hotel is still open. Let's all get a double-decker chocolate ice-cream cone, my treat," Myra said. "I think we deserve a re-ward for a good night's work."

"Smashing idea, old girl! Someone should alert Mr. Snowden and the others that our job is done, and we'll be joining them momentarily," Annie said.

"I just did," Nikki said, laughing.

"Did we do good or what?" Kathryn queried.

"Damn straight we did good," Yoko trilled as she bounced along, one knee sock at her ankle, the other one at midcalf. Somewhere along the way, she'd lost her broken glasses.

"I just love it when we win out. First string, my ass!" the ever-verbal Kathryn expounded. "I thought these guys were supposed to be *good*."

"They are . . . were good. They weren't expecting a sneak attack by women. It's just that we're better," Nikki said.

"And the reason for that is . . ." Isabelle said, the rest of the sentence hanging in the air.

In unison, the girls shouted, "Because we're women."

Avery Snowden caught sight of the women, all licking ice-cream cones. He shuddered as he tried to avoid them by scooting behind a thick fern. Son of a bitch! The women did pull it off. And they did it without anyone even knowing what was going on. If this level of expertise were maintained, he and his people would become expendable.

His perch behind the thick fern was suddenly disturbed by Cooper, who nudged his leg and barked. A playful bark, but a bark just the same.

"We saw you before Cooper did, Mr. Snowden," Yoko trilled. "No need to hide."

"Goddamn it," Snowden seethed as he made his way out the lobby doors and down the driveway, to where his people were waiting for him. Sometimes, he decided, the end really did justify the means.

Inside Myra and Annie's luxurious suite, between licks on their ice-cream cones, the women regaled their partners with a summary of what had happened down in the gardens of the famous hotel.

While young Dennis felt a little queasy, he managed to display approving looks of admiration, while Dishbang Deshi fought to control the contents of his stomach. Crushed windpipe, ear hanging by a thread, all those broken bones. And they were licking ice-cream cones as if they were at some young girl's sweet sixteen party. These women truly were vigilantes. He couldn't help but wonder who had trained them. Harry? The one named Jack, who appeared to be Harry's equal? Were they secret agents of the American CIA or the FBI?

The fact that they were here in China could mean CIA because the CIA didn't operate domestically in America. That's why they had the FBI. He wished he knew more. Then he canceled the thought, realizing that what he already knew was more than enough to cause him endless sleepless nights.

"So, Dishbang Deshi, what do you think of my little band of warriors now?" Harry asked.

"Well . . . I . . ." Seeing Kathryn headed in his direction with a cold gleam in her eye, he quickly said, "I am very impressed. And pleased. And . . . and . . ."

"Yes?" Kathryn drawled as she finished off her cone by popping the crunchy bottom of it into her mouth.

"You . . . um . . . ladies are to be commended. I am sure those . . . thugs out there put up a good fight, and the fact that you bested them tells me you all have . . . no equals."

Sweat beaded up on Dishbang Deshi's forehead at the expression he was seeing on Kathryn's face. When she burst out laughing he almost blacked out.

"And don't you ever forget it," Annie shouted from across the room.

Like I could ever forget this nightmare, Dishbang Deshi thought to himself.

"Okay, people, gather around. We need to discuss our departure for Macau tomorrow morning," Charles said. He looked over at Harry, and his voice softened. "We're one day closer, Harry."

Harry simply nodded and squeezed his wife's hand. One day closer.

Cooper let loose with three soft yips before he retired to his position by the door, where he snuggled down with his one-eared half-tailed rabbit.

Chapter 14

Promptly at ten o'clock the following morning, a gaggle of bellboys appeared with wheeled racks to deliver the group's purchases of custom clothing and handcrafted footwear from the previous day. Everyone rushed to find their designated orders, which were clearly marked. Now all they had to do was sign off on the delivery and redirect all the packages to a dead-drop address in Las Vegas, Nevada, home of Crescent China Tours, which Lizzie Fox had set up for them. The hotel would see to it that the items would be packaged into one order and shipped from the hotel to the address provided. For a fee, of course. An outrageous fee, according to Annie.

Harry was like a cat on a hot griddle as he shouted instructions in Chinese. Finally, Maggie,

Crescent China Tours' designated tour-group leader, signed the last sheet of paper, handed out tips to all the bellboys, then sighed with relief. "People, we are good to go. Everyone, make a final check of your rooms to make sure you aren't leaving anything behind. We will all assemble in the open courtyard to await our ride to the ferry, compliments of the hotel's green Rolls-Royces. Remember now, act your parts and do not deviate from the roles you've been playing."

"What about Mr. Snowden and his people?" Dennis asked. "Shouldn't we wait for them? What if they get lost, or they don't meet up with us on time?"

"They will be meeting us at the ferry, Dennis. Don't worry about them. We have it all under control," Charles said. Behind his back, Charles crossed his fingers, hoping that what he was saying was true. Snowden had yet to check in this morning. While Charles was worried, he wasn't particularly alarmed. Yet. Avery Snowden marched to his own drummer and, in all the years of his employment, had never failed him. Then again, there was always a first time for everything. Along the lines of the best-laid plans of mice and men . . . or something like that.

Maggie and Ted checked out the tour group at the front desk, offered a tip for the impeccable service, smiled, bowed, and then joined the group in the courtyard.

Maggie clamped her hat firmly on her head, making sure the plumed feather was straight up. Ted did the same thing.

While they waited for the green Rolls-Royces to arrive, Maggie and Ted both went into their tour-guide spiel.

"Okay, people, listen up! We are about to depart for the Macau ferry terminal, where we will be leaving by Turbojet. Travel time is approximately sixty minutes. We will disembark at the Macau Outer Harbor Ferry Terminal. Since the Turbojet leaves every fifteen minutes, there is no need to purchase tickets in advance. If Mr. Snowden is running late for some reason, he will simply take the next ferry. I do not think we need to concern ourselves with his late arrival. He and his friends are seasoned travelers, and it is my understanding that several of his party have been here before. As I said, I see no cause for worry or concern.

"We could make this short journey in first class, but this tour is on a budget, as are all travel tours, so we're traveling economy. This was all explained at the outset, but I feel I need to make a point of our economizing. I don't want any of you getting all pissy on me about accommodations." Yoko started to giggle, and the others joined in. It was hard for Maggie to keep a straight face when Cooper started barking to express his opinion. No one was sure if he was for or against first-class travel or economy. There were some things a bark simply could not succeed in conveying, and this was one of them.

"When we arrive in Macau, since we are all US residents, immigration should take us only a few minutes. I hope this is true. I'm reading this straight off a pamphlet. We all know our passports are current. And the visas here are good for thirty to one hundred eighty days. Not that we have visas, of course, those being unnecessary for US citizens coming to China. I'm just saying.

"Now, as to money. We all have Hong Kong dollars with us—we saw to that yesterday—so there is no need for us to convert to Macau pataca currency. The tradespeople actually prefer Hong Kong dollars, I am told. Any questions?" *God, I hope not,* Maggie muttered.

"And our rides approach," Ted called out cheerfully as the green Rolls-Royces appeared in a straight line, engines purring like contented cats.

There was still no sign of Avery Snowden or his people.

The ride to the ferry terminal was short, and there were no snafus along the way.

Once again, Maggie and Ted took center stage. This time, Ted took the lead as Maggie pretended to count heads and check carry-on bags while she let her gaze wander to the hundreds of people waiting to board the ferry. She could see no sign of Snowden or his people.

She looked over at Charles, who, to her mind's eye, looked worried, as did Fergus. If the others were worried, they weren't showing any signs or giving off any bad vibes.

"We'll be boarding in seven minutes, people. Line up, and remember who is in front of you and who is in back of you. Always, always, watch for the feathers. Once we are on board, snacks will be distributed. We do not have to pay for those. There will be no tipping on this ferry ride.

"When we reach Macau, our hotel van will be waiting to take us to our accommodations. We will be staying at the Wynn Macau on Rua Cidade de Sintra, NAPE, right here on Macau. We got a special rate because there are so many of us. Otherwise, this tour couldn't afford such accommodations. Just so you all know. Any questions?" *There better not be,* Ted's expression said.

"They're lowering the chain. Orderly fashion, people. Ted will go first. I will be last. Move, people!" Maggie said forcefully.

They moved.

"You know, Annie, in my opinion Ted and Maggie aren't half bad as tour guides. I'm starting to believe they actually are tour guides. If I were an outside observer, I would never question their professions, would you?"

"I wouldn't either. I've seen a lot of people looking at us. I can read speculation with the best of them. I think we're pulling this off. I really do," Annie said. "I also have not seen anything that is worrisome. Have you?"

"So far, so good. Each hour brings us one hour closer to finding Lily. It's been a long, roundabout process, but I think we've been doing everything right. Even Harry's old friend Dishbang Deshi is cooperating. Which, by the way, I find very amusing for some reason," Myra said.

Annie nodded. "You know, Myra, I am worried about something. Once we get to Macau, I am really going to need to talk to Bert. And then there's Kathryn and her current itch in regard to Bert. We need to be mindful of that because she can be a hothead when she wants to be, and God help anyone standing in her way."

"We'll figure something out. For now, let's just relax and enjoy this rather choppy ferry ride, knowing that once we hit Macau, we are one step closer to that mountain we have to reach.

"Yoko appears quite serene. Harry just looks tense and Cooper . . . Cooper just looks like . . . Cooper. That has to be a good thing."

"You do realize, don't you, Myra, that this mission almost solely depends on that very strange dog. It's like he has all the answers but can't tell us what they are. We are to follow him blindly. A dog! We're actually following a dog! It blows my mind."

"A dog with superior intellect, Annie. You and I are very tuned to the spirit world. I don't know whether Cooper is part of that world or not. What I do know is, I will follow that animal wherever he leads us, knowing that when we reach our destination, it will be all we hoped it would be."

The rest of the ferry ride was made in silence on the part of the Crescent China Tours group. The other passengers carried on and on about whatever it was they were jabbering about in Chinese.

When the ferry captain came on the loudspeaker to announce they would dock in seven minutes, Harry translated for the group.

"Everyone remain seated and we'll be last off the ferry," Ted shouted, to be heard over the bedlam as passengers gathered up their gear, babbling to anyone who would listen.

And then they were on dry land again. Directly ahead of them were Avery Snowden and his people, properly dressed in their Crescent China Tours clothing. He merely nodded to show they were all present and accounted for. It was now obvious they had taken an earlier ferry to be here waiting for the rest of the group.

Ted looked around for the Wynn Casino transportation that would take them to the hotel. Their transportation turned out to be two white Mercedes travel vans. Riding in the first van was Bert Navarro, who looked lazy and comfortable in the front passenger seat.

The minute Kathryn spotted her former lover, she grabbed Nikki's hand and pulled her in the direction of the second van. "You need to help me avoid him, Nikki. I don't want anything to screw this mission up and have everyone blame me. Please, spread the word to the girls. I'll take a seat in the back of this van and wait it out. Will you do that for me, Nikki?"

"Of course I'll do it, but you do realize that at some point you two are going to come face-to-face. What then?"

"I don't know. When we parted, it was over. He agreed to go his way, and I would go mine. And yet, here he is."

"But Kathryn, he was part of the mission Charles put together. He's here because he is needed. Bert has always been a team player, you know that."

"Then ask yourself what the hell he's doing here taking up a seat in the van. Is he going to talk to Annie and the others in front of a Chinese driver? I don't think so."

"Calm down, Kathryn. The minute we reach the hotel, I can corner him so you can get away clean. I can have Jack and Harry talk to him. Or better yet, Annie. I think you're overreacting, I really do."

At Kathryn's skeptical look, Nikki hastened to explain, "Do you really think the Bert we all know would do anything to screw up Harry's getting his daughter back? He would never do that. The fact that he's here tells me he needs to talk to Annie or Charles or someone, and he has something worthwhile to report. It is entirely possible that you're flattering yourself, Kathryn, in that you believe he's here to see you. I know how awful that sounds coming from me, but it is possible, Kathryn. Think about it, okay?

"I'm going to take the first seat up front so I can be first off when we get to the hotel. I'll get to him as soon as I can. In the meantime, relax."

"Okay. Okay. Of course, you could be right. I hope you are."

Nikki made her way to the front of the van and sat down across from the driver, a Chinese with a gap-toothed smile and wire-rim glasses. She smiled in return as she settled herself into the comfortable seat, where she tapped out a text to Annie and asked for her help as well as an explanation as to Bert's appearance.

Next to board were Avery and his crew. The last person on was Dennis, who made his way to the back of the van to take a seat next to Kathryn.

Conversation was nil as the Wynn van made its way to the casino hotel. The ride was short. Dennis was glad when it was time to step out of the van. Kathryn's anger bothered him because he didn't understand it. In the end, he decided that was probably a girly thing. He was learning, these days, more about women than he really wanted to know. When he hit the ground, he grimaced as he heard Maggie going into one of her never-ending spiels. He gritted his teeth and listened, knowing it was all part of the plan should there be eyes and ears on the alert.

"Okay, people, we are here. I know all of you can't wait to lose your money, but I caution you again to gamble wisely. Our journey is not at an end yet, and you don't want to have to call back home for additional funds.

"We are now at the Wynn Macau. It's fabulous, as you can see. It was built in 2006, so by now all the quirks have been smoothed out. The Wynn is the first Las Vegas–style resort in Asia. Mr. Steve Wynn of Las Vegas is the chairman of the board and the chief executive officer of this fine establishment. I think that fact alone will make us all feel at home.

"I'd like to start off by saying the population here in Macau is five hundred thousand. The hotel has six hundred rooms and suites, roughly five hundred table games on the main floor and over two hundred in the VIP. They have two hundred seventy-five slot machines that take up more than two hundred thousand square feet of space. They have four restaurants, an atrium, heated swimming pool, a spa, a salon, two lounge and bar areas, and a whole lot of other space for convention facilities. The names of the restaurants are Mizumi, Ristorante il Teatro, the Golden Flower, and the Wing Lei. I'm telling you this in case you want to mention it on the postcards you will want to send back home.

"Aside from the four five-star dining rooms that we will *not* be dining in, since we are on a budget, I am told there are four casual dining rooms that are quite splendid, and the food is top-notch. And, of course, if we find ourselves in other casinos, we can grab a bite to eat there.

"Okay, that's our lesson for today, people. Follow me and Ted. I'll check us in, then we can meet down here on the main floor in an hour so that we can begin our second adventure here in China."

Harry and Jack stepped to the side to allow the others to pass them in a single file. It was deliberate on their part, so they could inch their way closer to where Bert Navarro was standing alongside the other driver. As they shuffled forward at a snail's pace, Harry engaged the driver in Chinese while Jack grinned and stuck out his hand toward Bert.

It all looked casual enough if anyone was watching. When Jack inched forward he heard Bert hiss, "Urgent." A newspaper was thrust into his hand. He kept moving, aware that Harry was behind him. He heard the door to the van slam shut and heard rather than saw the vehicle move from under the portico.

As the line crept forward, Jack was aware of the intense conversation his wife was having with Kathryn. He could only pick up bits and pieces, but he managed to put it all together. Kathryn was angry about Bert, and Nikki was cajoling her into feeling shame because whatever it was she was worried about didn't happen.

"So, wise one, is Kathryn pissed that Bert ignored her, or is she pissed at herself?" Harry asked, tongue-in-cheek.

"How should I know?"

"Well, wise one, you claim to know everything there is to know about women. So what is it?" Harry cackled.

"Stuff it, Harry."

Cooper nudged Jack's leg and let loose with a soft yip. Jack tickled him behind the ears, to the big dog's delight. Just long enough for a thought to race across Jack's brain. *Read the paper, it's urgent.*

Thinking the newspaper was in Chinese, Jack handed the *Macau Daily News* to Harry, who flipped it open. He blinked, then blinked again before he let loose with a string of curses that made Jack blush. He felt the paper being shoved in his hands. He looked down to see a picture of Harry Wong, above the fold, and in color. He'd been wrong. The *Macau Daily News* was a Chinese English-language newspaper.

"Uh-oh!" was all he could think to say.

Harry bounded ahead like a steamroller. He stopped short, right in front of Charles Martin and Fergus Duffy, who were about to step into the elevator. Fergus gave Harry a shove and hissed, "Not here. Wait till we get to the room and calm down. That's an order."

Jack thought the ride to the twelfth floor seemed to take forever. He was almost afraid to look at Harry, who looked like he was about to explode. What the hell was his picture doing on the front page of the local paper? He wished he'd gotten more than a glimpse. Who knew Harry was here? Was their cover blown? He looked down at Cooper, who looked like he was used to riding in elevators every day of his life. That had to mean things were . . . copacetic—at least for the moment. Still, he crossed his fingers for good luck. Cooper let loose with a soft yip, indicating he was aware of Jack's concern.

The elevator pinged, and part of the group bailed out and headed down the hall. The others trailed behind, wondering what was going on. The elevator pinged again, and Avery Snowden and his crew raced to catch up.

Inside the luxurious suite, Harry snatched the paper from Charles's hands and started to bellow at the top of his lungs, "Do you see this? They know! The bastards know we're here! That I'm here! Me!"

Everyone started to clamor at once, asking what was in the paper and why Harry's picture was on the front page.

"It says I am here in China to defend my

martial-arts title as the number one martial-arts expert in the world now that Jun Yu is dead. The contest is one week from now!"

Jack suddenly felt light-headed. He cleared his throat. "Who . . . who are you defending your title against, Harry?"

"Who do you think, *Jack*?"

"Well, I don't know, Harry, that's why I asked." But he did know, and the knowing was making him sick to his stomach.

"Wing Ping, that's who."

Chapter 15

There was a moment of silence at Harry's bitter words, followed by an instant clamor, with everyone talking and shouting at once. The only one not caught up in the moment was Cooper, who searched for his one-eared rabbit with only half a tail, then carried it to the door, where he flopped down and went to sleep.

If Annie had had her gun, she would have fired it to impose silence on the increasingly loud cacophony of voices. Instead, she whistled sharply and was rewarded with instant silence. The crowd stared at her, their faces a mix of anger, frustration, and fear. "Everyone take a deep breath here! What exactly does that paper say, Harry? Please do not tell me all of this"—she said, waving her arms about—"was for naught."

"It's an AP wire article. It says I am here in China to defend my title now that Jun Yu has gone on to meet his ancestors. That's exactly how it is worded. I'm being challenged by Wing Ping. To turn this down would make me a coward in the eyes of the Chinese people and the sporting world. Because I now live in America, it isn't sitting well with these people, meaning the Chinese, that an American holds the title even though I am Chinese by birth. They believe, or whoever wrote this article believes, that the title holder should live in China as Jun Yu did, and that's why Wing Ping is challenging me. Does that make sense to all of you?"

"Let me see that paper!" Kathryn growled as she snatched the paper from Harry's hands. The women clustered around her as they all tried to read the brief article.

Dishbang Deshi held up both hands. "Does it say specifically that you are already here or is it an invitation for you to come to China? Your disguise fooled me, Harry. I'm sure it fooled the others, too. And Wing Ping has not seen you since we were youngsters at the monastery. Of course, there are pictures of you as you look now all over the place and on the Net for anyone who wants to take the time to search you out. If they made me out, it was at the café, and we did walk back to the Peninsula. I rather thought we were clever and pulled it off. Dishbang Deshi, meaning me, was never seen again once he walked through the portals of the Peninsula. For all anyone knows, I'm still a guest at the hotel."

"There is that little matter of thirteen missing men, thugs, scum, whatever you want to call them," Annie said. "I think that's what they are going with and blaming it all on Harry. Unless our rooms at the hotel were bugged."

"If the rooms were bugged, Snowden would have found the bugs. That's what he does. I'm thinking this is to draw you out, Harry. They *think* you're here. They aren't sure," Jack said as he looked over at Cooper, who cracked one eyelid and let loose with a soft yip. "See, Cooper agrees."

"This article says the tournament will take place on Song Mountain at the monastery," Alexis said as she read over Kathryn's shoulder. "The event of the decade is how it is being portrayed if I'm reading this correctly."

"If I'm reading this the way Kathryn is, and I think I am, this news has been plastered all over the Internet. We are all savvy enough to know that if you want something to get out to the masses, social media is the way to go. I'm going to text Abner right now to ask him to look into this," Isabelle said.

"Wait a moment, dear. Everyone, is this a good idea?" Myra asked. "Can these people monitor our calls and texts out of this country?

And how do we know this room isn't . . . um . . . bugged."

Maggie spoke up. "Because when I checked us in at the last second, I requested a totally different floor. Just to be on the safe side. There would be no time to bug these rooms since we came up here as soon as we checked in. Mr. Snowden's tactics rubbed off on me, I think."

Everyone in the room nodded to show their approval of Maggie's actions.

"To answer your question, Myra, so what if I call or text Abner? He's my husband who stayed behind. I can send a text or speak in code that only Abner and I understand," Isabelle said as she pressed in digit after digit, not caring about the time difference.

"This tournament will bring in millions of dollars. That's US dollars. The smart money, the Chinese money, will be on Wing Ping. They'll do everything they can to destroy your reputation, Harry. They'll start with your changing your name from Wong Guotin to Harry Wong when you left for the States.

"Your Chinese name means 'polite, firm, strong leader.' They'll say you gave up that fearsome name to become American, with the name Harry. I have no idea what the name Harry means, but when it hits print, it won't be anything nice, I can guarantee that much," Dishbang Deshi said.

"This is today's newspaper," Nikki said. "If

I'm reading this right, the tournament is set for next week. They're expecting thousands of people to attend. It will be the event of the decade. This article sounds like it's been confirmed and is already a done deal. Like you already agreed to defend your title, Harry. How are you supposed to . . . agree or disagree?" Ted asked.

Dishbang Deshi held up his hand. "This is my opinion, and only my opinion, but I think Wing Ping is hoping that Harry is a no-show. Then he takes the title by default." He turned to Harry and winced at the pain he was seeing on his old friend's face. "If it's any consolation, Harry, I don't think Wing Ping is prepared for combat. He's been with the triads too long. He's gotten sloppy. He hasn't had a good life, and there is his background, which still haunts him. He's hoping you won't show. Like you say, he was born to the art; but over time, that art has faded and disappeared. I'll stake my life on it. You, on the other hand, work at your craft, your profession, on a daily basis. You can take him, Harry, I know you can."

Harry shook his head. "Why would the monks allow this to happen? How can they give in to these . . . these people?"

"Harry, the monks are a peaceful people. They fight only for good. I'm sure the infiltration was insidious, and they didn't realize what was happening until it was too late. And now they're under siege. They have no options, surely you can see that," Dishbang Deshi responded.

"My daughter . . ."

Cooper opened both eyes and yipped as he stared at Jack just long enough for Jack to say, "She's safe, Harry. They want you to think otherwise. They're using her as bait to get you to do what they want. And that means you show up, they scare you by saying you'll make some kind of stupid statement like you bow to the superior force, meaning Wing Ping, and they will let you have your daughter back. And then you go home in disgrace, and Wing Ping wins whatever the hell you win at one of those tournaments. I'm right, Harry, I know I am. If Cooper thinks or . . . *knows* that Lily is safe, that's good enough for me, and it sure as hell should be good enough for you, too.

"I think that means that the monks got her away in the nick of time. We just have to figure out where that place of safety is, and that's where Cooper comes in."

Harry looked over at Yoko, who nodded in agreement with what Jack had said. "You're right, Jack. But . . . I do not plan on hanging around here for the next few days to gamble and to keep on pretending. I want us to leave for the monastery first thing in the morning. Better yet, right now. Maggie and Ted, as the so-called tour leaders, can come up with a reason why we're leaving ahead of schedule. I do not think there will be a problem since the rooms were paid in advance, and the hotel can re-rent the rooms."

"But I was supposed to meet with Bert to discuss . . ." Annie started to say.

"Well, that's not going to happen, Annie. Send him a text or something giving him the go-ahead on your plans to open a casino here. That is why you were meeting, isn't it?" Kathryn said, her voice so cold and angry the others shivered. "I'm with Harry here—we need to move and to move quickly. In the next few hours if that is possible. The other side, if we are being watched or under surveillance, will not be expecting this change of plans, especially not so quickly."

Nikki held up her hand, her eyes on Jack. "Kathryn is right. We should leave now if we can. How difficult is it to change our tickets to Song Mountain?"

Maggie was busy typing before Nikki finished talking. She mumbled something that sounded like, *Do not unpack. Yet.*

Ted knew it was going to happen, so he stood up and said, "I'll go down to the desk to explain our situation and arrange for transportation to the airport."

There was no argument from anyone in the group. The wheels were in motion, and they all knew that when that happened, you needed to be ready at the drop of a hat.

Jack looked over at Cooper, who had his

half-tailed rabbit with only one ear between his teeth. He was as ready to go as anyone else in the group. "Attaboy, Coop!"

Cooper let loose with a series of sharp yips, which meant, Let's get this show on the road; as you can easily see, I am ready.

Ninety minutes later, the entire group was assembled and in line at the Macau International Airport for the next flight to their destination. There was no sign of Avery Snowden and his people. While anxious, none of them were worried about his absence. Avery Snowden knew their destination and would arrive either before or shortly after they did. Spook tradecraft.

As it turned out, the seven-hour plane ride proved to be uneventful. As Dennis put it, the only thing of interest was the noodle soup they were served twice, along with a strange-tasting tea that he said he hoped he would never have the misfortune to drink ever again.

On their arrival, they were once again all pleased and relieved to see Avery Snowden and his people, who promptly led them through customs and immigration without a problem.

Avery explained that he and his people were the last to board and the first ones off the plane, and that's why he knew what steps they were to take before heading for Song Mountain. "It would appear that all travel going up to the mountain is being carefully monitored, but the surveillance for the return is very lax."

"Problems?" Charles asked quietly.

"Not sure," was Snowden's curt response. "As you can see, there are police everywhere. It's almost like they're looking for someone in particular. As in Harry or Dishbang Deshi. I could be wrong, but I don't think so. We all just need to act like stupid American tourists. That's how the Chinese think of us. Just talk and laugh and act silly. They expect it. Whatever you do, don't make eye contact with anyone.

"We're headed for something similar to a bus depot. They call it a car barn or something like that. We board and continue to act excited. Be careful where you point your cameras. Meaning, take pictures of each other, and if you're lucky, you might snag something in the background. I can't stress enough for you all to be extremely careful."

Isabelle whispered to Alexis, who then whispered to Nikki, who passed the message along until everyone knew that Abner said that all the social media were going crazy with the news of Harry Wong defending his title. Tumblr, Facebook, and especially Twitter were awash in messages, tweets, and the like. Tickets for the event were said to be going for as much as five thousand dollars each. The airlines could not fill all the travel requests for those wanting to fly to China to attend the event. He went on to say in his text that groups were hiring private jets, and even the private sector was running short of planes for hire.

"You feeling the love, Harry?" Jack quipped.

"Yeah, I am, Jack." Harry actually laughed, leaving Jack stunned at his response. Harry must be up to something.

Out of the corner of his eye, Jack watched two red-capped police officers approach. They honed in on Cooper and his one-eared half-tailed rabbit. The men laughed and pointed at the dog and his security toy. Quicker than lightning, Yoko, sporting new glasses that made her look extremely childish, rushed to Cooper and dropped to her knees to hug him. She crooned and mumbled something to the dog that made his tail wag furiously. The two police officers laughed again and moved on past the little group.

"Good job, Cooper," Yoko whispered in the dog's ear. "These people do not understand how Americans feel about their pets, that they're part of a family. Like I said, good job, Cooper." Cooper's tail continued to swish back and forth as Yoko made her way back to stand in line with Harry.

"That was close, honey. Good thinking," Harry whispered. "In some ways, Chinese police are like you girls. They kick ass and take names later."

"Why, Harry, that's one of the nicest things you've ever said to me. Tell me more," Yoko cooed.

Harry flushed. "Aren't you supposed to be my daughter or something? Stop that right now. You know how ticklish I am. You need to move up to Annie and Myra. Those guys are on their return hike. Be careful."

"Always, Harry. You too."

A small clutch of Chinese women boarded the train behind the Crescent China Tours group, six in all. They carried no bags or luggage. All wore colorful fanny packs and appeared to be in their early to midtwenties, but as Jack said, it was hard to guess anyone's age.

Jack watched out of the corner of his eye as Avery Snowden and his people separated and somehow managed to insinuate themselves among the six young women. It was a move the women did not appear to like. Sharp words ensued. Sharp and loud enough for the tour group to take notice, which they did instantly. Which was Snowden's intention.

On the alert now, the group took their seats, which were not preassigned with the ticket purchase. They did their best to cluster together so there were no strangers sitting near or next to them, something else that angered the six women with the colorful fanny packs.

Snowden and his people played the part of obnoxious Americans, while the tour group followed his instructions about laughing and giggling and telling jokes. Cooper moved closer to Jack, who looked down at the dog to see his mood. He reached for the one-eared rabbit with half a tail and stuffed it in his pocket when Cooper growled deep in his throat. Only Jack heard the sound with all the laughter going on. He lowered his hand to rub Cooper's head to let him know he had to be alert.

The train was crowded, with mostly middle-aged men. To Jack's relief, there were no children in their compartment car. He looked across the aisle and willed Harry to turn to look at him. He nodded slightly and let his gaze go to the six young women, who were now scattered at the far end of the car. Both men let their eyes do all the talking as they singled out Avery Snowden and the way he had positioned his people as close to the six young women as possible.

As the train lurched forward, the loudspeaker came to life. Harry translated the message, which was to sit back, enjoy the trip up the mountain, and food would be served shortly.

"Oh, great, more noodle soup," Dennis muttered. "I hope they throw in a fortune cookie while they're at it."

"Dreamer," Espinosa said out of the corner of his mouth. "I can tell you your fortune right now without a cookie."

"I don't want to know it, Espinosa. I can figure it out on my own," Dennis snapped.

Jack hated squabbling, so he leaned back and stared out at the landscape. All he could see was hard rain. He knew the rain would be cold. Cold, hard rain in a foreign country. How much worse could it get, he wondered?

Much worse, he decided before he closed his eyes even though he knew he wouldn't sleep. Over and over, he played every scenario—good, bad, and indifferent—as to how things would go once they got off the train.

Jack cracked one eyelid to see where Avery Snowden was. Middle of the compartment car, halfway between Charles and Fergus. He shivered when he remembered Yoko's telling him that some of the most lethal kung fu experts in China were women. He had no reason to doubt her information. Were there six kung fu experts at the front of the car? Cooper seemed to think so. And whatever Cooper thought was good enough for him.

Chapter 16

They were under siege.

To a stranger it might not seem like things at the monastery were normal as monks dotted the landscape going to and fro, but there was a tension in the air that belied the serene tranquility the monastery had known for generations. The monks normally made their rounds in groups as they saw to the daily running of the monastery. For weeks now, they found themselves walking alone, fearful of the eyes and ears that seemed to be everywhere. Conversations, when there were conversations, consisted of discussions of the students, the weather, and the tasteless food that appeared on plates at mealtimes. No one ever raised his eyes to look at the strange men who dined with the Abbot in the dining hall. Nor did they look at them in the halls or on the grounds.

The monks did, however, whisper at night behind closed doors when the lights were out. They used primitive methods from the old days of communicating that only they understood. They used sign language, taps on the wall, sounds that imitated birdcalls. Even the students weren't aware of what the wily old monks were doing.

Communication with the outside world was nil. Even Brother Dui, who helped the Abbot in the office, was unable to filter out much information for Brothers Shen and Hung. But he had an idea that he said would work. When the tradespeople came to pick up the eggs from the henhouse, a note could be slipped to the person picking up the eggs. Two notes, actually, Dui said, one so the egg man would understand what he was to do, the other note to be delivered the old way, by runner. Or, as Brother Hung whispered to Brother Shen, "We go back to the Dark Ages and make it work for us." He went on to say that the high-tech gurus who had gained control of the monastery wouldn't have a clue about the old ways of communication.

The word was passed from monk to monk, who smiled secretly and, to a man, thought that perhaps all would be made right in the end.

But as Brother Shen said, "We are still under siege. We are not free to be who we are."

Those somber words offered no consolation to any of the monks.

Brother Dui was out of breath due to excitement at the information he'd suddenly come by. The excitement was because he didn't know what to do with the information he had to share. Who should he go to first? What reason could he come up with that would appear legitimate to the eyes constantly watching him? He finally decided he didn't want his heart to explode out of his chest, so he made the decision to tell the first monk he came in contact with. He hoped it would be Brother Hung or Brother Shen. And he would use the monks' old sign-language method of communicating, which would alert whomever he talked to that they needed to meet somehow, somewhere to discuss a matter of extreme importance.

Brother Dui suddenly felt the weight of the responsibility that now rested on his shoulders. The matter was so important, and he didn't like the feeling.

Because he didn't know what to do, Dui walked aimlessly up one hall and down the other. From time to time he stopped by the schoolrooms and looked and listened to the students and their teachers. He missed Hop, Gan, and little Lily. He as well as the other monks all

formed strong bonds with the students and
built up memories that lasted a lifetime. He
could still remember their fathers, Jun Yu and
Wong Guotin, and their friend, Dishbang Deshi,
and the mischievous pranks they would try to
play on the teachers even though they were always caught in the act, much to their dismay.
Since the three youngsters were unfailingly
contrite until their next prank, the monks
turned away to hide their smiles as they remembered their own school days. He sighed mightily
as he wondered where Gan and Hop were. He
knew through the monastery grapevine that
Lily Wong was safe. How sad that Jun Yu had
gone to meet his ancestors, leaving his wife
and two children fatherless. Jun Yu, he knew,
had been a good man. A good father and husband. He had been honest and honorable, just
as Wong Guotin, now Harry Wong, still was, according to Brother Hung.

Brother Dui felt himself bristle with anxiety
as an idea spun around in his head. First, he
had to figure out where Brother Hung was at
this hour of the day.

Brother Dui continued his trek down the
various hallways until he came to the library, a
favorite place of solitude for Brother Hung.
He walked in and looked around. He could see
no sign of the fellow monk he was seeking or
any of the other senior monks. But he did see
strangers, who stared at him with vile-looking
expressions. Brother Dui looked away and left

the library. He headed to the great room, where a beautiful fire was blazing in the monster fireplace. Brother Hung was sipping tea as he stared into the flames. Brother Dui called a greeting as he fixed himself a cup of tea. He turned around and tripped over his own feet. He went down so fast he was stunned. Brother Hung rushed to his aid as the two men at the door laughed out loud.

With Brother Hung's back to the door, Brother Dui was able to slip the note he'd scribbled in the bathroom into his hand. Brother Hung deftly palmed the slip of paper, then helped Brother Dui over to a seat by the fire. He checked the monk's ankle so he could whisper.

And the important information Brother Dui transferred was now ready for the pipeline. Wong Guotin, known to most of the world as Harry Wong, was on his way up the mountain along with a tour group and Lily Wong's mystical dog Cooper, which they all knew about. All this was thanks to the intervention of the American and Chinese embassies by way of some Americans who owned casinos in Macau, something that was beyond his comprehension.

The very air, the electricity in the monastery, changed at that precise moment in time. No one could say exactly what happened or how it happened, but things changed. The monks' steps were no longer sluggish, their heads were raised high, and there was talk and some laughter. The dining-room dialogue was a mixture of different languages that their captors didn't understand. The monks were no longer afraid. The lines were drawn, and, as Brother Shen put it, "Now we're on the winning side." No one saw him cross his fingers, because his hands were hidden in the folds of his robe.

It was bitter cold. The tour group stood among the hordes of people intent on traveling to Song Mountain. Everyone was grumbling and complaining to one another as they shuffled their feet and clapped their hands together for warmth.

Ted, who was the tallest of them all, stood on his toes to see if he could figure out what the delay was. He shook his head to indicate that he couldn't tell.

"This is bullshit!" Harry exploded. "I've had enough of this crap. Either we move, or we find another way to get to Song Mountain. I'm done with this."

"Easy, Harry. This is China," Jack said, as though that was all that was needed to explain their current situation. "The object here is not to call attention to ourselves, and that's exactly what you're doing. People are staring at you and the rest of us, so simmer down till we can figure out what to do."

Harry looked around. There were too many people. Way too many people. He'd read somewhere on the plane ride over that on a good day, fifty people visiting the famous monastery on Song Mountain would be considered higher than normal. It looked to him like there were seven or eight hundred people clustered in the area where he was standing.

"No trams are leaving, and no trams are arriving. We've been here for over an hour," Charles said. "I hate to say this, mates, but something is not right."

Dishbang Deshi suddenly appeared next to Jack and Harry. "Listen to me. I wormed my way up a little and got into a conversation with several men who are as disgruntled as we are. They say there are men at the station, not police, who are refusing to allow the trams to leave. These people are fearful. No one is being told why they won't allow the trams to move. They say that the men are bandits who have no authority to direct the tram traffic."

"Then we should call the police," Harry said.

"Do you really want to do that, Harry?" Dishbang Deshi asked. "I don't think so. You've been gone too long from this country. Do you want me to give you chapter and verse about why that is not a good idea?"

"No, he doesn't want you to do that, Dishbang Deshi. Is there another way to get up the mountain?"

Charles moved closer to Annie and started to whisper. She nodded as she pulled her mobile out of her pocket. She tapped furiously, the bottom line was simply, ASAP.

The crowd members started stomping their feet and shouting what sounded like Chinese obscenities.

"Of course there are other ways. But here's the thing. These people are locals. We appear to be the only tourists. The locals must know that the other ways are just as blocked or as congested as this one; otherwise, they wouldn't still be standing here. That's why they suddenly started to protest."

"So what do we do?" Jack asked.

Dishbang Deshi flapped his hands in the air. "I do not know. I'm a silk merchant. I'm not up on all this subterfuge and spook business. That's your forte."

Twenty minutes later, a deafening silence came over the crowd. Off in the distance, they could hear the wail of police sirens. It was a sound recognized the world over.

"Back away, back away, this is going to get ugly really quickly!" Dishbang Deshi shouted to the tour group. "Hurry, hurry!"

"What the hell!" Jack muttered. "What's going on?"

Charles smiled. He shouted to be heard over the clamor. "I had Annie send Bert a text telling him to get in touch with the authorities in Countess de Silva's name. She told him the casino deal was off unless the embassy intervened and allowed her friends from the Crescent China Tours group to visit Song Mountain. She asked him to enlist the aid of the other American casino owners, which he obviously did. Money, especially American dollars, talks over here. I imagine those sirens we're hearing are the local police, who will make short order of the thugs who are preventing us and all these other people from going up the mountain. I will also take that one step further and say those miscreants are in the employ of Harry's nemesis, Wing Ping. Ah, the people are scattering. Stand still so the police can see we belong to the tour group. Don't say anything. Let Harry or Dishbang Deshi do the talking if talk is needed," Charles warned.

Annie looked down at the mobile in her hands. She poked Myra to lean closer so she could read the message on the small screen that Bert had just sent.

Exhibition will be streamed live from monastery to the Wynn casino. Does Harry know? Macau has been inundated with martial-arts aficionados. All hotels filled, people being turned away. Airlines adding extra flights. Someone named Wing Ping is the odds-on favorite. You

all need to tell me what is going on so I can
help. If all this is really true and not some
cockamamie scheme, I say we put some serious
money down on Harry. This place is going
crazy. There is also some crazy talk going
around that billions will ride on this exhibition.
It's not computing. I don't know if it's trash talk
or not. Dixson just sent me a text that said
Vegas is going wild. Anything I can do, let me
know. Here's the thing, the odds here in China
are 20 to 1 on Wing Ping, and it's just the oppo-
site in Vegas.

Myra reached for the mobile and handed it to
Charles, who quickly read the text and handed it
back. He held up five fingers. Annie wiggled her
eyebrows and sent off a text that read, Countess
Anna de Silva bets five million on Harry Wong. If he
wins, I'll donate the money to the monastery. I like
those odds. Spread that rumor as fast as you can. Get
back to me. Gotta run, the tram is boarding.

The local police had formed a barricade and
were inspecting papers and identities. Maggie
and Ted moved to the front of the line and held
out the group's passports, which were scruti-
nized carefully before permission to board was
granted. There was no sign of the illegal stop-
page, and more than half the people who had
been in line were now gone, obviously not wanting any kind of confrontation with the local
police.

"It's about time," Harry seethed as he ush-

ered Cooper ahead of him and into the tram
car.

"We're almost there, Harry. Don't go blow-
ing it now. Hey, check this out, big guy!" Jack
said, as he handed over Annie's mobile with
Bert's message. Harry grinned. He turned
around to see where Annie was and gave her a
thumbs-up for her support. She laughed out
loud.

The mobile traveled backward so all the girls
could read the message. When it was Kathryn's
turn, she read the message, her lips tightening
as she passed it on, then stared straight ahead
as her mind raced.

Nikki patted her arm, and said, "It doesn't
mean anything where you and Bert are concerned. This has nothing to do with you, and if
you think it does, you need to stop flattering
yourself, Kathryn. Get your emotions under
control, or you're going to be sitting on the sidelines." Hothead that she was, Kathryn didn't respond but continued to stare off into space.

Then it was Isabelle's turn to pass her mobile from one member of the group to another
with the latest text from Abner, which simply
said that the sports world was going crazy, and
Vegas in particular, as they were trying to buy
the rights to the martial-arts exhibition. Vegas,
he said, was already full of fans, experts, and
media types. There was money to be made by

the bushel. Unlike the situation in China, the smart American dollars were on Harry Wong.

When the mobile reached Harry's hands, he read Abner's message and smiled. He was still smiling when he slipped into a deep sleep, Cooper wedged into the seat next to him.

Chapter 17

Chaos ensued when it was time to depart the tram, with Cooper barking his head off as he danced around the small waiting area. It was all Jack and Harry could do to calm him down. Even the offer of his one-eared half-tailed rabbit, which Harry pulled out of his pocket, where he had hidden it after Jack passed it off to him, failed to calm the jittery dog. Harry shrugged and secured the stuffed animal in one of his cargo pockets and closed the flap. He knew his very life would be at risk if he lost the tattered rabbit.

A fine, cold mist was falling as Maggie led the group over to a big white bus that said SHAOLIN MONASTERY on the side in bold red Chinese letters. At least that's what she thought it said.

Once again, they all trooped inside for the twenty-minute ride to the monastery at the top of the mountain. They were informed by the driver, as soon as they took their seats, that there was no heat on the bus. Cooper, who had grown quiet, voiced his opinion with a sharp bark that made the driver's hands shake on the wheel.

"Almost there, Harry," Jack whispered.

"This is not going to be a piece of cake, Jack. You know that, right? That business back at the tram, that was just the beginning. What's your best guess as to what we'll find once we actually hit the monastery?"

"Reinforcements. How many, I don't know. How many monks are in residence? How many students? You know the monastery, what's your best guess?"

"Sixty-seven monks plus the Abbot. At this point in time, I simply can't be more definite. That's what it was the year before Lily came here. The last I heard, there were one hundred eighty students, but that was the last semester. It could be more, or it could be less. I don't know how many people Wing Ping would need to . . . to keep everyone in line. The monks won't give him any trouble, nor will the students if the monks caution them. If this had happened when I was there, we would have done nothing. It's all about instant obedience. Wing Ping would know that, so he might be going with a skeleton crew.

"There is something else, Jack. The monks live a holy life. They live to do good and to help mankind. But"—Harry held up his hand to show he had more to say—"back in the day as we students got older, we realized that the monks had a way of communicating with each other in secret. At the time, we didn't know what sign language was, but that's what they were doing. I'd bet my life on it."

"So, let me get this right, Harry. Are you saying even though that scumbag Wing Ping thinks he is in control of the monastery, the monks are actually in control and will revolt when the time is right?"

"In a manner of speaking. Back in the day when I was here, they didn't have computers and phones. They used runners. Much the way the American Indians did during their time. It would always be the young novitiates that did the running. Fleet of foot, that kind of thing. I guarantee that those monks know we are on the way and are just waiting for our arrival."

Jack shook his head to clear his thoughts. "If all you say is true, that has to mean, at least to me, that Lily is safe. That the monks spirited her away. Probably right after your old friend Jun Yu arrived to snatch his kids. Why did you go so nuts then?"

"Because I wasn't thinking properly. I reacted the way a father would react. I forgot to look inward to my teachings. And then there's

Cooper. Aside from my inward teachings, Cooper was really all the proof I needed to convince myself that Lily is safe. Go on, Jack, say it before I have to beat it out of you. I'm putting all my beliefs and hopes on a dog. Cooper is not just any dog, Jack. I thought we agreed on that. He's . . . he's . . ."

"Yes," Jack drawled.

"He is what he is. We can speculate from now till the end of time and probably never come up with an answer that satisfies us both. We simply accept it."

Jack nodded and bent over to scratch Cooper between the ears, just long enough for a thought to enter his mind. *Finally you're getting it.* Cooper cracked open one eye and stared up at Jack. Later when he told Nikki, he said he could almost swear Cooper was grinning at him. "I'm telling you, Nikki, my blood ran cold there for a minute." And Nikki had just smiled and smiled. And at that precise moment, somewhere not far away, he could hear a dog bark. Even though he was not a rocket scientist, he knew Cooper's bark, could recognize it miles away.

"We're here!" Maggie shouted from the front of the bus. "And if I am not mistaken, there is a . . . let's just say for the moment a welcoming committee of a dozen or so scrawny-looking men. I don't see any yellow-garbed monks. Ted and I will take the lead here. Even though I

think our cover is blown, let's all continue to
play our parts. Gather all your gear, people."
She jammed the straw hat with the plumed
feather snug on her head. Ted did the same
thing.

The weather was foul, the cold mist that had
been falling back at the tram stop now an icy
rain. One of the scrawny men, dressed in a shiny
black slicker, made motions with his hands to indicate they were all to turn around and get right
back on the bus. Being American, the group
pretended not to understand.

That's when Cooper rose on his hind legs
and let loose with an unholy bellow of sound.
The black-clad figure stopped and stepped
back as Cooper raced toward him just as the
monster doors to the monastery opened to
allow a gaggle of monks to emerge, all jabbering in different languages. They rushed forward, reached out to the tour group, and pulled
and tugged them forward into the monastery.
Cooper showed his teeth in an ugly snarl as he
advanced on the welcoming committee of
scrawny men, who decided it might not be wise
to antagonize the strange-looking animal.

Alexis and Espinosa were the last in line and
saw the greeter in the black raincoat hit the
speed dial on his mobile phone.

Once inside, they all knew they were prisoners. Of a sort.

Brother Hung stepped forward and in a low

whisper in English asked where Harry Wong was.

Cooper nudged Brother Hung's leg and growled as he nudged him forward.

Harry held out his hand. The old monk clasped it tightly in both his hands. "I knew you would come. I just didn't expect you to . . . is it a disguise?"

"It is. And these are all my friends. Tell me, where is my daughter? Is she safe?"

"She is safe. She will remain safe until it is time for you to take her back to your home in America."

The relief on Harry's face made the old monk smile. "And who is your friend?"

Dishbang Deshi held out his hand the way Harry had. "It is good to see you again, my esteemed teacher."

"Ah, I see. Master Dishbang. An excellent disguise. I never would have known either of you. As you can see, the others do not recognize you. Remarkable. Absolutely remarkable. We are under siege here. But we are in control. These idiotic people just don't know it or refuse to accept that fact."

"How many are there, Brother Hung?" Harry asked.

"We counted fifty. They are spread all over the monastery. Chi Xongin, our current Abbot, is an imposter. He is in charge of these thugs. He has been hiding out in the offices. His meals are taken to him. We have not seen him in days. Brother Dui, who has always done the clerical work in the office, says he is on the computer and his mobile phone all day long. Come along to the dining hall, so we can show you our hospitality. None of these thugs understand English, but the Abbot does. Be careful. Tell me you have a plan, Harry, to . . . to liberate us and the monastery."

"We have a plan, Brother Hung," Harry said somberly. "You're sure my daughter is safe?"

"As safe as if she were in her mother's arms. I assume that little schoolgirl in disguise is Lily's mother."

"She is."

"I had Yuke Lok spirit her away the moment I realized what was happening. You remember Yuke Lok from when you came to visit, right? She is what we call Lily's big sister. As you know, the older girls look after the younger ones just the way it was when you were here with your big brothers looking after you and the younger boys.

"We do not like living like this, Harry. Those people are desecrating this beautiful monastery. They bring evil here. Why? Why are they doing this to us? Do you know?"

"It's Wing Ping. He wants to be number one. But more than that, he wants revenge on all of you and the monastery itself for expelling him and shaming him and his family. He wants it all

back, and this is the only way he *thinks* he can
do it. I am convinced he killed Jun Yu. If he
didn't do it, he had someone else do it for
him. I was not aware of what became of him
and how he chose to lead his life after he was
sent home from the monastery, until Dishbang
Deshi told me. It's a miracle that Jun Yu was
able to send his family to me. They, by the way,
are as safe as they can be. They will be sad for a
very long time, but they will acclimate to their
new life with all the help we can give them. Jun
Yu said he tried to get Lily but couldn't. Failing
to acquire Jun Ling and the children had to
enrage Wing Ping. He wants . . . needs to reclaim his old life and bring honor back to his
family. At least that's my take on the whole
thing. Nothing else makes sense."

"So you will fight him?" Brother Hung asked
quietly.

"It's the only way for all of you to reclaim the
monastery. If I were to go wherever it is you
have Lily sequestered and leave, Wing Ping
would do terrible things to all of you and this
beautiful monastery. We both know that. I
can't walk away and leave you to his tender
mercies. It goes against all you have taught me
during my days here. But . . . I think I might
have an idea. I need to think about it and discuss it with Yoko and my people before I say
anything more."

"But, Wong Guotin, Wing Ping was born to

the art. Tales of his expertise are all over China. These past years he has goaded Jun Yu to fight him, but Jun Yu refused. They called Jun Yu a coward. He was not, as you know. This is the result."

"So I guess the next move is Wing Ping's. Either we wait him out, or we take matters into our own hands. I think the people in my group here"—Harry said, waving his arm about— "are capable of taking all fifty of them out and securing the monastery. There are no weapons here, are there?"

The old monk shook his head. "You should know better than to say a thing like that. Even Wing Ping would not dare bring a weapon onto this sacred ground. He considers himself a weapon, as do all those . . . those people he sent here. Look around, Wong Guotin, we have gotten old. True, we have some younger brothers here, but the majority of us are old and, while not useless, we won't be of much help. I heard you when you said your group is quite capable of taking care of these intruders. How can that be, Wong Guotin? There are more women than men."

The sudden burst of laughter at the long dining table brought color to the old monk's cheeks. "I meant no disrespect, Wong Guotin."

"And none was taken. You have no worries where these females are concerned. They can all take care of themselves."

Brother Hung's voice dropped to a whisper, "But . . . but two of them are . . . *old*. Like most of my brother monks."

"I heard that!" Annie said, amusement ringing in her voice.

"I did, too." Myra giggled.

Charles and Fergus both wiggled their hands in the air to show the monks they, too, were in the game. Brother Hung's face turned even redder.

Cooper took that particular moment to move front and center to weigh in with his opinion. He tossed his head from side to side before he let loose with a god-awful howl, before he trotted back to his place next to Harry.

"There is old, and then there is *old*, my teacher. Trust me, you have no worries where my friends are concerned."

"I see, I see. This then," Hung said, to indicate the entire group, "is your clan. Your force."

"I like the word *army*," Dennis said boldly. The others hooted their approval as the monks suddenly started setting food down on the long table. It was simple food—hot, nourishing, and smelled wonderful. The group fell to it, jabbering and gesturing as they chowed down.

"Just so you know, that was the last of our food. We have a few staples and a little food in our freezers, but this is it. Part of Wing Ping's plan is to starve us. No supplies are being brought in. His people have consumed most of the food we had in store since they've been here," Brother Shen said quietly.

As one, the group looked guilty. Annie apologized for their hearty appetites, saying had they known how dire the situation was, they would have curbed their food intake. Brother Hung waved away her words. "What we have we share. We are not novices when it comes to doing without. As I said when you arrived, we have been under siege. The only person permitted to go back and forth is the egg man. We do not even know why that is, unless the man is in the employ of Wing Ping. Or that he and his people at the base of the mountain have a fetish for eggs."

Brother Shen wiped his hands on a pristine white apron as he looked around at the guests sitting at the table. "We need a plan. Do we have a plan? We want to help, but until you tell us what we can do, our hands are tied." He went on to tell them about their original plan to give the egg man two notes. "It was all we could come up with. But if the egg man is in the employ of Wing Ping, then we cannot involve him."

"That will be easy enough to figure out when he arrives," Jack said. "We'll just give him the old American third degree and wait for him to either fall apart or offer to cooperate."

Kathryn raised her hand to show she wanted to speak. "What would happen if the monks sent word that they wanted a sit-down with all the men here in the monastery? If they come to the table, we take them out. Don't look at me like that! We can do it. They won't give us women a second thought. We turn the tables on them, lock them up somewhere, and force Wing Ping to come here in person. With, I suppose, another endless supply of men to do his bidding. I think we can do it. What do you all think, people? The sooner we get this show on the road, the sooner we can head back home."

Nikki agreed, her voice ringing the loudest, to the monk's dismay. Yoko whistled sharply, an earsplitting sound that made the monks cower and move closer together as they stared first at Yoko, then at Harry. Dennis thought it was funny and burst out laughing. He did a jig of sorts, still laughing, until Ted told him to bottle it up.

Harry and Dishbang Deshi looked over at the line of monks, who appeared to be standing at attention. They slowly ripped at their various disguises until they looked once again like Harry Wong and Dishbang Deshi. "How do you communicate with the intruders?" Harry asked.

"We don't. They just follow us around and shout orders. I will say that none of them have laid a hand on any of us. I want to believe it is out of respect, but I simply do not know whether that is true."

The girls were now ripping at their wigs and

shedding the extra clothing and padding they'd been wearing. Yoko tossed her glasses into the flames of the kitchen fireplace, along with the hated knee socks. While she didn't look any bigger or smaller, she once again looked like Yoko. She grinned at the others, who simply grinned back.

"Are we all agreed that we will . . . um . . . take them on?" Myra asked.

Every hand in the room shot in the air.

"Brother Hung, it is up to you to invite all of Wing Ping's men to the arena. All of them. Jack, Dennis, and Yoko will go with you." Cooper barked. "And, of course, the dog." Cooper barked again. "Sorry, Cooper. Jack, Dennis, Yoko, *and Cooper* will accompany you." Harry looked down at Cooper and hissed, "Show-off." Cooper barked happily as he trotted off.

"And if they don't or won't do as I ask?" the old monk asked fretfully.

Harry laughed. The old monk shivered as Cooper let loose with another happy bark.

Dennis was so giddy that he was being included in the initial takedown, he almost blacked out in excitement. That Harry thought he was good enough to accompany Jack and Yoko had him floating on a cloud of pure bliss.

"What? Are you waiting for a bus? *GO!*" It was an iron command from Annie and Myra at the same moment.

"Hold on here a minute," Jack said. "Do any

of you think there might be a little bit of a problem since Dennis, Yoko, and I do *not* speak Chinese?"

"True, but Brother Hung does speak Chinese. He can do all the talking," Brother Shen said. "He has been our spokesperson with these people since they first arrived."

Cooper let loose with several happy yips as he danced around Yoko's legs.

"If the dog isn't worried about the language barrier, then you don't need to worry either," Harry snarled. "Go already!"

"Well, since you put it like that, Harry, I guess I'll just take my little merry band and the dog whose name is Cooper and head out to save the monastery and return or not return as the case may be."

Harry couldn't resist a parting shot. "Don't come back unless you are victorious."

Cooper stopped in his tracks, but he didn't bark. He simply looked up at Harry as much as to say, stupid is as stupid does. The thought raced through Jack's brain at the speed of light. "See, even the dog whose name is Cooper knows we will be victorious. O ye of little faith!"

Everyone in the dining hall started to talk at once, the decibel level so high, the fine hairs on the back of Annie's neck started to move back and forth. She whistled sharply for silence. "Let's all sit down and get with the plan."

"We don't have a plan," Maggie said.

"I know that, dear. We are going to make a plan right now at this table. So, everyone please sit down, and let's get to it."

"It's about time," Kathryn grumbled.

"Amen!" Nikki said.

Chapter 18

The foursome, along with Cooper, exited the dining hall and emerged into a wide corridor that smelled strongly of incense. The little group was quiet, all of them looking over one shoulder to see if anyone was following or watching them. "No eyes that I can see," Yoko whispered.

"I don't see anyone either," Jack said. "Are you and the others free to walk around at your own leisure?" he asked Brother Hung.

"No, not at all. Someone, usually groups of two or three, monitors the halls. Something must be going on. I would assume that the interlopers who have been occupying the monastery are gathering somewhere to discuss what to do with all of you. Us as well, I would think. It is

possible, of course, that those inside are waiting for orders from Wing Ping. I simply do not
know. Nothing like this has ever happened to
us before, so there is no precedent."

"Let's head for the offices so we can speak
with the imposter who claims to be your Abbot,"
Jack said forcefully. "Where is it located from
where we are right now?"

The words were no sooner out of Jack's
mouth than the bells from the center bell
tower in the courtyard outside the entrance to
the monastery started to ring. They all stopped
to listen. "Why are the bells ringing?" Dennis
asked in a jittery voice.

Brother Hung looked around. "I do not
know. This is the first time that the bells have
rung since these people arrived. We ring the
bells only when there is an emergency of some
sort. Our captors do have people on guard
outside. The weather might have worsened, so
it might be a call to come indoors. Or possibly it's
a call for them all to gather. Quickly, go around
the corner, and the office is to the right."

Cooper sprinted forward at the speed of
light just as though he knew exactly where to
go. His long, plumed tail swished importantly
as Jack advanced and, with one quick motion,
thrust open the door. Jack saw at a glance that
there were four people in the room. One man,
supposedly the bogus Abbot because of his yellow robe, was sitting at a computer, with a man
to his right, one to his left, and a man Jack

identified as Brother Dui stapling papers into
a neat pile.

"I take the Abbot, Dennis left, Yoko right.
Coop, guard the door!" Jack hissed.

The element of surprise worked. The en-
counter was over before any response by the
invaders had a chance to get off the ground.
Jack looked at Brother Hung. "We need something to tie them up. I don't suppose you have
any duct tape, or even know what that is, do
you?"

Brother Hung stood rooted to the floor,
stunned at what he had just seen. Who were
these people Wong Guotin had surrounded
himself with? He shook his head to clear it
and said as smartly as he could, "Of course we
have duct tape. It is in the closet. Dui, please
fetch it and . . . and do what they say." His gaze
went to Yoko; he was as impressed as he could
be with what he'd just seen her do. She winked
at him and smiled. Brother Hung was so flustered, Cooper nipped at his leg to let him
know he was to get with the program.

And at that precise moment, the doors burst
open and a small army of men rushed into the
room. To Jack's dismay, every single one of the
intruders assumed a fighting stance. He risked
a glance at Dennis and Yoko, who were frozen
in place. What confused him even more was
that Cooper was silent. "Stand down, guys,"
Jack said under his breath, his lips barely moving.

"I count nine," Yoko whispered. "These three are bound. Stand down my ass!"

"My ass, too," Dennis hissed.

Cooper remained silent, watching the men, who were jabbering, their hands pummeling the air around them.

"They want us to take the tape off their people," Brother Hung said.

"Well, that's not going to happen anytime soon," Jack said. "We don't give an inch. They have no weapons."

"Like we give a good rat's ass what they want," Dennis said defiantly.

Cooper remained silent but watchful. Jack wondered what the hell the dog was all about at that moment. He stared at Cooper long enough for a thought to ricochet through his head. On the count of four was the thought. *Four?* He looked at Yoko and Dennis. "On the count of four!"

"They want you to shut up," Brother Hung said. "Do not talk! They said they will kill you if you keep talking. They do not understand English."

"One."

"Two."

"Three!"

"FOUR!"

Cooper lazily got up as though he was stretching his legs. Then he was in the air, as were Yoko and Dennis. No slouch himself, Jack reacted and lashed out, Brother Dui trying to help him by swinging a stapler at one of the attackers, before he wisely, Jack thought, ducked under the desk. But a moment later, to Jack's amazement, Brother Dui had a metal wastebasket in his hands, which he dropped over the head of one of the attackers. Then he yanked at the phone and beat on the bottom of the can with all his strength. The attacker managed to get the basket off his head, but he was so disoriented that he started to stagger across the room. Brother Hung's leg shot out and tripped him, knocking him to the floor. Dennis moved, dodged an attacker, and stomped on the man's neck, all the while yelling, "Tape this jerk up!"

Yoko dusted her hands together as she eyeballed Dennis. "You did good, kiddo. We barely broke a sweat on this one. Nine down, not bad. What do you think, Jack? Will my husband be happy with us?"

"I don't think your esteemed husband could have done it any better. Yoko is right; you did good, kid," Jack said. "Cooper, you little devil, we couldn't have done it without you. You did good, too, Coop. Okay, enough praise. What's our next step?" All eyes turned to the two monks, both of whom were wearing blank expressions. Jack knew in that instant they would be no help. "Okay, drag them all into that big bathroom. We lock that door, then we lock the door to the office and go about our business. Hung, you tell anyone who asks that the Abbot himself locked the doors and said no one was to go inside the office. Tell them the moment the bells rang, he and his two partners ran down the hall and out another entrance. It's not much, but for now I think that will work."

"Where are we going now?" Dennis asked.

Cooper was back on his feet and sauntering to the door. Yoko opened it. "Wherever he goes, we follow—it's really that simple."

Hung finally came out of his stupor. "Do you Americans always follow the whims of . . . of this creature?"

Cooper stopped long enough to glare at the old monk. "Excuse me, I meant to say do you always follow . . . *Cooper's* orders and go where he goes?"

"Yep," the three said in unison. Cooper barked once, just loud enough to acknowledge the old monk's gaffe.

"Absolutely remarkable. Do you not agree, Brother Dui?" The younger monk nodded although he looked perplexed.

"It looks like Cooper is taking us back to the dining hall. I thought we were going to go to the arena, or at least tell someone we all wanted to meet there," Dennis said as he trotted alongside Yoko.

"I guess Cooper has other plans." Jack turned to Brother Hung. "I have a question. Your oldest class of students, are there any young men advanced enough in their studies so that they can fight? Men whom we can enlist to help us? In case we are significantly out-numbered."

"I knew you would ask me that question sooner or later. The answer is yes and no. Certainly, they are not of the same caliber as Jun Yu, Dishbang Deshi, and Wong Guotin. And certainly not Wing Ping, when he was their age. None of the three students in attendance now have come close to the prowess shown by those four. We hold the first three alumni up as models and try to avoid any reference to that monster, Wing Ping, except as an example not to follow. The students all strive to match the expertise of the first three. But none of them even come close.

"Having said that, in a real-life situation, they might surprise us all."

"Where are the students right now?" Jack asked.

"At the back and at the other side of the building. What do you want me to do?"

"We're almost to the dining hall. Turn around, and if anyone asks, pretend that the Abbot told you to go to the three students and take them to the dining hall. Can you do that?"

Brother Hung looked around nervously. "I can certainly try. I *will* do as you ask."

"Do you want to take Cooper with you?"

"Um . . . no, I think . . . he is better off with you. I will go now. Be careful."

"Always." Yoko smiled at the old monk, who

jammed his hands into the folds of his robe so that the others couldn't see how badly he was trembling.

Dennis stopped at one of the paned windows to look outside. "Weather doesn't look good. And is anyone noticing that it is getting colder here?"

"I don't think they heat the hallways, Dennis. We aren't going outside, so cross that worry off your list. At least for now. Okay, I see the door to the dining hall. Move it, guys!"

"I didn't see a lock or bolt on the dining-hall door," Yoko volunteered. "Do you all think that maybe just the office has a lock? I remember thinking it was very shiny, like perhaps newly installed. Maybe when these gangsters moved in, they installed it for their own reasons."

Jack had no idea, because he hadn't paid any attention to the shiny lock. He shrugged as Dennis thrust open the door. Cooper let loose with his victory greeting.

"Talk! What happened?" the group shouted out, as if their voices were controlled by a group mind.

Jack brought the group up to speed quickly, ending with, "Brother Hung is on his way to the student quarters to fetch his three star pupils." At Harry and Dishbang Deshi's puzzled looks, he explained, "They're bodies. A show of force. I have to be honest here. Brother Hung said they are . . . not nearly as good as you guys were. I took that to mean, even on your bad days they can't measure up. Like I said, a show of bodies, and as students, they speak English. At least I assume they do. Brother Hung was quick to point out that possibly they might rise to the occasion when they see it is a life-and-death matter. I hope he's right."

"Are we going to fight it out here in the dining hall?" Dennis asked.

"Ask me something I know the answer to, kid. I know what you know. For the moment, I think we just sit here and wait for someone to come blasting through that door."

Harry chewed on his bottom lip as he stared at Dishbang Deshi. "Something's wrong. Do you feel it, my old friend?"

"I do. If they have the army we think they have, we should be surrounded by now. We cut their numbers by . . . a dozen. If you're counting, that is. By now they should be missed. And that number includes the fake Abbot himself and the goons he had with him in his office. We should build the fire up and perhaps make tea for everyone. Tea is a calming agent, as we all know."

Fergus tended to the fire while Charles headed for the monster range to prepare tea.

"So we sit and wait, is that what you're saying?" Annie questioned.

"Unless you have a better idea," Maggie snapped irritably.

"Someone should do the dishes," Isabelle said.

"I will," Alexis said. "I'll wash, you dry. Shouldn't you have heard from Abner by now?"

"Yes, and I'm worried that he hasn't been in touch. I don't know what that means."

"Probably means he doesn't have anything worthwhile to report," Ted said.

"Where's Cooper?" Nikki asked.

"Sleeping under the table. That's a good thing right now. It means we're safe for the moment," Myra observed.

Charles was pouring tea into little white bowls when the doors to the dining hall opened to admit Brother Hung and his three students. Introductions were made. "Meet Wen Ho, Chang Li, and Yong Park." The students bowed, their faces a mix of awe, respect, and excitement. Especially when Harry and Dishbang Deshi were introduced.

"Hero worship at its finest," Jack muttered under his breath.

"What is going on outside?" Yoko demanded of Brother Hung.

"Nothing. I saw no one. I was not accosted. The three men guarding the students gave me no trouble when I told them the Abbot wanted to see these three in his office. One of them has a cell phone. I saw no sign of weapons. They are treating the students well. None of them seemed overly anxious. Aside from the three men standing guard, everything appeared normal."

"Maybe the weather has something to do

with things," Maggie said. "Mother Nature, as we all know full well, is notorious for throwing monkey wrenches into the best-laid plans. Or"—her voice changed from sounding fretful to outright angry—"it is night now. Maybe they're waiting for the witching hour or something to wage a full-scale attack."

No one offered up a comment. The huge dining hall turned silent again.

Harry paced, Dishbang Deshi right behind him. "I say we call Wing Ping. We have the Abbot's phone. We speak Chinese. What do you think, Dishbang Deshi?"

"What I think is that Wing Ping is waiting for you to call him. He wants to be in control. Right now, we have a standoff. It's just my opinion, Harry, but I think we should wait it out, make him come to you. Not us, you."

Harry nodded. "You're right, Dishbang Deshi. As hard as it is to do, we'll wait him out. By now, he has to know we've taken out some of his men. They haven't reported in. Twelve men suddenly going silent will not go unnoticed for long. He's probably weighing his options right now. At the moment, I just don't know if the bad weather out there is in his favor or ours. We still haven't figured out what the ringing bells was all about."

"A call to arms, Harry. That's the only thing it can possibly mean. Somewhere in this holy monastery are a group of malcontents bent on destroying us. Obviously, they are waiting somewhere inside this holy place for further instructions."

Harry gulped at the tea in his cup, then held the cup out to Charles for a refill.

The large dining hall returned to silence.

Two hours went by without anything happening. The group was actually starting to doze off when, without fanfare, without any warning from Cooper, the great doors opened and five men entered the hall. The door was closed quietly by the last man in the little group.

"Standoff," Dennis said through clenched teeth.

Cooper stirred, rose to his feet, stretched, and then meandered over to where Harry, Jack, and Dishbang Deshi were standing.

"Who has the eye?" Nikki hissed.

"I do," Yoko hissed in return, her lips barely moving.

The leader of the five-man group looked around until his gaze settled on Harry Wong. He motioned for him to step forward. Harry didn't move. The hoodlum leader motioned again as he started to jabber in Chinese. Harry remained still and mute.

The leader shed his quilted jacket, which looked to be soaking wet, and pulled a gun from the back of his loose black trousers. None of the other four made a move, their eyes ricocheting around the room at all the women.

Brother Shen and Brother Hung reared up,

their voices raised in anger. "You dare to bring a firearm into this holy monastery! You dare to do this!" they cried in excited Chinese that Dishbang Deshi interpreted for the others.

"This might be a stupid question, Harry, but do you think that creep knows how to use that gun, or is it just for show?" Jack asked, his face squeezed into deep frown lines.

Before Harry could respond, the gunman laughed, a foul cackle of sound. "I speak English, and yes, I know how to use this gun. I will shoot all of you one by one if you don't remain quiet and do as you're told."

Jack looked down at Cooper, who appeared to be yawning. *Yawning? Cooper?* The dog half turned to Jack in time for his thought processes to catch the word *four* filtering through his brain. "*Four*," he shouted. "Who has the eye?" His tone was high-pitched but still conversational.

"I do," Yoko said quietly.

"One!"

"Two!"

"Three!"

Cooper flew through the air and had the gunman's wrist clamped between his teeth before any of the other invaders could respond. The gun clattered to the floor.

And then they were all moving in every direction, arms, legs, human torsos sailing through the air. Out of the corner of his eye, Jack saw that Espinosa had the gun and was holding it as if it were a poisonous snake.

Cooper was still holding on to the gunman's wrist until Harry came up from behind and put a chokehold on the man. Cooper released his captive, looked around at the melee, then retired to his space under the massive table. He closed his eyes but cracked one open when he heard Harry say, "Great job, Cooper. You had the eye that time! Next time, though, don't say four when you mean three!" Cooper went back to sleep.

"Bad news, people," Ted said.

"What now?" Jack bellowed.

"We're out of duct tape, that's what," Ted snarled.

"We have rope," Brother Shen said.

"This might be a good time to think about producing it," Dennis said through clenched teeth, his eyes on Espinosa and the gun.

Brother Shen scurried off to what was probably a pantry off the dining hall. He returned with a coil of yellow nylon rope that he handed over to Harry. To Espinosa's relief, Jack reached for the gun and stuck it under his belt at the small of his back. His shirt covered it.

"We can gag them with the dishcloths," Nikki said as she fished through drawers that lined the huge sink next to the stove.

"You sure you want that gun, Jack? I'm a better shot than you are," Annie said. To give more weight to her words, she added, "And these sexist idiots will certainly not expect me, a woman, to have a gun." Jack thought about it for a moment or two and realized Annie was right; and she really was a crack shot. He handed it over. Annie, in turn, stuck it in the small of her back just the way Jack had. She now felt in control again. It was the little things, she thought, that made it all worthwhile. She felt like shouting, bring it on, I'm ready but she kept the thought to herself. No sense getting ahead of herself. When the time came, she would be ready for anything that Wing Ping and his bullyboys could bring.

Chapter 19

Charles shuffled his feet as he took a step backward to stand alongside Fergus Duffy. His lips were barely moving when he said, "Tell me what you see, Fergus. What I see is that things are going to start going south any minute now. The girls didn't come halfway around the world to sit in a dining hall with a bunch of low-life bottom-feeders. Your beloved is just itching to pull out that gun and plug someone center mass. My own beloved is about to stomp on someone, and at this point I do not think she cares if it's one of the low-life bottom-feeders or one of us. Kathryn . . . she's a ticking time bomb. The others are getting more agitated by the second. Any ideas?"

Fergus rolled his eyes as he took in the scene around him. Charles was right, and he winced at what he thought the outcome might be. "This is how I see it, Sir Charles. You are the undisputed leader of this little group, so you better start acting like you know what you're doing. A little guidance will go a long way, I'm thinking. And while there is always the possibility that I could be wrong, I don't think I am. The ball is firmly in your court now. The question is, are you going to put the ball in motion, or are you going to stand here and play with it?"

"When did you get so smart, Fergus? You're right on all counts. Buckle up! I expect some fireworks."

Charles reached into his pocket and withdrew the whistle that he was never without. He gave it two sharp blasts, blasts that were so shrill that Cooper reared up and barked.

"Listen up, people! As you can all see, we are in a bit of a crisis mode here. I can also see that you are all champing at the bit to dive into things headfirst, but you are not looking closely enough at the consequences such an action will provoke. I have some ideas about a course of action and its consequences, so let's all sit down at the table like the reasonable adults we are and *talk*."

Charles noticed a certain sense of relief grip all members of the group as they scurried to take seats at the table. Isabelle, still carrying the dish towel, sat down and looked across the table at Yoko and Kathryn, both of whom looked like angry bees ready to sting someone

or something where it would get the most results.

The moment Charles had everyone's attention, he raised his hand for silence. "For
starters, Isabelle, contact Abner and find out
what's going on in the sports world and what
the latest is on this . . . this impending compe-
tition. We also need a weather forecast for this
region. Ted, you and Espinosa take care of
that. Annie, I want you to get in touch with
Bert to see what's going on in Macau in the
gaming industry. I want information ASAP.

"Jack, I want you, Harry, and Dennis to go
back to the office where you left the Abbot and
his men. Fetch them all here. Take the gun
you gave Annie so that you can manage all
twelve of the men in the office. We need everyone in one location.

"Brother Shen, you are in charge of the fire.
Keep it blazing—it's cold in here. Keep the
teakettle filled and brewing. Brother Hung, I
want you to interrogate our . . . guests. Kathryn
and Nikki will assist you. With threats and
physical violence if necessary. Can you do this,
or should I assign that role to Harry and Dishbang Deshi or our three new students?"

Brother Hung bowed low. "I can do what
you ask. I will do it willingly."

"Fine. Fine. Now, do we know where the rest
of the monks are being sequestered?"

Brother Shen responded, a sparkle of excitement in his eyes. "We do not actually know with

any certainty. Scattered about the monastery would be my guess. I don't see them being of any help to any of us. First and foremost, their thoughts and actions will be with the students, and we consider ourselves lucky so far that these people have not threatened or harmed them." Charles nodded that he totally understood.

"What do you want me to do?" Dishbang Deshi asked, his frustration that he had been left out of the mix obvious to all.

"I would like you to make some calls, send some texts, to see what you can find out back where you came from. Right now, we are flying blind, as the saying goes. We need all the information we can get."

"This whole thing sounds like a Mexican standoff," Kathryn grumbled.

Cooper stretched lazily before he headed for the exit. When he reached the massive double doors, he turned and barked.

"Time to go. We don't want Cooper getting antsy," Jack said, sprinting across the room, Harry and Dennis on his heels. A second later they were gone.

"All right, then, who has the weather?"

"Storm front. Ice storm. No one is coming up the mountain, which also means none of us are going to go down the mountain anytime soon. It's expected to continue for the next few days," Ted said, clicking at the keys faster than any of them could blink.

"That has to mean we only have to deal with those in the monastery. I say we round them up one by one and haul their scrawny asses right here into this dining room. We can make them talk," Kathryn, the hothead in the group, said loudly enough that her voice carried to the far end of the dining hall, where their newest captives sat lined up, bound and secure, in a neat row.

The women's clenched fists shot in the air, Annie's the highest. "Bring it on, girls, and let's show them who is in control here. We came here to rescue a little girl, and the more time we waste, the longer that's going to take."

Dishbang Deshi blanched at this show of bravado. He thought about his sweet, outspoken American wife, and wondered if as she got older, she would turn out to be like these take-charge women. He blinked to push away the unwelcome thought as the word *bloodthirsty* came to mind. This time he shook his head to clear his thoughts.

"I haven't heard back from Bert yet," Annie said sourly. "I just sent off another text, and one to Dixson Kelly back in Vegas."

The monster doors of the dining room opened. Cooper ran into the room, looked around, paraded up and down in front of the bound captives, and growled deep in his throat before he took up residence under the table.

Pulling, shoving, and pushing the twelve captives from the office, Jack shouted, "Do you believe these guys! They didn't want to come with us. This slimeball," he said, pointing to the bogus Abbot, "tried for a crotch kick when I untied his feet so he could walk here."

"And . . ." Nikki said sweetly.

Jack laughed. "They're up there somewhere in the middle of his stomach. See how green he looks. A man from China looking green is something you don't normally see. I think he's in quite a bit of pain right now. After what happened to him, none of the others so much as breathed a complaint when it was their turn."

"Oh, boohoo, too bad, too sad," Maggie said as she gave one of the captives a mighty push so that he stumbled and fell to the floor. Dishbang Deshi dragged him across the room and added him to the neat line of bodies. Fergus quickly tied his ankles together. Captive number two was set in line by Ted and Espinosa, who then went back and manhandled nine of the others into place.

Meanwhile, Jack hauled the bogus Abbot over to the table and plopped him down. None too gently. The man's eyeballs rolled back in his head. When he was finally able to focus, Jack went at him. "Listen to me, you smelly son of a bitch. Because I am only going to say this once. Tell us what's going on. Where is Wing Ping? What's the plan? Nod your head to show me you understood what I just said, and don't pretend you don't understand English. I'm going to take the tape off your mouth, and then you talk. If you don't, Wong Guotin here is going to pull your tongue out and stuff it up your scrawny ass. Nod if you understood my last statement."

The bogus Abbot nodded, his eyes full of panic. The moment the tape was ripped from his mouth, the Abbot squealed, "I know nothing. I just follow orders and do as I am told, as do the others. I hear rumors. We all hear them and talk about them, but we have no concrete facts. I cannot tell you something I don't know. Please, be merciful," the man said pitifully.

"Right now, this very minute, you need to ask yourself why I don't believe you," Jack said, his tone cold and ominous.

"I don't know about the rest of you good folks, but I am nowhere near buying the crap this guy is trying to sell me. Forget yanking his tongue out. Give him over to us," Kathryn said, waving her arm in the direction of the girls. "If there's anything in that pea brain of his, we'll get it out of him."

The girls rushed over to form a circle around the bogus Abbot the minute Jack had him up and on his feet. They pushed and shoved him until he was beyond the long table and in front of the roaring fire, which looked hot enough to roast a buffalo.

"Have at it, girls," Jack said agreeably.

"Strip all of them down till they're butt naked," Nikki said, taking charge. "That means you men. We'll start to work on this one, a little bit at a time." She winked roguishly at the Abbot.

Cooper raised his head, looked around, then let loose with three yips of pure joy. He didn't go back to sleep, though. He rested his massive head on his paws and gleefully, it seemed to anyone who looked at him, watched the proceedings.

"Well, this is certainly going to answer one of life's little secrets," Annie said.

"What's that, dear?" Myra asked.

Annie giggled. "The secret to what they wear under those robes!"

"Jockeys or briefs?" Yoko laughed outright. Harry openly cringed.

And the bets were on. Half for jockeys, half for boxers, and one independent—who said, "Nothing as in nothing." They all hooted again with laughter.

"Oh, man, I would talk so fast, my teeth would fall out," Dennis said in a jittery-sounding voice. "No guy wants a bunch of women to . . . you know . . . see his package."

The girls laughed again, Myra the loudest and longest.

"You guys use kitchen shears?" Kathryn bellowed. Like a good surgical nurse, Brother Shen slapped them into her hands before she could draw a breath. "Guess that means I have the honor. Ah, they're in the modern world here, a Velcro closing. Looks like a Fruit of the Loom T-shirt. American all the way. Okay, girls, ready for the unveiling?"

"Ooooh, we are soooo ready," Nikki replied, giggling. "Aren't we, girls!"

"Well, I certainly am," Yoko cooed. She turned to Harry and cooed again, "Honey, pay attention. If you ever strip, willingly or unwillingly, I will kill you!"

"Jesus, Harry, I think she means it. You might need to get some reinforced zippers or something," Jack said out of the corner of his mouth.

Harry had to vent because he felt light-headed, so he used his favorite expression when he was at odds with Jack, "Eat shit, Jack!"

"That goes for you, too, Jack," Nikki trilled.

"And you, too, Espinosa," Alexis singsonged.

"I don't care, Ted. You want to show off your jewels, go for it," Maggie said, laughing so hard that she doubled over.

The bogus Abbot grew round-eyed at the jocularity displayed by these crazy women at his expense. He could see his colleagues smirking behind their gags. He closed his eyes in misery.

"Well, so much for your mystery, Annie," Kathryn said, peering closer at the Abbot's underwear. "I don't know what to call what he's wearing. Looks like an old lady's panties."

"They're Depends," Dennis said. "I saw a commercial on TV where a bunch of men, and women, were marching down the street strutting their stuff. 'They're Depends! And they don't leave lines under your clothing.' That was a big selling point." Authority rang in his voice, so no one disputed the young reporter's knowledge.

All the women eyed the embarrassed Abbot by walking around him and pointing to his underwear. Finally, the big question came. "Which one of us gets to take it off?" Annie giggled. "I think the holder of the shears should just . . . you know . . . snip away."

"Aha! I can do that! Absolutely I can do that! In fact, I actually want to do that!" Kathryn said, making snapping sounds with the shears.

"Then when you're done, what should we do, dear?" Myra asked with a smile in her voice that was contagious. All the women started to giggle.

"How's this for off the top of my head," Yoko volunteered. "We brand his ass, both cheeks, and then . . . and then we lay the fire on his . . . whatever you call his package in Chinese. There won't be anything left of his eeney meeney, itsy-bitsy you know what." The girls clapped with enthusiasm.

"Holy shit!" Jack muttered under his breath. "I sure as hell hope you never get on her bad side, Harry."

"Eat shit, Jack."

"You already said that. You need to be more original in your retorts."

"Oh, gee whiz," Dennis said. "They aren't going to really do that, are they?"

Cooper reared up and barked, a shrill sound that grated on everyone's ears.

"The boss has spoken, kid. That was your answer unless you want me to clarify it for you," Jack said.

"Um . . . no, that's okay. I read somewhere that the smell of burned flesh is hard to get out of your nose."

"It's not like they have a lot of fat on their asses. They're all on the scrawny side, so it will be one, two, three, that kind of thing," Espinosa said, weighing in.

"It's still going to stink," Dennis said stubbornly.

"Get over it, kid," Ted said.

"How are we doing over there, guys?" Isabelle called out, just as Fergus finished tying up the last of the dozen captives Jack, Dennis, and Harry had brought from the office. All the captives were buck naked now, trying their best to cover their private parts. "Nothing interesting here," he quipped to Annie's delight.

"The poker is almost ready," Nikki called out.

The bogus Abbot's knees gave out as tears rolled down his cheeks. Alexis grabbed for him and jerked him upright. "Talk, you pissant. What's your part in this caper with Wing Ping?"

"Ticket sales. The money end of the exhibition," he blurted. "That's all I do other than sometimes relaying messages to the men. I swear!"

"It's not an exhibition, you creep. It's a fight to the death, and you know that," Kathryn bellowed as she pushed him closer to the fire. Alexis and Isabelle each had to take one of his arms to hold him in place.

"No! No! Wing Ping just wants to be number one. That's what he said. He said no American should hold the title. Only a Chinese deserves to hold the title."

"You're lying!" Nikki screamed as she took the red-hot poker out of the fire to examine it. "It's not quite ready. We want the brand to go *deep*. To the very bone." The Abbot's knees buckled again. From the far corner of the room, mewling sounds could be heard. No one paid any attention.

"Where is the bastard?" Annie asked quietly.

"I don't know. I have never seen him, never met him. I and all these men here in the monastery deal with a man named Wei Ming. He is the only one who has seen or talked to Wing Ping. I will say he is an evil man. All of us are fearful of him."

"Where is this Wei Ming?"

"I don't know. With Wing Ping, I would think. He is his right-hand man. I heard rumors, we all did, that Wing Ping promised to make him rich if he aligned himself with Wing Ping. They know that you have captured many of their men. But he doesn't care about that. He has many men waiting to replace those who are captured. It's Harry Wong they want."

"Where are the rest of your people? How many are left? Are any outside?" Myra asked. The Abbot shrugged.

"Poker's ready!" Nikki called out cheerfully.

"Let's do it!" Kathryn said, spinning the Abbot around so all Nikki had to do was run the red-hot poker across his buttocks, which she did with a flourish. The scream was primal. The other captives wailed, knowing that they were next.

Cooper barked his approval.

"American men don't whimper and whine. They take their punishment like the men they are. You know where the next one goes, so speak up now or forever hold your peace," Kathryn blasted the Abbot.

Tears streaming down his face, the Abbot's eyes were full of hate as he glared at both Nikki and Kathryn. "When I want a meeting to discuss an order from Wing Ping, I call the one named Chen Fang. He brings everyone to the office and we . . . we talk."

"Call him right now and tell him to round everyone up and bring them here. In Chinese, please. No whimpering, no wailing. One word out of place and this poker goes straight up your ass and out your throat. Do you understand me?" Nikki said. She looked over at Harry and Dishbang Deshi and told them to listen carefully to what the bogus Abbot was saying. Both men nodded.

Yoko walked over to a side table, where all the cell phones waited. She picked up one, looked at it, then handed it to the Abbot. But not before Jack inspected it and gave a nod of approval.

"Do it!" Nikki ordered. "Try to sound like the voice of authority. If you screw up, it's all over." She handed the phone over. In the end, Kathryn had to hold it because the man's hands were shaking too badly. His eyes were on the smoldering, red-hot poker Nikki held in her hand, but his voice was clear and firm when he told Chen Fang to bring everyone to the dining hall. Kathryn tossed the phone to Yoko, who placed it back on the table.

"What should we do with him?" Isabelle asked.

"Sit him down over there with his friends," Myra said.

"*Sit?*"

"Uh-huh."

"Hey, you, Mr. Abbot! Get your skinny butt over here and sit down by your friends," Isabelle shrieked as she struggled to keep a straight face.

"That looks . . . painful," Dennis said as he stared at the Abbot's backside.

"It does, doesn't it?" Jack said, tongue in cheek.

Chapter 20

The call made, the great dining hall turned silent. From time to time, the group could hear what sounded like stifled sobs coming from the captives. They ignored the sounds.

Cooper got up, stretched, and walked around the big room, finally settling himself in front of the line of bound captives. He lowered his head to rest on his paws but didn't close his eyes. The men started to mutter until Nikki swung the hot poker in a wide arc. Instantly, absolute silence prevailed.

"How are we going to handle this, Charles?" Jack asked. "Do we wait at the door, admit them one by one, what? We don't know how many there are. Harry, ask the Abbot how many he thinks there are."

Before Harry could get his tongue to work, the Abbot spoke, his words spewing forth at lightning speed.

"Possibly thirty. I really do not know. They come and go, trade places, some outdoors, most inside."

"They will probably try to rush us, would be my guess," Fergus said.

"Well, we can't allow that to happen," Annie said. "Do any of them have weapons?"

Again the Abbot spoke. "No weapons. Just the one you confiscated. And I would like to go on record that I personally objected to the firearm. I respect this monastery and the holy men who live here. I speak the truth!" the Abbot wailed.

"And yet you allowed yourself to be used by these men. You impersonated a holy man, you lied, you cheated, and you would have allowed Harry Wong's daughter to be kidnapped. Only the quick thinking of Brother Hung, who managed to get her to safety, prevented you from achieving your goal. You would have allowed that travesty, using a little child! All in the name of money!" Myra shouted.

Tears rolled down the Abbot's cheeks. His voice was strained and full of pain. "Unless you live here, you will never understand the fear a man like Wing Ping can instill in a person. I have old parents, and he threatened them. I have no wife or children of my own, but I do have brothers and sisters who have families. We all know what happened to Jun Yu. I think I speak for all of us in this room. The others who are coming I am not so certain about, because I do not know them."

Charles surprised everyone by saying, "I believe him. I know a thing or two about China, as does Fergus. We also know people like Wing Ping."

"Charles is absolutely right," Fergus said.

No one said they agreed or disagreed with Charles's statement and Fergus's affirmation. To everyone's surprise, Cooper remained silent but alert.

"What does that mean, Jack?" Dennis asked nervously. "I mean about Cooper's not barking."

"I think it means Cooper is in agreement that the Abbot is telling the truth. I'm no seer, Dennis. That's just a guess on my part," Jack said.

"I know, I know. That's what I was thinking. So in an actual showdown, these creeps would really be on our side, right?"

Jack laughed. "Kid, do you *really* think any of them are in a position right now to help anyone, even themselves?"

His voice still jittery, Dennis looked Jack in the eye, and said, "I guess that was pretty stupid coming from me. It's just that I've never been in a situation like this. These guys are *Chinese!*"

Cooper let loose with a yip of sound that startled everyone since they couldn't hear Jack and Dennis's conversation.

"Let it go, kid. As you can see and hear, Cooper agrees it was a stupid question. We need to —" Whatever Jack was about to say was cut short when a hard pounding could be heard at the door.

Charles moved quickly as he motioned for the Brothers Hung and Shen to open the door. He held up his hand, then chopped it down to mean they should open the door. They did, and men rushed in. Jack tried to count them, as did Harry.

"Twenty-eight," Jack said.

"Twenty-nine," Harry said.

"Wrong. Thirty-one," Dennis said.

Cooper barked.

"Thirty-one it is!" Annie said, brandishing the gun that Jack had returned to her. She fired one shot at the ceiling. The shot was so loud in the cavernous dining hall that it sounded like a bomb going off. It had the desired effect. The men froze in position. Their expressions said it all. A grandmother with gray hair shooting a gun! Unheard of in China.

"I am going to make a speech. Harry, will you translate, please. Tell them first of all not to move or I will plug them right between the eyes or . . . between their legs, whichever they prefer. I'm not choosy." Annie waited while Harry made the translation.

When he was finished, Annie said, "Now point out that nice line of captives that we have secured on the far wall." Harry obeyed. The man named Chen Fang stepped forward and started to give Harry some Chinese lip. Annie shot him in the knee. Chen Fang's bellow was a sound none of them had ever heard before. Harry shrugged as Dennis and Ted dragged the screaming, squealing man over to the line of captives. They left him on the floor because, as Ted laconically said, "He isn't going anywhere anytime soon."

"Now what?" Kathryn demanded.

"Herd them over to the line with the others. Explain to them clearly that they can do it quietly or they can cry in pain, it's their choice," Annie said. "What are they muttering about, Harry? Tell them to shut up so you can tell them what I just said."

"They're cursing you in Chinese, Annie," Harry said cheerfully. "I'm telling them what you said, but I'm not sure they want to hear what I'm saying."

Annie let loose with a snorting sound. Cooper barked twice. Annie brought up the gun in her hand, fixed her sights on a man directly in front of her, and sighted the gun, eight inches below his waistline. The man scurried to the line and sat down as though he were a misbehaving schoolboy. And then, to Annie's delight, he folded his hands. She whirled around and pointed the gun again with the same, as she put it, awesome results as all the men who had rushed through the door scurried, even pushing and shoving their partners to get into the line with the others.

"You do such good work, Annie! I'm proud of you!" Myra gurgled.

Everyone clapped their hands. And then the boys rushed to help Fergus and Charles tie and bind all of their newest guests together.

"We're getting a full house here." Nikki laughed.

"We sure are," Yoko said as she winked at a flustered Harry.

Cooper closed his eyes and appeared to go to sleep, but it was all a ruse, since everyone in the room who mattered knew that Cooper never slept.

"Done and done," Fergus said as he took his place at the table with the others.

"What do we do now?" Nikki asked. "Just wait for the weather to clear? Or we could give some thought to having that guy Chen Fang call Wing Ping's right-hand guy, Wei Ming. I think it's a good idea," Nikki added, and the others agreed.

"To say what?" Maggie asked.

Kathryn laughed out loud. "To tell him they're being held prisoner. What else? Or we could have him say the exhibition, the fight, whatever you want to call it, is off. I was kicking something around with the girls earlier, and what if we have Isabelle contact Abner and have him do the social media thing all the way. Say the fight is off. That Harry has no interest in defending his title, either in China or the States, with someone who isn't even listed in the world rankings and whose ability is only a matter of hearsay. That means Wing Ping. We think that should put his jockeys in a knot. He'll be incensed and have his hands full trying to hold back all the bad publicity that announcement should generate. Unless he succeeds in countering, he'll look like a silly fool those in the sports field will laugh at. We think it will work, but we are open to discussion. We don't have anything else to do at the moment, so why not?"

A babble of sound ensued until Charles blew his whistle. "One at a time. We do this the democratic way—we each get a vote. All in favor of getting in touch with Wei Ming, raise your hand." Every hand at the table shot into the air.

"Everyone in favor of having Abner do the social media counterattack."

Again, every hand at the table shot high in the air.

"Let's do it, people! That means you, Isabelle. Get cracking and ask Abner how long it will take before we see some results," Kathryn said, her eyes blazing with something the others had never seen before.

"Well, I guess that takes care of that, now, doesn't it? Chen Fang over there appears to be in a great deal of pain. Do we want him making the call and saying what happened, or do we want one of the others who speaks English to make it?"

They all kicked that idea around for a few minutes, and finally agreed that Chen Fang, in pain, wailing, and cursing, should make the call. Or as Espinosa put it, his English was better than that of the others. "Keep that gun on him, and he's all yours, for whatever that's worth."

"I'm not calling Wei Ming. When this is over, he'll hunt me down and kill me. Call him yourself," Chen shouted bravely.

"Not if we kill you first," Yoko said playfully, wagging her finger under the man's nose. Right now, you are looking at an either/or. With us, you stand a better chance of surviving by making us happy by cooperating. It is your choice, however. We're Americans, and we believe in democracy and freedom of speech."

"Oh, dear, do we have to go through this again," Annie said as she whipped the gun out from behind her back. She lazily walked over, tossing the gun from her right hand to her left. "I'm John Wayne's older sister, Chen Fang. Do you want to make the call or do you want me to . . . ?"

A string of screeching Chinese permeated the room. The group of Americans all looked at Harry. "You don't want to know what he's saying," Harry informed them. "The bottom line is that he's willing to make the call."

"Is there a doctor here in the monastery? Shouldn't someone be taking care of that guy's knee? What if he bleeds out?" Dennis asked.

"We do have a man of medicine here at the monastery. Not a doctor like you have in America or the big cities in China. He deals in herbs, but he also knows how to dress wounds. I'm sure he will know how to remove the bullet in the man's knee. Shall I go to the office, try to restore our system, and call him? If I can activate it, we can use the loudspeaker system to tell him he's needed here in the dining hall. He could be anywhere in this vast monastery, and it could take many hours to locate him."

"Yes, yes, do that, please. We'll hold off calling Wei Ming until the medicine man gets here. I think we can all agree on that," Charles said, as the others nodded their agreement. "In the meantime, girls, write out on paper what you want Chen Fang to say."

"What did you say, Annie?" Myra whispered so as not to distract the others.

"I'm mumbling to myself, Myra. Bert still has not responded to my last two e-mails. That is not like him. I sent Dixson Kelly an e-mail, and he just responded, again, saying he hasn't been able to reach Bert either. He also said he sent off queries to Big Al at the Sands and Todd at the Wynn, and he got no responses.

But, then, he just sent them, so we need to give him some time. I'm worried," she said flatly.

All eyes turned to Kathryn, who stared them all down. "What? Why are you all looking at me like that? I'm not Bert's keeper. I'm not his anything anymore. You all need to accept that and move on, as I have. I can't make him respond to an e-mail or text message.

"Surely, you all know that? Where's the restroom in this place?" she asked in a choked-sounding voice.

"Out the door, down the hall, and make a left. It's the second door on the right," Dennis said.

"I'm not even going to ask how you know that," Jack muttered. This kid never ceased to amaze him and the others as well.

"I saw the door out of the corner of my eye when we went to the office. I'm a reporter, I'm trained to see things and put them together. That's what reporters do." Dennis's voice held just a trace of defiance.

"And Dennis is right," Maggie said. "As a rule, we reporters sometimes see and hear things others would pass on. It's a kind of instinct on our part. With time and practice, we hone it, then we live by it. Dennis is a good pupil. He's very observant."

"Okay, okay! At least we all know where the restroom is, thanks to Dennis here," Jack said, clapping the young multimillionaire reporter on the back.

Cooper barked his approval of the compliment, then sauntered to the door and waited. Harry opened the door and followed the dog out to the main lobby, where he opened the massive doors. Cooper walked out and was back within minutes. He looked up at Harry and waited. "What?"

Cooper turned and pawed the heavy door.

"Right! Right! Lock it!" Harry slid the heavy metal bar across the double doors. Safe! Cooper yipped his approval as he started the trek back to the dining hall.

In front of the great doors, Harry stopped and dropped to his haunches. Cooper placed his paws on his shoulders so that man and dog could eyeball each other. "I wish you could talk, Cooper. I wish I understood really what you are all about. My imagination, I know, doesn't . . . it's like you're not real, that you're human to some extent. How do you know . . . is it dog instinct that's superior to human instinct? I need to know. I want to know. I feel like . . . like you're part of me and Lily, and I don't understand why that is. Help me out here, Cooper."

Cooper nuzzled Harry's neck, then licked at the tip of his nose. He made soft noises in his throat, sounds Harry had never heard him make before. "Okay. Maybe someday I'll figure it all out. Right now all I care about is that you have our backs and that Lily is safe. Do I at least have that right?"

Cooper let loose with two joyous yips.

Inside the dining hall again, Charles asked about the weather. Harry just shrugged. He didn't see any sense in telling Charles or the others that he hadn't noticed if it was raining, sleeting, or snowing because his thoughts were elsewhere. No point at all.

While they waited to see if Brother Hung would be successful in restoring the monastery's electronics and for the medicine man to be found, the group talked in low tones as they worked on a script for Chen Fang to use when he called Wei Ming.

Kathryn returned to the table and stared off into space, while Isabelle sent one text after another to her husband, Abner. From time to time she smiled, and once she actually giggled. Annie, looking like Mother Doom and Gloom, kept her fingers on the speed dial as she tried to locate Bert Navarro.

"Something's wrong," Annie whispered to Myra.

"Yes, I know. I feel what you're feeling because I am feeling the same thing. I know Bert can take care of himself. He came up through the ranks of the FBI and was director for a time. But that was back in the States, where we play by the rules. This is China, and things are different here. Not to mention Bert has some emotional baggage he's toting around. Just keep trying to reach him, and anyone else you can think of who might know something about where he is and what he's doing. Unless you have a better idea," Myra said softly, her eyes as worried as Annie's.

"Therein lies the problem, Myra. I don't have any other ideas. I don't know what else to do. Like you said, this is China. Even though we were assured that these special phones can't be hacked, I'm not so sure. For all we know, we've been monitored, spied on, and God knows what else since we've been here. I'm really worried, Myra."

"I know, dear. I am, too. But let's not let on to the others. They have enough going on right now without worrying about Bert."

Annie nodded, her eyes going to Kathryn, who was staring into the flames as though mesmerized. She wondered what the young woman was thinking right this minute. Then she corrected herself. Right now, she didn't want to know what Kathryn was thinking.

Time wore on, hour after hour, until the dining hall doors finally opened and Brother Hung ushered in a little round man with owlish glasses, who looked around as though he had been dropped onto some alien planet in another galaxy. He carried a canvas medical bag in one of his hands.

The group watched as the little medicine man examined Chen Fang's kneecap, clucking his tongue in distress as he did so. He rummaged in his bag and came up with a thick green leaf and shoved it between Chen Fang's clenched teeth. "Chew and swallow." Hung translated the medicine man's instructions. Within minutes, Chen Fang was out like the proverbial light, allowing the medicine man to poke and prod at his knee. In the quiet room, the bullet made a sharp sound when he dropped it on the floor.

"Whatever that leaf is, I want a bushelful," Ted said with a straight face.

And on and on it went for another hour. They were just settling down with fresh tea when the medicine man pronounced Chen Fang alive but in a world of pain. He left a handful of leaves in a little canvas sack for Brother Shen and said that the minute Chen Fang opened his eyes, Brother Shen was to shove a leaf in his mouth until a medical doctor could tend to the man. He gave his assurances that Chen Fang would not die and left the room as fast as his fat little body could take him.

"I'm relieved," Dennis said.

The others ignored his comment and concentrated on Isabelle and the exuberance she was showing. She held up her phone and whipped it around. "Okay, people, tell me my husband is the smartest man in the universe! Take a look and see what he's done in a little over an hour."

"What? What?" they all chorused as one.

"He turned the whole fight, exhibition, whatever they're calling it, upside down. He

canceled it and said the promoters would re-
fund all the ticket sales. There's a war going on
stateside, and it's going to reach this side of
the world very quickly. Give it another thirty
minutes, and Macau will have an uprising, and
Wing Ping will have round eyes."

Annie looked at Myra, who met her gaze
with unblinking intensity. Their thought was
the same—Bert.

Chapter 21

"How's Chen Fang going to call that snake if he's out cold?" Ted asked.

"Obviously, he isn't going to until he wakes up," Charles said.

"So what should we do in the meantime?" Myra asked.

Tongue in cheek, Charles said, "What you do best, my dearest one—scheme and plot."

"That wasn't the least bit funny, Charles," Myra sniffed.

"You're right, it wasn't funny at all. I was just making conversation. It's getting late, we're all stressed, and until there is something concrete we can do, I suggest we take turns trying to catch a little sleep. I'm sure the brothers can fetch us some bedding. We men will take the first watch, and you girls sleep. Four-hour shifts, if that meets with everyone's approval."

The women all started talking at once, with comments ranging from I'm not that tired, to How do you expect us to sleep under these circumstances? to I'm too wired up to sleep. Charles wagged his finger in the air to indicate he meant business as the Brothers scurried off to fetch the required bedding.

Annie was pacing the huge room, her fingers tapping out text after text. The incoming texts caused her to pick up her feet and move faster. She was scowling and muttering as she made her way around the room in circles.

Isabelle was doing the same thing Annie was doing, but instead of scowling, she was laughing and giggling at what she was seeing on her special phone. Finally, she clicked off and turned to the girls. "Oh, you are going to love, love, love what I'm going to show you. We really need to give Abner some kind of prize for what he's done. I'm telling you, you are going to . . . to . . . just . . . Especially you, Harry."

"It would help, dear, if you told us what Abner sent you that we all need to see," Myra said quietly.

"I know, I know, it's just . . . I'm just flabbergasted at what he's done. I mean I know he's good—excellent, actually. No, that's wrong, he's the best hacker in the good old US of A. Maybe the world," Isabelle cried out jubilantly. "And he did it all in a little over two hours.

TWO HOURS, people." She waved the special phone in the air to make her point.

"It's only going to take me two seconds to lay your ass out on this tile floor if you don't shut up and tell us what's on that damn phone." Kathryn screeched so loud that the captives sat up straight to see what was going on. Chen Fang still slept peacefully, as did Cooper the mystic dog, who didn't react to Kathryn's outburst in any way whatsoever.

Isabelle backed off, her jaw dropping at Kathryn's eruption. "Jeez, Kathryn, get a grip, will you? A few minutes of drama and excitement aren't going to change things right now. Besides, I'm proud of what my husband did, as we should all be, because half a world away he is saving the day. Do me a favor—in fact, do us all a favor—and just shut the hell up for a while. None of us needs your surly attitude right now."

Kathryn let loose with an unladylike snort as she crossed her arms over her chest and turned her gaze to the dancing flames in the monster fireplace. Her mouth was a thin, tight line of anger. She did remain quiet as she looked around at the startled expressions on the faces of her colleagues.

"Okay, okay, everyone gather round. First things first, though. As I told you before, Abner did the Facebook, the tweet, the Instagram, the everything, then he did YouTube. I don't know how he did it, but the YouTube ditty is a cartoon of Wing Ping dressed in his trademark *American* cowboy hat and *American* cowboy boots, but in the cartoon he's a scrawny chicken or maybe a rooster, can't be sure. But it's hilarious. Abner said that so many likes came into Facebook it shut down, and he was receiving something like six hundred tweets a minute. Vegas is going nuts. The YouTube video is being shown at all the casinos. He's waiting right now for this part of the world to weigh in. Okay, here's the video." Everyone but Kathryn crowded around Isabelle to look at the small screen.

Belly laughs and hysterical eye-wiping filled the big dining hall, with Harry laughing the loudest.

"Well, if anyone wants my opinion, I think this just cinched the deal that there will be no exhibition," Annie said. "Harry, you look great as an avenging chicken."

"Oh, honey, Abner got it all just right," a giggling Yoko said to her husband.

"So how is Wing Ping going to counterattack against all of that?" Nikki asked. "Looks to me like he has really lost face and has become a laughingstock. The punch line to a bad joke. Especially in America. What happens when all of that makes it here to China, assuming it hasn't already? Especially in Macau, where they were going to mainstream the event." She was careful to look everywhere but at Kathryn, who had zoned out in front of the dancing flames.

"Chen Fang is awake," Fergus called. "If you want him to make his call, this is the time. I'll prop him up so he can speak normally. Where's the script?"

"Right here," Myra said, handing it over. "I'm thinking it might be a good idea to do a dry run to make sure he's comfortable with all the words. In Chinese, right? Harry and Dishbang Deshi can listen to make sure he isn't going to try to sneak clues or something into the conversation."

"Excellent idea, old girl," Charles said happily. "Go at it, Harry!"

Glassy-eyed and disoriented, Chen Fang stared at the people gathered around him. Out of it or not, he understood the gravity of the situation he was in. All the proof he needed was seeing Annie holding the gun and pointing it at his nether regions. He nodded slightly to show that he understood what was expected of him.

"Wait! Wait! Maybe we should show him the chicken video so he can see he's on the wrong end of things. With these people, you never know," Jack said.

"Excellent idea, Jack." Nikki beamed.

Isabelle raced around the table, turned on the special phone, and dropped to her knees so she was eye level with the glassy-eyed Chen Fang. "Watch and weep, you little weasel," she said, and laughed as she pressed the button for the video to start. Chen Fang's expression went from anger to horror to disbelief and back to horror as he struggled to find the words he wanted to spew. When he finally got his tongue to work, his bottom line was that they were all doomed and they would all be going to meet their ancestors the minute Wing Ping made his way to the monastery. After which he kept muttering the word *chicken* over and over until Espinosa clipped him on the side of his head. He shut up immediately.

Harry and Dishbang Deshi had Chen Fang go through three tries at the script. They were finally satisfied the third time around. Fergus held up one of the thick green leaves that acted as a narcotic and waved it around. "Tell him he doesn't get this until he delivers a perfect speech. Stress that there is to be no improvising on his part."

"It's a go on the count of three." Harry held up first one finger, then the second, and finally the third, and Maggie pressed the button for the call to go through. They all listened but couldn't understand a word that was being said, so they concentrated on Harry's and Dishbang Deshi's expressions, which clearly showed that Chen Fang was following orders.

Fergus slipped the thick green leaf between Chen Fang's lips, and he gobbled it like a starving man. In a matter of minutes, Chen Fang was in another world.

"We assume Chen Fang did his part. What did that guy Wei Ming say?" Charles demanded.

"Threats. Chen Fang will be dead when Wei Ming gets his hands around his neck, and so will all the others for failing Wing Ping. He, along with Wing Ping, is on the way up here now that the weather has cleared. Two hours, possibly three. He's bringing *armed* men with him. Wei Ming said the reason for the arms is now that we've used social media to bring disgrace to his master, meaning Wing Ping, there are no rules. He's going to kill Harry one way or another. The last thing he said was you, Harry, are hiding behind a bunch of women's skirts. He said that shows what a coward you really are."

Cooper reared up, barked three times to indicate that statement was entirely untrue. Harry threw his arms in the air. "What can I say?"

"Nothing, sweetie," Yoko cooed. "I don't want you to worry, we'll protect you, won't we, girls?" It was meant as a joke to lighten the moment, but all Harry did was scowl.

"With our lives," Annie said, brandishing the gun in her hands.

"We have a few hours to barricade all the entrances to the monastery and to make sure the students are kept safe. We only want the front entrance to go live. We can control things that way," Charles said. "It is possible, is it not, Brother Hung?"

"Yes, yes, you men come with me. You three

also," he said, pointing to the three male students, who were watching what was going on with disbelief. "The only weapons, if you want to call them weapons, are the bamboo poles we use when fencing. Against firearms, they will not be much of a deterrent, but it is the best we can do. As I said before, we are a peaceful, holy people. And you do not know how many men Wing Ping is bringing with him."

"All true, all true," Charles said. "Go quickly to secure the monastery and the students. We'll stay here and map out a plan of action. Please, be quick about it."

"Oh, man, this is excitement with a capital E," Dennis babbled as he raced alongside Jack. "Hey, how come Cooper isn't with us?"

Jack looked around. The kid was right, Cooper was nowhere in sight. "Guess he felt like we could handle it on our own. Smart dog."

They were back in the dining hall in a little over an hour, secure in the knowledge that the monastery was as safe as they could make it.

Inside the dining hall, everyone seemed to have a task of some sort, as human bodies moved and raced around. "How about an update?" Espinosa asked.

"Aside from your lean, mean, muscular bodies that are weapons themselves, we have four fire tongs currently roasting in the flames. The dozen bamboo poles you brought with you have to be whittled so that one end is a spear. We have one gun, which Annie is in charge of. We are boiling pots of water on every burner on the stove. That's it as far as our arsenal of weapons go," Charles said, a wicked gleam in his eyes. "I do not think there will be many firearms. This is the worst country in the world to pick one up. At a minimum, I say three. I can't even guess at this point how many men Wing Ping will bring with him. Take into consideration the short notice, possibly ten to thirty, possibly more depending on what Wing Ping promised them. Get the knives, people, and start your whittling."

Brother Shen raised his hand to speak. Charles nodded.

"Many of our brothers are expert archers. We have many bows and arrows in the arena. Should we fetch them?"

"Now you tell us! Why didn't you mention that when we were racing around the monastery?" Jack snarled.

"Because I just thought of it," Brother Shen said smartly. "Hung and I will fetch them. As well as the archers themselves. Unless you think they will not be useful."

"Go!" Jack thundered.

Nikki moved the pokers sitting in the hot embers. "Who has the eye?" she called over her back.

"I do," Myra responded, her eyes dropping to the watch on her wrist with the oversize numerals. "We're at two hours and seventeen minutes. We still have some time on *our* clocks.

How should we best use that time?" No one responded to her query. She looked over at Annie, who looked mad enough to chew iron and spit rust. Her eyebrows asked the question.

Annie shrugged. "I'm not getting anywhere. Isabelle, what is Abner saying about what's going down in Macau?"

"A little action. The local police tried to shut down the streaming-chicken video, but it had already aired thousands of times. People are stampeding to get their money back from the ticket sales. Unfortunately, the promoters cannot be located. No one has seen Wing Ping. He's had no luck contacting Dixson Kelly, so he hacked into his e-mail. Dix is not responding to texts or phone calls. Neither is Bert. Right now, he's hacking the Wynn and the Sands. He just signed off." Isabelle chewed on her lower lip as she tried to make sense out of what her husband had just communicated to her by way of text and what it meant to all of them.

From that point on, the only sound to be heard in the huge dining hall was the sound of knives striking the bamboo kung fu spears until the huge doors opened to admit Shen, Hung, and five fit-looking younger brothers, each of them carrying a bow, and a leather sack, filled to the brim with arrows, attached to their backs.

"Our fittest warriors," Shen said proudly as he introduced the younger brothers.

Charles looked over at Fergus and said under his breath, "This is as good as it's going to get." He looked over at his wife, whose eyes were glued to her watch as she counted down the minutes. He hated the worry he was seeing on her face. Then he looked at Annie, who winked at him.

Suddenly, he felt better, relieved for some reason. Maybe things really would work out in their favor. And if they didn't, it wouldn't be for lack of trying. All things considered, being in a foreign land where there were no rules, they were doing okay.

For the moment, anyway.

Chapter 22

Time dragged on, the occupants in the great dining hall champing at the bit for something, anything, to happen to relieve the tense atmosphere.

Annie huddled with Myra, her fingers incessantly tapping the keys on her phone with no results. They conversed in low whispers as to why that was and what was going on in Macau. Nikki doodled on a pad in front of her, the same pad they'd used to craft the script for Chen Fang's phone call to Wei Ming. Alexis and Isabelle talked about Myra's upcoming New Year's Eve party, noodling about whether or not it would come off and about what kind of sparkly outfits they would wear to the gala. Maggie and Ted, along with Espinosa, looked at the pictures Espinosa had taken, trying to

decide which ones would be best for the article
they planned to write for the *Post* when they
got back to Washington. Jack and Dennis talked
football, specifically whether or not this was
the year the Redskins' owner, Dan Snyder, would
be forced to change the team's name, while
Fergus and Charles kept their eyes on the restless captives. Yoko and Harry whispered to each
other about their daughter, wondering how
she would adapt to being back in the States
and what to buy her for Christmas this year.
They speculated about the change in her and
how this adventure would play out in her life.

Cooper watched it all, his great head resting
on his paws under the table. He appeared un-
concerned, as did Kathryn, who was transfixed
with the dancing flames in front of her.

"Incoming text from Abner!" Isabelle shouted.
"Oh, wow! Wait till you guys see this! Once
again, my husband gets the prize! I'll give you
the short version. The American embassy is talking to the Chinese embassy about the American tour group, Crescent China Tours, being
held hostage in a Chinese monastery by a Chinese national by the name of Wing Ping. It
goes on to say that this Wing Ping character
concocted this whole kung fu charade to get
even with Harry Wong, the former number
two martial-arts expert in the world who rose
up to the number one spot with the murder of
Jun Yu, who had held the title of number one
for many, many years. It goes on to say that

Wing Ping was kicked out of the Shaolin Monastery for reasons not being disclosed. Abner isn't saying if the article, and he did not send the entire text, outright accused Wing Ping of murder, but it sounds like that to me."

"Holy crap!" Dennis yelped.

"Beats anything I could come up with," Jack muttered.

"Anything else?" Charles asked.

"Another text is coming in. Hold on," Isabelle said as her eyes raked the text in front of her. "Okay, it says the local police here are searching for Wing Ping. Macau is going crazy. Money crazy, that is. No other explanation. Oh, oh, wait a minute, the promoters can't be found, just as they can't be found in the States. That's the end of it. Abner said more to come as things develop, and, before you can ask, yes, he went to the AP wire services with the story. He used your name, Annie; otherwise, he said no one would carry the story."

"You're right, the boy gets a prize," Annie said.

The dining hall reverted to silent mode for another twenty minutes. The room as a whole tensed when Cooper barked and raced to the huge double doors. He threw back his head and howled an ungodly sound before he moved to the side of the great doors.

"I could be wrong, guys, but I think it's showtime!" Jack said, just loud enough for everyone to hear.

"That's gunfire!" Charles said. "*Automatic* gunfire! They're strafing the entrance doors. Stay away from the doors, people!" he shouted. "We rehearsed this ad nauseam, so you all know what to do."

It could have been a choreographed exercise as the five archers lined up, bows and arrows at the ready, while the bamboo poles were raised simultaneously, those holding them in a shooter's stance.

Kathryn was off her chair in a nanosecond as she raced to where Nikki was guarding the red-hot fire tongs. "About time you came back to the present."

Kathryn grinned. "You can kick my butt later, Nikki. I told you I wouldn't let you down."

"I knew that, Kathryn," Nikki said quietly. "No matter what, you are one of us, and we all know. We also understand. Who has the eye?" she shouted.

"I do, and I'm keeping it!" Yoko bellowed.

Annie finally gave up and shoved the cell phone she'd been working for hours into one of her many pockets. "You a betting woman, Myra?" she hissed.

"You know I am. I did more or less like Yoko's scenario, or Plan C, as she called it." Annie laughed. "I hope we don't have to resort to that, but on the other hand, it should certainly prove interesting if we're forced to put the plan into operation." In spite of herself, Myra laughed out loud. The others looked around to see the cause of Myra's laughter and instantly realized why. In turn, wide grins split across their faces. Not so the boys, who simply looked pained and angry.

Jack had his eyes on Cooper, so he missed it all. He moved closer to the big dog, Dennis right behind him. He was close enough to stroke his head. "This might be a good time for you to . . . you know . . . let me know how this is going to work out. Like four, not three, that kind of thing," he muttered. He could feel his thoughts whirling and twirling until he settled into one thought. *Nine men with the first rush, one automatic weapon, two handguns, clubs, Harry's adversary and five men bringing up the rear.*

Doable.

He roared his thought to the tense room. Harry simply nodded as gunfire shattered the beautiful carved doors to the great dining hall. The moment they sagged and hung drunkenly on the massive hinges, the stampede began, and all hell broke loose. Bamboo spears shot forward as arrows sailed through the air. Bodies leaped and spun in midair, howls of pain from the interlopers who had come into contact with the red-hot fire tongs filled the great hall.

Last man standing—a wild-eyed, snarling Wing Ping. And that was by design. The sisters and the boys dragged the intruders to where the other captives were being held. Fergus and Charles worked frantically to bind them to the

others, not caring about their wounds or the
words spewing from their mouths.

This, then, was going to be the showdown
between Harry Wong and Wing Ping.

Jack, Ted, Espinosa, and Dennis quickly
used all their muscles to shove the long, heavy
table and benches out of the way to clear the
space for whatever was going to go down.

Harry yanked the belt from around his waist
and kicked off his shoes. Wing Ping moved
closer to the center space that had been cleared.
Harry held up his hand. "Isabelle, show Mr.
Wing the video and the article Abner sent you."
Isabelle scurried to the middle of the room
and held up her phone so that Wing Ping
could see what they had all seen earlier.

"It's over, Wing. They're coming for you. If
you're smart, you'll get out of here right now."

Wing Ping pushed his American cowboy hat
farther back on his head, all the better to see
Harry. Then he looked down at his cowboy
boots. He looked up and showed his dentally
challenged grimace in a vicious snarl. His eyes
spewed hatred as he lashed out at Isabelle, who
deftly danced out of his way.

"So that's the way it's going to be, eh? Okay,
cowboy, let's see what you got!"

And the game was on. The watchers were
breathless as they saw both men duck, parry,
strike, and give each other as good as they had
in them.

Jack mentally had himself in Harry's position, knowing exactly what his next move was going to be. Harry went for the Ridgehand Strike and hit Wing Ping squarely on the head, knocking the weird-looking cowboy hat to the floor. Dennis quickly kicked it out of the way as Harry followed up with a Reverse Punch and clipped Wing Ping with the palm of his hand right below his chin. Wing Ping went down but was up in an instant. Harry went with a Front Thrust Kick but was taken down with Wing Ping's Side Snap Kick.

"Get up, Harry! Don't make me help you out, you wuss," Jack bellowed. Harry staggered to his feet and let loose with a Roundhouse Kick that sent Wing Ping sailing across the room. Wing Ping scrambled to his feet and literally skidded across the room, his side punch missing Harry by a hair. Harry whirled about, then was in the air, his legs spread wide to clinch Wing Ping between his knees. Both men landed with a loud thump on the cold tile floor, but Harry's hold on Wing Ping's neck never faltered. Wing Ping gagged and struggled to breathe. He managed somehow to bring one hand up in a feeble gesture to tap Harry on the arm, the sign that he surrendered. Harry nodded but didn't release immediately.

Cooper barked. Jack yelled to release. Yoko screamed at Harry, telling him not to kill his opponent. Finally, Harry released his hold on Wing Ping and rocked back on his heels. "Killing you is too good. Let someone else do

it. Here's the thing, Wing Ping. I gave you the
chance to ride off into the sunset the way
American cowboys do, but you opted for this.
Somebody tie up this piece of trash!" he bellowed.

"Wait! Wait!" Harry said. "Somebody record
this, please." Ted held up his phone and nodded.

"You killed Jun Yu, didn't you? Say it, you
bastard, I want to hear the words. Nikki, show
him the poker!" Wing Ping tried to shrivel into
himself as the poker was lowered to the soft
spot between his legs.

"I didn't! I didn't! Wei Ming killed him. It
wasn't me," Wing Ping screamed.

From the other side of the room, the in-
vader who must have been Wei Ming bellowed
at the top of his lungs, "You ordered me to do
it. I just followed your orders. I believed you,
you rat-faced weasel. You said this was a piece
of cake, a walk in the park, all those American
terms you love so much, along with that stupid
hat and boots. You hated Jun Yu, tell them. You
wanted me to kill his wife and children, too.
You tried to kidnap Harry Wong's daughter."

"Tell me that what Wei Ming said is true,
Wing Ping, or you get the poker. Someone pull
his pants down." Kathryn gladly obliged. "One
more chance or you're branded for life."

Nikki's hand, holding the red-hot poker,
slowly descended, at which point Wing Ping
screamed, "It's true. You're no warrior, Wong

Guotin. If you were, you would have defended your honor and killed me. You're a coward," he spat.

All Harry could do was shake his head in disgust.

Yoko was having none of it. "If my husband is a coward, why is he standing while you're on the floor staring up at him?" In a voice none of them had ever heard from Yoko before, she looked at Nikki and Kathryn, and said, "Give him something to remember us by."

Neither Nikki nor Kathryn had to be told twice. Both red-hot pokers came down at the same time. The smell of burning flesh filled the room before they danced away, wicked grins on their faces. Yoko gave a thumbs-up, to her husband's chagrin. Then he relaxed and whispered in his wife's ear. She smiled from ear to ear.

Harry looked down at Cooper. "Okay, it's done. I want my daughter!"

Brother Hung stepped forward. "She is on her way. She should be here by first light. She is well and looking forward to seeing all of you. Especially this magnificent animal named Cooper."

Cooper lowered his head in a low bow, it seemed to everyone. "You're a big ham, Cooper!" Jack said. The thought ricocheted around his brain in a second—*It takes one to know one.* Cooper barked and barked as he strutted around the great dining hall, enjoying the praise everyone heaped on his furry shoulders before he found a spot under the table. This time he closed his eyes and truly went to sleep.

"What's our next move?" Maggie demanded.

"Helping us fix our doors," Brother Hung responded smartly.

"I have a better idea," Annie said just as smartly. "Since all of us here are constructurally challenged, how will it be if we leave enough money with you so that professional carpenters can repair these aged, beautiful doors." Brother Hung was most gracious in his acceptance.

"We need to get to Macau as soon as possible," Annie said.

"We leave the moment my daughter walks through what's left of these doors," Harry said. "We can help you shore up the doors in the meantime." Once again, Brother Hung gracefully accepted Harry's offer of help.

"I guess it's up to us women to restore this kitchen to what it was before we arrived," Alexis said. "Not that our place is in the kitchen, it's just that we do it better. Everyone agree?"

"Damn straight," Myra said.

"First, before we do anything, I want a cup of coffee. I cannot drink that shitty tea one more time. I know there is coffee here somewhere, we just have to find it. Search, people!" Annie ordered.

They finally found a can of American Max-
well House coffee behind a stack of wooden
bowls in the large pantry. Annie smacked her
lips as her taste buds went to work. "And the
cream they have here is *real.*"

It was all so real, they drank pot after pot
until dawn started to break, at which point
Cooper stirred and raced to the wide center
hall.

"Harry, I think your daughter is about to arrive. Cooper went out to greet her," Annie said
gently. She swore later that never in her whole
life had she seen anything more beautiful than
Harry's and Yoko's smiles.

The young girl named Yuke Lok walked
into the kitchen, holding Lily's hand, Cooper
at her side. They were in agony as they waited
for the ritual that ensued, the graceful bows,
the Chinese greetings, more bows, then Lily
let loose with a whoop of joy, and screamed,
"Mommieeee, Daddyeeeee!"

There wasn't a dry eye in the room. And
then Lily was on Harry's shoulders as he waltzed
her around the room as she laughed and
laughed. Cooper barked his pleasure when Lily
was once more on the ground. She followed
him over to the big table and crawled under it.
She hugged the big dog and whispered to him
as the others watched, somehow knowing that
the dog was whispering right back.

Lily crawled back out from under the table

and ran over to her father to stick her hands in each of his pockets until she found what she wanted. A wide smile on her face, she carried the two treasures she was holding over to Yuke Lok. "My daddy says you always have to keep a promise. He's right. He brought them all the way from America for you." She held out the butterfly pin and the cherry red lipstick.

Yuke Lok stared down at her little sister's offering. "But how . . . you had no way of telling your father . . ." Cooper barked, and Lily laughed out loud. "It's magic," she whispered to Yuke Lok."

"That was so sweet," Nikki said to Kathryn. "Did you see that?"

"I did, and you're right. Time to go, everyone!" Kathryn shouted.

"Good-bye, China!" the group shouted as they all gathered up their belongings to head to the shored-up entrance. Outside, the same bus that had brought them to the monastery waited for them, this time carrying one more passenger, Lily Wong.

The good-byes were brief but heartfelt. Brother Hung gasped at the amount of American currency Annie stuffed into the pockets of his yellow robe, but he simply bowed. And then he did a very American thing—he hugged her and Myra as well.

And, finally, they were ready to board the bus and head down the mountain to the airport that would take them to Macau.

"Well done, people!" Charles said "We can now return to the States via Macau, knowing that once again we persevered and prevailed."

"Hear! Hear!" they all shouted as the big bus raced down the hill on the first leg of their journey back to the States.

Epilogue

Though the sky was clear, the air was frigid, and the wind was shrieking and howling as the group boarded the bus that would take them to the bottom of the mountain, where they would start the first leg of their journey back to the States.

The members of the group partnered up and took their seats, mindful of Brother Hung's words that the bus was a bit ancient, without heat or seat belts. They didn't care; all they wanted to do was leave the monastery as fast as possible.

For the most part, the group was quiet. Charles and Fergus, at the front of the bus, conversed in low tones, anxious, fretful tones that turned to anger. "This is the first time Avery has failed me. I'm starting to think the Chinese pulled him in. Otherwise, some way, somehow, he would have found a way to get in touch. I'm not sure the monks are capable of . . ."

"Go ahead, mate, say it. Disposing of Wing Ping and his minions. I agree with you. I also find it hard to believe that he couldn't outwit these cartoon characters who pose as police."

Charles fiddled with his mobile, then blinked when a text appeared from Brother Shen. It was short and curt. ***Your people are here.*** Charles showed it to Fergus. He leaned toward the aisle from his seat, his fist shooting in the air. "Mr. Snowden arrived. We know nothing more at this point." The collective sigh of relief wafted all the way to the front of the bus.

Charles leaned back and closed his eyes. He felt light-headed, almost giddy with relief that Snowden, for whatever reason, had not failed him.

"This isn't the way we went up the mountain," Fergus said suddenly. "This is a different road."

"One of the monks said in passing that you go up one way and go down another way. I don't know why that is. We were all on an adrenaline high when we traveled up, but I do recall thinking it was rather steep. Perhaps it iced over.

"And we never did figure out how Wing Ping made it up to the monastery. At some point we'll figure it out, and it will turn out to be so simple, we'll feel silly for not realizing whatever the explanation is. Does that make sense, Fergus?"

"This might be a good time to tell me what is *really* bugging you, mate. We did what we came here to do, and now we're on our way home. What could be better?"

"We aren't home yet, Fergus. There is that little business of Bert in Macau. Annie still hasn't heard a thing. *That* has me very concerned." All Fergus could do was nod in agreement.

In the back of the bus, Dennis fidgeted in his seat next to Jack. "Okay, okay, what is it, kid? We pulled it off, we're on our way home, so what's bothering you?"

"That snake, that Wing Ping. He wanted to fight Harry to the death. That's bothering me. It should bother you, too, Jack."

"It didn't happen. We're good here, Dennis. You should know Harry would never, ever kill anyone. Now, that's not to say he wouldn't hurt someone bad enough that they wished they were dead, but to actually kill someone, no!"

"What's going to happen to him? Wing Ping, I mean. This is . . . China, not the United States, where that guy Snowden has superpowers, or at least it seems like that. Like I said, this is China."

"You know better than to ask that, kid. We do not ask. That's our number one rule. Whatever happens to him will be well deserved. He had Harry's friend killed. Jun Yu's wife and children are now in a strange land without a father and husband. He has to pay for that. Somehow, some way. And if you did know, how would that help you?"

"I don't suppose it would. It's the reporter in me. I want to know the why, the how, and the outcome. I'm nervous right now, so I might say whatever pops into my head."

"You need to get over that real quick, kid. It is what it is. Whatever happens to him, he deserves it. The first rule is that we never, ever, *ever* ask that question. Relax and stop fidgeting. That's an order."

Dennis chomped down on his lower lip but did as he was told.

Jack leaned back and followed his own advice and closed his eyes. He longed for warmth and to be high above the earth in American airspace. It couldn't happen soon enough for him.

Twenty minutes later, the old bus came to a halt outside the same building from which they'd started their journey. Even in the bus, they could hear the babble of voices coming from a group of people in uniform.

"I was afraid of this," Charles said. "I was expecting a police presence but not of this magnitude. We'll let Harry and Dishbang Deshi take care of this." He turned to alert Harry, but Harry and Dishbang Deshi were almost to the front of the bus.

"Let us do the talking," Harry said, as the driver, one of the monks on this trip, nervously opened the door.

"Of course I am, mate. We have papers, credentials, the best money can buy," Fergus whispered. He looked over at Annie, who simply nodded. The nod meant her plane had left Hong Kong and was en route to Macau. "We need to get out of this country as fast as possible. But first we have to make it to Macau."

"Tell me something I do not already know, Fergus. Even you should realize we are not going to be cleared to leave this area until those . . . those . . . crackpots say we can. Right now, we have to leave it up to Harry and Dishbang Deshi to get us out of this."

At that moment, a fat little man of middle age, wearing drab olive green with a matching cap, stepped forward, his hand outstretched. Harry nodded and handed over his legitimate passport and visa. Dishbang Deshi did the same thing. A fast and furious dialogue followed, along with several bows and a lot of arm waving. There were no smiles, no nods of understanding. Finally, Harry stepped forward and was literally eyeball to eyeball with the fat little man. He did some hand pointing and held up his hand as he ticked off his fingers.

"I think he's trying to find out about Avery, and the fat guy is saying he doesn't know anything about such a person. I'm thinking that's a good thing."

Charles looked down at his mobile and the incoming text. He wanted to shout with joy, but he didn't. "It's from Avery. He has the situation in hand. He said there are Chinese police on his trail, but the monks will take over. The police were unable to get up the mountain because of the ice. So we're good on that score. Pass the word, but do it quietly."

The group shuffled their feet as the dialogue between Harry and the fat little official continued. And then a strange thing happened. The fat little man motioned for Harry to stand next to him, so he could have his picture taken. All the uniformed men clapped their hands and wanted their pictures taken with Harry, who gladly obliged.

And then they were free to board the tram that would take them to the airport for the short flight that would land at Macau International Airport, where they hoped they would find the answers to the mystery surrounding Bert Navarro.

Ninety minutes later, the plane landed in Macau, with the passengers offering up high-fives to each other. They used up another twenty minutes securing a van that could accommodate all of them. Their destination, the Sands Hotel and Casino, where Bert had last been seen.

Isabelle looked down at the mobile clutched in her hand. "I know where he is! Abner found him! I'm talking about Bert! Oh my God! Oh my God! Listen to this. Bert beat the house at the Sands. He was on his way to the Wynn with his winnings, so Todd, who manages the Wynn, could pay off all the ticket sales for the fight that never came off and for which the Wynn was on the hook. I don't mean Bert was carrying money, but he had something from the Sands that the Wynn would accept. He was waylaid on the way and left out in the street. Easily recognized as an American, he was taken to the hospital, but whoever beat him up took all his identification. Abner says he has a dislocated shoulder, broken ribs, his face looks like pulp, and they think some damage was done to his kidneys. He's in bad shape but will recover. They have him listed as a Chinese-American named Lu Fu. He's in a private hospital called Hospital Kiang Wu. The good thing is, he was not taken to the one public hospital, and Abner says that none of the hospitals in Macau are internationally accredited. But he's alive, and that's what matters."

A cheer went up from the group. No eyes turned to see what if any reaction there was from Kathryn Lucas.

"First, we go to both casinos. Then we can decide what we should do about the hospital," Annie said, taking charge. The others agreed as they clamored into the van that would take them to the Wynn Casino, where they could get the real lowdown on Bert Navarro.

"I say we get something to eat before we do anything," Ted said. "Let's take a vote!"

One look from Annie was all it took for Ted and the others to realize they could wait until she gave the okay to chow down. "Business first" was how she put it.

The Wynn Casino and Hotel was no different from any casino and hotel back in the States. The bells and whistles were the same. The customers, mostly Asian, chattered and squealed just like the gamblers back in the States. The carpets looked the same, the blinding white lights the same, the security prowling the aisles the same.

Annie looked around, then turned to the group, and said, "Since we're a contingent of Americans, I'm thinking all we need to do at the moment is to stand still, and the head of security will find us. Oh, I think he's headed our way as I speak. At least he fits Bert's description of his pal Todd.

Annie stepped forward, her hand outstretched. Todd was a big man with a brush cut, steely gray eyes, and a salt-and-pepper mustache. At a quick glance, one would put his weight at around 190 when in truth he weighed 230 pounds. He was as light on his feet as a dancer. The smile he offered up never reached his eyes because his eyes were everywhere in

the room. He was doing the meet-and-greet,
but at the same time he was taking care of business. Annie appreciated that. They shook hands,
introductions were made, and then the number one question was asked. "How is Bert?"

Todd ushered the group away from the
crowds toward a bar area called the Halo Bar.
He motioned for them to take a seat while he
ordered drinks on the house for all of them.
Bowls of pretzels and chips dotted the tables.
The group as one grabbed and crunched until
the cold, frosty bottles of Tsingtao beer arrived
and, in just moments, were quickly replaced as
the gang gulped and swallowed.

Annie walked away from the group and
looked up at the tall man staring down at her.
"Your man is okay, Ms. de Silva. Believe it or
not I just found out myself, forty minutes ago,
via a text by somebody named Abner Tookus.
By okay I mean as well as he can be with the
beating he suffered. The Sands replaced his
winnings, and we're in the process of repaying
ticket sales. Bert was extremely upset about all
of that. For a guy with his credentials, I am having trouble believing he allowed himself to be
blindsided the way he was. But that's water
under the bridge, as we say back in the States.
Just so you know, Bert and I go way back. We've
been friends for years.

"There's a lot of flak going on over at the
Sands, with Bert having beaten the house as
badly as he did. Big Al, who is also a friend, as-

sured me that he did it fair and square. But there are some out there, I am sure, who will say that is not the case. What I've just told you is the sum total of what I know.

"Al says he doesn't know any more than what I've just told you. Bert is in good hands. Al and I both have some of our best security watching over him. Just in case. You never know, this is China.

"By the way, if you and your contingent of people are thinking about going to the hospital, don't. It's different over here, ma'am. Let's not make any waves. If you want to send him a message, give it to me, and I'll see that he gets it.

"Since the exhibition was called off, there has been a lot of rumbling going on, some idle, some serious. We're always mindful of the triads and the tongs here because, as I always say, this is China. Take my advice and get out of here as quick as you can."

Annie struggled for a smile but failed. "My plane is ninety minutes out. As much as I don't want to, I will take your advice. Tell Bert to get in touch when he's able to. Should I leave money for the hospital bill?"

"Will do. That's not necessary. Al and I took care of that already. Over here, you pay in advance, plus tip plus bribe. You know how that goes. Now if I might make an observation, your people seem hungry. How about a dinner in my private dining room for all of you. You did say you have ninety minutes. Deal?"

"Deal," Annie said, as she offered up her hand. She motioned for the others to follow her, which they did gladly.

The meal was a scrumptious affair—jumbo prawns, thick Kobe beef steaks, baked potatoes, and a luscious green salad. The biscuits, Espinosa said, were so light they could float on air. The Tsingtao flowed like water.

A bevy of waiters were about to serve a delicious five-tier chocolate mousse cake when Todd appeared, and shouted, "Now! Everyone move!"

Within three minutes flat, the group was in the casino van and being transported to the airport, where they made a mad scramble for the stairs that were being lowered to the ground. They bolted forward, pushing and shoving until they were all on board.

"Wheels up in ten seconds," the pilot shouted. They were slicing down the runway before anyone was seated and belted in. They were airborne in less than thirty seconds.

"What the hell!" Jack shouted.

Everyone had something to say at the same time. They stopped talking when the pilot's voice came over the loudspeaker. "Sorry about the rush, folks. Someone named Big Al called and said to get all your asses airborne as quickly as possible because . . . a detaining party was on the way to take you all in for questioning. I hope that answers any questions you might have. So, folks, lean back and enjoy the ride.

Our hostess for the trip is named Sara, and she will be serving beverages in just a few minutes."

It wasn't until they were at a cruising altitude of thirty-five thousand feet that the group started talking and asking questions of one another. It was Myra who looked around and asked where Kathryn was.

"Restroom probably," Nikki said.

"Nope, both are vacant," Maggie said.

"Maybe she's asleep in the back," Alexis said.

"She's not back here!" Dennis shouted.

"Did she get on the plane?" Annie asked hoarsely.

Pandemonium broke out. The end result was that no one could remember seeing Kathryn board the plane. "It all happened so quickly. Harry and I were concentrating on getting Lily and Cooper on board. I just wasn't paying attention," Yoko cried.

"We left her behind?" Fergus said, his expression as shocked as everyone else's.

The girls started to wail. The boys started to curse under their breath until Charles let loose with a sharp whistle that created instant silence. Even Cooper stood at attention.

"Let's give some thought to the possibility that Kathryn deliberately stayed behind to maybe . . . perhaps, visit Bert. I'm aware of that situation, as are you all. Before we jump to con-

clusions, let's be sure we didn't leave her behind versus she stayed behind on her own."

"But this is . . . was China. Is she safe?" Dennis asked.

"I don't know, son. I wish I did," Charles
said.

"We can't go back," Nikki said in a choked
voice.

"No, dear, we can't," Myra said.

"But . . ." It was all Isabelle could get past
her lips. "I was so sharp with her. I should have
minded my own business. She had so much to
say to me when Abner and I hit our rough
patch. I guess I was trying . . . never mind." She
dabbed at her eyes, then closed them.

Myra looked over at Charles. "Send Avery a
text, dear. Make sure he understands this is a
crisis." Charles nodded as he tapped on the
keys. It was all he could do.

Fergus waved away the hostess with her tray
of drinks.

Myra looked up at Annie, whose eyes were
filled with tears. "We never left one of ours behind before. I don't know what to feel, Annie."

The words were no sooner out of Myra's
mouth than Cooper decided to do his wild-
hair sprint up and down the aisle, barking so
loudly that everyone covered their ears with
their hands, except Jack, who narrowed his
eyes and concentrated on the sound of the
shrill barking. When the dog finally came to a

frenzied stop next to him, his tail wagging furiously, the thought went through his head at warp speed. Kathryn was standing inside a hospital room with tears rolling down her cheeks.

"You sure about that, Coop?" The big dog let loose with a single bark.

"Okay, then! Yo, people, listen up! I have good news!"

For the first time the menfolk are stepping out of the pages of #1 New York Times *best-selling author Fern Michaels's beloved Sisterhood series and into the spotlight . . .*

DOUBLE DOWN

After years of standing by their women, the Sisterhood's significant others have also become loyal friends. And now Jack Emery, Nikki's husband, has enlisted Ted, Joe, Jay, Bert, Dennis, and Abner to form a top-secret organization known as BOLO Consultants.

Jack has two missions in mind. The first: offering some behind-the-scenes help to Nikki's law firm as they take on the all-powerful Andover Pharmaceuticals. Andover's anti-leukemia drug causes terrible side effects in young patients, but a class-action suit seems doomed to fail. BOLO Consultants have a prescription to cure that. Meanwhile, Virginia's lieutenant governor has a sideline as a slum landlord, and his impoverished tenants are suffering. Tyler Sandford believes his status puts him above the law. But when the Sisterhood and their allies decide to get involved, no one is beyond the reach of true justice . . .

Turn the page for a special look!

A Zebra mass-market paperback and eBook on sale now.

Jack Emery propped his chin on his cupped hands and looked out the window of the Bagel Emporium at the blustery weather outside. His thoughts traveled back in time to a year ago, to the last day that Emanuel Macklin was seen. A lot had happened in the past year. Much of his life, and the lives of his friends, had been turned upside down. And sometimes he had a hard time coming to terms with the way all of it had happened at what seemed to be the speed of light.

He was a free agent these days. Right after the first of the year, he'd left his wife's, Nikki's, law firm, with her reluctant approval, supposedly to write a book. It was something that never happened. He'd done some consulting work for a few months, but that hadn't worked either. He'd then stepped into his old shoes at the district attorney's office, prosecuted two cases, and walked away. He'd won both cases but they were both on appeal. Some smart-ass defense attorney would come up with some frigging loophole, and the bad guys would be right back out on the street. So, disillusioned, he'd thrown in the towel and walked away, frustrated and angry at a criminal justice system that seemed to coddle the criminals and leave the good guys, the victims, to fend for themselves.

Jack's eyes were glued to the redbrick building across the street from where he was sitting. His building. Well, not totally his. He, along with Ted Robinson, Joe Espinosa, Harry Wong, Bert Navarro, and Jay Sparrow, owned the building. They'd invested the bonus money they'd gotten years ago when they worked for Hank Jellicoe, money that none of them had ever touched until a few months ago, when he convinced his little band of avengers that this was what they needed to do. *This* meaning buying the six-thousand-square-foot brick building, refurbishing it, and going into business together. Into a business that was completely off the grid. And today was move-in day.

In a shopping bag at his feet, he had a bottle of champagne, crystal wine flutes, and a jug of tea for Harry so they could christen their new business in—he looked down at his watch—

ten more minutes. Next to the shopping bag was Cyrus, a huge, sleek, 140-pound black German shepherd, who was his new best friend forever. Cyrus was two years old and, as far as Jack was concerned, half human and half dog. Cyrus was so in tune with Jack, he knew what Jack was going to do before Jack knew himself.

Four months ago, he had stopped in for his morning bagel while Cyrus waited outside. While he waited in line for his coffee and bagel, the door opened, and a man bellowed, "Everyone on the floor!" As he was dropping to the floor to obey the robber's orders, Jack saw a black streak clear the door with inches to spare. In the blink of an eye, all 140 pounds of ferocious dog propelled the robber to the floor, then sat on him. Jack, in a lightning move, scooped up the gun the man had been brandishing while Domingo Lopez, known to his patrons as Ding, called the police. Cyrus was the hero of the day, and, as Ding said, "I don't care what the Health Department's rules are, Cyrus can come in here anytime." His patrons agreed, and everyone else looked the other way. Jack reached down to pat the magnificent dog on the head. Cyrus nuzzled his hand.

Jack returned to his thoughts as he stared out the window. The weatherman had predicted a possibility of snow flurries later in the day. It was, after all, December, so snow flurries were to be expected. Just like last year, when the same prediction led to three weeks of arc-

tic air and so much snow that the District had
to shut down because there was nowhere else
to move the white stuff.

So much had happened during that short
period of time. Charles Martin had flown the
coop, Jack and Nikki had hit a rough patch,
and he'd resigned, to her initial chagrin. But
in the end, she agreed because she just wanted
him to be happy with his life. During the past
year, her twelve-member all-female law firm
took on six new associates and seven new para-
legals. The expansion was needed to deal with
three class-action lawsuits that would make the
firm *kazillions* of dollars. If the workload didn't
kill everyone first. All they had to do was work
twenty hours a day to make it happen. Sometimes, he didn't see or talk to his wife for days
at a time. What the hell kind of life was that?
Things were still sticky between the two of them,
but they were both trying to work it all through.
Alexis Thorn, Joe Espinosa's significant other,
had given Espinosa the boot shortly before
Valentine's Day, saying she preferred her job
to a relationship, and she hoped that he understood that she couldn't do both. Espinosa did
not understand, any more than Jack did. They'd
cried into their beers way too many times the
last ten months.

Maggie Spritzer was back at the *Post* as the
EIC after John Cassidy resigned because he
didn't have enough time to go fly-fishing. It
had taken a lot of sweet-talking on Annie de

Silva's part to get Maggie back in harness, but, finally, all the perks Annie dangled in front of Maggie won her over, and she was once again calling the shots at the *Post.* Not a bad thing, Jack had decided at the time. Or as Ted put it, "She's out of our hair for now."

Jack's little "guy group," as he called it, had three new exclusive members and one long-distance member. The other members referred to it as "an off-the-grid spy group," whatever the hell that meant. The name conjured up all kinds of weird images and possible scenarios. Bert Navarro was the long-distance member. Dennis West, cub reporter and Ted Robinson, hero worshipper, as well as a new billionaire, Abner Tookus, hacker extraordinaire, and Jack Sparrow, who out of necessity was called Jay for a little while, were the latest recruits to the off-the-grid avengers club.

Jack let his thoughts wander to Myra and Annie, who had settled in for the long winter ahead. The last time he'd checked with Myra, she was knitting. *Knitting.* She'd said she was making a scarf that was two miles long, and she needed a wagon to carry it in. Or, as Annie put it, one long line of colored yarn filled with sloppy stitches. Annie said she was taking cooking lessons and brushing up on her pole dancing. She had mumbled something about feathers on shoes, or maybe it was her white cowboy boots that she always wore, but he hadn't understood a word of what she was saying. What he did understand was that, unlike the others, who were running themselves ragged, she and Myra were bored out of their minds.

Women! He would never understand them. Never!

Isabelle Flanders Tookus was still in England, designing a new-age city, and had no downtime available for Abner, which pretty much left him at loose ends and ready to dive into the guy group. Yoko, it appeared, at least according to Harry, was happier than a pig in a mud slide with her plant nursery and raising Lily, which left precious little time for Harry, who these days was meaner than a wet cat on a treadmill.

Kathryn Lucas, fiancée of Bert Navarro, thrived on driving the open roads in her eighteen-wheeler, making two stops a month in Las Vegas for, as Bert put it, booty calls. He also said theirs would be the longest engagement in history because Kathryn had no intention of ever marrying again. Bert said he was okay with the engagement because he had no other options, and he loved Kathryn heart and soul.

Cyrus raised his head, then reared up. He'd heard the sound of Harry's Ducati before Jack had. "Okay, big guy, do your thing while I pay the bill." Doing his thing meant going from table to table to offer up his paw and, with luck, get a little treat from his friends at the other tables. When he finished his rounds, he barked, and Ding came out from behind the counter and handed the big dog a monster dog treat. Cyrus barked, offered up his paw, and waited for Jack to open the door. Ham that he was, Cyrus turned and bowed. The patrons loved it and always clapped. Jack said, "You are the biggest ham I've ever seen, Cyrus. Hero worship is a sin. Do you know that?" Cyrus barked, waited for a break in traffic, and raced across the road to greet Harry, who obligingly ruffled his ears.

"Hi, Harry!"

"Hi, Jack!"

"Let's walk around back so we can all go in together. I want us all to oooh and aaah at the same time. Ted just turned the corner, and I think I saw Sparrow come in from the other direction. Haven't seen Abner yet, though. Oops, there he goes. How's it going, Harry?"

"It's going, Jack. You?"

"It's going, Harry. You up for this gig?"

Never long on words, Harry said, "I'm here."

"Let's do it!" Jack said as he picked up his feet and raced to the back alley behind the newly remodeled property, where the guys were waiting for them. Cyrus barked a greeting, then offered his paw. It was a ritual that had to be observed, or Cyrus would bark relentlessly until the others made it happen. Satisfied that he had all the attention he needed, the big dog stood back while Jack allowed the retina scanner to check his eyeball, then listened for the hydraulic hiss of the door opening at their new, off-the-grid digs.

Books by Bestselling Author
Fern Michaels